BITTER SWEET

Brian Raftery

SEAVIEW
PRESS

Inquiries should be made to:
Seaview Press
PO Box 234
Henley Beach SA 5022
Telephone 08-8235 1535; fax 08-8235 9144;
e-mail seaview@seaviewpress.com.au

Seaview Press is a division of A.C.N. 075 827 851 Pty Ltd.

Printed by Copy Master:
234 Currie Street
Adelaide
South Australia 5000

ISBN 1 74008 027 0

To my brother Rodney

Whose latter days were bittersweet

He kept his sorrow to himself

His joy he shared abundantly

Would that I could be so strong!

Contents

Chapter 1

War's end

It was the 10th of May in the spring of 1945. The mid-morning sun over Germany bathed the mountains in its seductive warmth. Rolf Bauer's back was getting sweaty. The luxuriant rays cut through his threadbare vest. He guided the heavy paintbrush up and down in long, rhythmic strokes. Rolf's whole arm ached. The tired barn walls beneath the old Bavarian farmhouse sorely needed sprucing after six years of neglect. I'll finish it in two days, he thought, as he stood back and surveyed his work. The paint was about ten years old and had sat in the barn gathering dust since before the war. It had taken half an hour of stirring to get some life back into it. Everything had stopped for the war. Like the landscape and its people, this old tin had seemed to have some inertia about getting moving again. He applied the paint sparingly.

Soon he was covered in specks and splashes of the dull red colour that so characterised the buildings in the region. He peered across the valley and could see other dwellings in exactly the same red, all heavily faded and crying out for a fresh cloak of paint. Rolf dipped the brush again and went back to his strokes. He hoped he would have enough.

Rolf was troubled that sunny morning by unfamiliar rumblings in the distance. A bit like thunder, the noise would start and stop intermittently. Each time it seemed a little closer. He had started the painting job at first light, just after he had fed the hens and put the cows out to pasture. He had left the four sows in the barn, grunting over an armful of old cabbage leaves.

The rustic Bauer farmhouse, built in traditional fashion atop the winter holding barn for animals, was a warm and inviting place. Adorned with sturdy window boxes all round, a wood fire burned constantly, for heating and cooking.

Heavy oak shutters gave protection from the winter snows. The farmland below was divided into several paddocks extending down the valley to a clay-dirt roadway. The paddock closest to the road was exposed to the chill winds that often whipped up the valley, so Rolf had planted a copse of evergreen shelter trees back in a previous summer. He knew every bit of the farm and was damn proud of the way the pasture had responded to the successive spreading of manure each spring.

Rolf was only 19. His left leg caused him to wince whenever he climbed the ladder. He had grown accustomed to his slight limp, the legacy of a farm accident when he was barely five years old. Though he often mourned his lack of mobility, his mother was secretly thankful that this small imperfection had prevented her son being conscripted into the Wehrmacht. Were it not for his impairment, Rolf would have been an ideal candidate for the ranks of the regular army, or, indeed, the SS. He stood over 188 centimetres tall, with broad shoulders and thick forearms—freckled and strengthened by years of toil in the fields. Generally, he walked with a straight back and his head held high, a subconscious habit, perhaps to offset his limp. Rolf's hair was blond and curly, framing a handsome face, tanned by the sunshine and spotted with a few freckles. It was a gentle face—quick to smile and slow to anger. He might have looked like a fine soldier, but he had inherited his father's peaceful nature and didn't have a fighting bone in his body.

At the end of the farmhouse, Rolf's father, Joachim Bauer, tinkered with their rusty tractor. The old man had been trying to start the engine for two hours. His arms were covered in grease and grime, but his efforts were unsuccessful.

'Father, did you hear those noises?' shouted Rolf.

'Sure. Of course I did. It sounded like trucks or a bulldozer. Too far away to tell, really.' The older man brushed his wispy hair back with a greasy forearm. Now, his forehead was blackened as well. He continued, 'How's the paint supply holding up?'

'Oh, I've got enough, I think. I keep using turps to thin it out.'

'Well, keep at it and don't worry about those noises. Let's just mind our own business and keep working. You must finish that job by tomorrow.' Joachim immediately regretted being so abrupt with Rolf. Why couldn't he be a little kinder to his children? He resolved to do so.

Rolf just nodded, arched his back in a slow stretch, and went back to his duties. He felt a twinge of pity for his father, who had suffered internment during the war. Rolf remembered well that devastating day when his dear father, a former lecturer in languages at Salzburg University, had been brutally taken from their home. He'd been forcibly transported to Dachau concentration camp on the outskirts of Munich. For 18 months he'd been incarcerated there, because he'd made the mistake of defending human rights. The prisoner huts at Dachau had been hellholes. Inmates had been cramped in small wooden bunks, one above another, with little bedding, even in the middle of winter. Tuberculosis and dysentery were rife in such appalling conditions. When Joachim had arrived at the camp, only four of the 30 huts were used as infirmaries. Eighteen months later, the number had risen to 13, all jam-packed with skeletal souls, clinging to life in the harshest of conditions. As a political prisoner, and a German citizen, Joachim at least had been spared the 'human experiments' carried out with murderous frequency.

During his internment, he'd been forced to work on the new, showpiece autobahn between Munich and Salzburg. Throughout this forced labour, without the protection of winter clothing, he had suffered from constant exposure to the weather.

Having served his time, he was at home now, but in poor health following this ordeal.

At 57 years of age, Joachim was a tall and frail figure with a gaunt look, and a slow, deliberate walk more befitting a man in his 70s. His thinning hair was all grey. He rarely smiled and never laughed. A tired and weather-beaten face bespoke many years of anguish. The past few years had taken the strength from his body and the humour from his soul. He was a far cry from the energetic farmer who'd successfully combined lectures and agriculture before the war. Moreover, his personality had changed. Now he was stern and abrupt—even to his own family. He rarely smiled. The old man knew that his days were numbered. Sooner or later, his frail body would succumb. Desperately, he toiled to rebuild the farm for his family. Every night he prayed that God would bless him with a few more years to provide a secure future for his three loved ones.

Rolf himself had spent half his life on this little farm, nestled on a green hillside near the Austrian border, not far from the picturesque village of Berchtesgaden. He loved farming and felt he belonged on the land. It was his life—the isolation of it all, the soil and the animals. He marvelled at the miracle of germination and relished the self-sufficiency of farm life. Rolf remembered, as a child, the simple pleasure of going with his father to the produce market down in Berchtesgaden on a Saturday. He also loved having coffee, cake and conversation in one of the village cafes on a Sunday afternoon, with his parents and sister Marianne.

Rolf stretched again and looked up from where he was brushing. The ladder shifted, forcing him to lean on his bad leg. He winced, and nearly painted over a window. Grimacing, he regained control only to lose it again as the ladder moved once more. The leg was always getting in the way, he thought. It had kept him out of the army and away from friends, but he preferred to keep separate from most people. Rolf liked the life that farming had given him.

He glanced up again towards the towering, snow-capped mountains of the Obersalzberg. These peaks were awesome. He loved to explore their rugged beauty. But he chose not to venture too high, because in the distance at the peak of the 2000-metre Kehlstein mountain was the Eagle's Nest. Many machine-gun nests and anti-aircraft batteries had surrounded it for years, to protect the Fuhrer's summer fortress. Like the rest of his family, Rolf thought the Eagle's Nest, which had taken over three years and millions of marks to build, had been a waste of money when so many of his countrymen were struggling to survive.

Earlier in the day, when he had pulled the wooden ladder from its storage slot in the barn roof, Rolf had first heard the unfamiliar rumbling noise. Unusual sounds were not uncommon in the mountains; indeed, noises were often magnified as they echoed between the granite ridges. He frequently heard the distant chatter of small-arms fire from soldiers patrolling the whole area below the fortress nestled in the white peaks of Kehlstein. He also heard the wailing sirens and muffled explosions as white-smoke generators spewed their contents upwards. These were triggered to minimise visibility, so that British pilots couldn't locate the Eagle's Nest they desperately wanted to destroy. So he was accustomed to odd sounds, But this distant rumbling was something new.

On the weather front, things were looking up a bit, he thought, even though the past few years had been so trying for all his family. Today, his beloved mountains were drenched in sunshine. A pair of jet-black starlings scurried about nearby, fossicking for nesting material. Rolf grew hungry from his toil. He had a voracious appetite and when he noticed the smell of paprika, he knew his mother had put on another pot of his favourite meal—goulash.

Rolf heard the door slam and the clink of crockery. That would be his sister Marianne bringing coffee out to her father.

'Do you want a cup, Rolf?' she asked, poking her head around the corner.

'No, I'm fine, thanks, I've got some cider here.'

In a voice loud enough for Rolf to hear, Marianne went on, 'Father, perhaps when Rolf has finished painting his overalls, you could get him to splash a bit on the walls as well.'

Rolf grinned to himself and went back to brushing, determined not to give his cheeky sister the satisfaction of any reaction.

The 12 cattle which had been in the barn moved about in the nearby top pasture, relishing their newfound freedom after winter isolation. They took their fill of the lush, spring pasture and swished their tails at hovering insects.

Further down the valley, at the lower extremity of the farm, a white Arabian stallion belonging to Rolf's young sister pranced elegantly. The proud and noble animal seemed an incongruous sight in this country humbled by the ravages of war.

Like all his family, Rolf delighted in observing the capricious whims of nature with the changing of the seasons. Each year throughout the war he had managed to plant some grain as well as good crops of potatoes and cabbages. The farm was fairly self-supporting. Luckily, the hillside property and most of the surrounding farms had escaped the bombing of recent months. Both the British and American planes had concentrated on the Ruhr Valley and the industrial cities to the west—way over on the other side of Germany.

Rolf didn't like to dwell on the war, even though it now appeared that the conflict was finally over. For five years, he had tracked its progress on a small radio that provided good reception when the weather was clear. Only the previous night, he had heard more encouraging news, that the war that had so ravaged Europe was finally drawing to a close. Apparently, towards the end of April, Italian partisans, while trying to escape to Switzerland, had captured Mussolini. Rolf was pleased to hear that the Fascist dictator was now strung up by his heels in Milan, alongside an aide and his mistress, Clara Petacci. It was rumoured, too, that the Fuehrer and Eva Braun had committed suicide in Berlin around the end of April, just after Adolf Hitler had handed full power over to Admiral Doenitz.

Rolf thought that perhaps the Third Reich, that had been supposed to last for a thousand years, had finally come to an end. The most encouraging news he had heard had been a short transmission as he was getting dressed to feed the hens. It was a brief news flash, broadcast in several languages: an unconditional surrender might have been signed at a small schoolhouse in the French town of Reims, where Eisenhower had his headquarters. Rolf had listened intently for a while longer, hoping for some confirmation of the capitulation and any additional news. He had heard something further about General Jodl and Marshall Friedeburg signing for Germany, then the radio had started to crackle and had faded out altogether. Maybe, at last, the whole thing was over. He certainly hoped it was. Reflecting for a moment, he realised that there had been no bombs now for about three days. Besides, a neighbour had told him that American land forces had entered Berchtesgaden.

Despite wartime damage and widespread poverty, eastern Bavaria remained a beautiful part of the world. Its rugged mountain peaks and green valleys were lined by rushing streams, invigorated in the months of spring by the melting snow. The centrepiece was the beautiful Konigssee, a clear mountain lake, regarded by Bavarians as one of the most picturesque waters in Germany. The locals were outraged that so much of this delightful landscape was now showing the savage scars of war. As well as the craters that pockmarked the countryside, there were ruins everywhere. Most roads had been damaged by military traffic. Almost all the bridges had been bombed, despite the fact that there was little industrial production in this part of Germany.

Back in 1934, Rolf's family had been forcibly displaced from their century-old home in the old Obersalzberg village. The dreaded Martin Bormann had bought up, taken over and then razed all the dwellings in the village, as part of his grand plan to clear the area beneath the mountain peak where he would later build his 'birthday present' for Hitler.

Rolf continued his painting. He could hear his father's raucous cough occasionally and the singing of Marianne. She was planting pelargonium cuttings in each of their window boxes.

Rolf heard that rumbling noise again. This time it was closer and a more angry and menacing sound. He paused to listen. As it continued, he became apprehensive. Apprehension turned to fear. A cold chill swept over his body as he recognised the unmistakable sound of tanks. *Wasn't it over yet?* Shaking all over, he scampered from the ladder, wincing in pain when his foot slipped on one of the rungs. He re-positioned the ladder so he could get on to the roof. It was pitched steeply to prevent snow building up, so he had to be careful.

Clambering onto the nearest gable, he crawled up to the highest point and peered to see over the roofline. In the valley below he saw a convoy of three tanks and three open Jeeps making their way in his direction. Each tank belched black smoke as its tracks tore into the dusty road.

'I knew it was tanks,' he muttered to himself. Rolf peered through the haze of smoke and dust. Even at this distance he could make out the single white star of the United States Army emblazoned on the bonnets of the dusty Jeeps.

'Mother!' he shouted, scooting down the ladder at breakneck speed. 'Tanks and Jeeps out there. All American! Coming straight for us.'

'How many?' Joachim asked.

'Three big tanks and three Jeeps.'

'Well, let's keep calm,' the older man replied. 'There's not much we can do anyway.'

'At least I'll bring the cattle in,' said Rolf as he rushed to herd his 12 precious charges into the safety of the barn.

Joachim flung open the barn doors. His wife, Brigitte, and daughter, Marianne, moved out to the grassy verge in front of the farmhouse. They stood and watched as the tanks approached. The earth trembled. Eventually the noisy monsters halted in the shade of some tall trees by the road. Abruptly, one of the three Jeeps, with two soldiers on board, left the group and charged towards them.

Joachim and Rolf joined the women at the front. Joachim put a reassuring arm around Brigitte's shoulder. The family of four watched as the Jeep approached, its engine roaring in protest as it started up the hillside.

In mute anxiety, they waited. Then each of them gasped. Out of the woods in the bottom paddock their beloved white stallion flashed across the ground as if it were trying to race the Jeep.

'My God!' Brigitte cried. 'We forgot about Kaiser!'

The face of 17-year-old Marianne went white and she doubled in anguish. She felt nauseous at the thought that her lovely white horse was in such danger. Suddenly she darted forward, but was restrained by Rolf. He put his arm around his sister and offered some words of comfort.

'Don't worry, Marianne, Kaiser will be fine. He can escape into the trees if he needs to.' Even as he spoke, though, Rolf himself became worried. The Jeep had stopped at the bottom gate to their property and the ever-friendly Kaiser was trotting over towards the soldiers to satisfy his curiosity. One of the troops got out of the vehicle to open the gate while the other stepped towards the horse—unslinging his rifle as he walked.

By this time, Marianne was frantic. 'Papa, they're going to shoot him.'

'Mari, settle down. Why would they want to kill him?'

By now one of the men was only a metre way from Kaiser, who had halted just the other side of the fence. The soldier pulled a short bayonet from a scabbard on his belt. Fearing the worst, Marianne covered her face with her hands and squirmed into her mother's shoulder.

'Tell me what's happening, Mama,' she said, 'Tell me, tell me!'

After a few seconds of anxious silence, Joachim said in a calm, reassuring voice, 'It's alright, it's alright. I told you so. He's only stopped to pat him.'

Marianne turned around and breathed a huge sigh of relief as she saw a soldier patting Kaiser's head. The other used his bayonet to cut a handful of grass tussocks from the roadside.

Rolf also felt relieved, because he was the one who had cared for Kaiser during these past six years, to get him safely through the war. This had been no mean feat, because, apart from soldiers, there had been so many misfits and strangers around.

The family watched for another couple of minutes with mixed feelings of apprehension and relief at the intrusion of the foreign troops. At length, the two soldiers reboarded the Jeep and continued their journey up towards the farmhouse. The vehicle stopped two hundred metres away, and one of the men began talking on his radio.

'Why did they stop, Papa?' Marianne asked.

'Be quiet a minute, child,' Joachim replied sternly. He was perplexed about what might occur.

Rolf was the first to spot what was happening. The Jeep had radioed one of the tanks. It had started to back out of the trees onto the middle of the roadway. When the tank stopped, its 76mm gun turret was slowly turned around and up so that it was directly aimed at the farmhouse.

'I'll get a sheet,' Rolf said. He dashed inside. Instead of going through to the bedroom, he yanked the white lace cloth from the kitchen table. Plates flew everywhere. He raced outside and waved the cloth frantically.

The Jeep moved forward slowly and came to a stop about 50 metres away. The two men alighted and moved forward with their rifles extended.

'Do any of you speak English?' the older one demanded sternly.

'We all speak good English,' Joachim replied. 'My name is—'

'Is anybody else in the house?' the soldier interrupted sharply.

Rolf stepped forward a couple of paces and said, 'Listen, gentlemen, take it easy! There's no-one else in the house. What exactly do you want from us?'

'We're only interested in enemy forces,' the older one replied. He went on, 'If there's no soldiers here, you have nothing to fear from us. Dutchy! A quick check of the house and barn. That machine shed over there too.'

They all waited silently until the younger soldier gave the all-clear.

Joachim said, 'Sir, may I now introduce myself? My name is Joachim Bauer. This is my wife Brigitte, my son Rolf and my daughter Marianne. I used to be a language professor and my wife was a schoolteacher. We all have a good command of English.'

'Mr Bauer, thank you! My name is Lieutenant Mark Briggs and this is Sergeant Larry Holland. We are from the 101st Airborne Division of the United States Army. Be advised that effective immediately we're imposing a curfew on local movements. You may leave this dwelling only between noon and 2 pm until this whole area is secure. Do you understand this order?'

'Yes, yes, of course we understand,' Joachim replied abruptly. 'But where do you go from here? The whole area above us was bombed last month, so I don't think you'll find much resistance anywhere.'

'Oh, we'll just check out the area a bit further up the mountain.'

'God be with you, then,' Joachim said. A worldly-wise man, he knew enough about warfare to realise that the three huge Sherman tanks below were, first and foremost, offensive weapons probably destined to do a lot more than just check out the area. Joachim went on, 'There's been too much killing already, so I hope you get things settled down quickly.'

'Sir?'

'Yes, what is it?' Joachim replied.

'Mr Bauer, we have to wait an hour or so. My men must tighten a loose track on one of the tanks. Could we take some fresh water from your tank? We're right out of drinking water.'

Knowing that the troops could take whatever they damn well pleased, Joachim nodded in approval and gestured to the rest of his family to move back into the house.

The two soldiers returned to the Jeep and radioed back to the others. Soon two men in a Jeep laden with jerry cans came up the hillside. They started to fill them with the clean drinking water.

Rolf looked out the window, then said to Joachim, 'Papa, should we give them some of our goulash? There's plenty there and they probably haven't had a hot meal in weeks.'

'Yes, no harm in that, I suppose. We need all the help and protection we can get from the Americans. There's a lot of plundering going on.'

Rolf went outside and made the offer to the lieutenant, who agreed in an instant. The four soldiers thoroughly enjoyed their meal and the oven-fresh bread. Sharing a meal together diffused the chill of the situation.

Marianne warmed things up further by bringing out a few bottles of homemade beer. The troops were pleased to meet a family who spoke English so well. As they chatted away, Marianne noticed that the two who stared at her occasionally seemed to be no more than 18. They asked lots of questions about Bavaria and brought the family up-to-date on the war situation.

Sergeant Holland did most of the talking. He said, 'We've been in Germany for only seven weeks but it seems like a lifetime. Always wanted to come to the Continent myself. But not like this. We landed in Italy and worked our way north across the Brenner. Being in the mountains was the worst. Those flamethrowers ... thought we'd be cooked alive.' He rubbed his arm, obviously remembering some wound or burn. 'We've seen so much bloodshed and destruction. War's a horrible, horrible thing. Thank God it's nearly over now. Thing is, it's not just the soldiers who die. We've seen women and children dead everywhere. Dead dogs and cattle. Even dead birds! I've got two young children. Hope to hell they never have to go to war. I'm actually a musician. Jazz. But all that's out the window now that my hearing is gone. Got blasted by a grenade from one of those Jerrys—sorry, you know what I mean.' He looked down and absently rubbed his arm again.

Sergeant Holland went on to confirm that Germany had indeed signed an unconditional surrender in the small town of Reims on the morning of 7th May. Furthermore, by midnight on the 9th May, an official cease-fire had come into force.

Rolf decided that these Americans were likeable—hardly the monsters that had been portrayed in local propaganda!

After a while, Lieutenant Briggs quietly took Joachim aside.

'Mr Bauer, you seem to be a man of peace. I'd like to ask a big favour of you. Before I do, I must tell you that you have every right to refuse. If you decline, that's fine. We'll be on our way quietly.'

Joachim leaned closer, his face puzzled as he wondered what this stranger could possibly want from him.

'Sir, I have in my party a badly wounded soldier. He took a hit from a sniper a few miles back. He's only a kid with a round stuck in his hip. I can't take him forward into further fighting. We've got absolutely no medic support at the moment. I realise you've every right to refuse, but I'd be truly grateful if I could leave him in your care for a few days. Just until my unit returns or I can send some kind of transport for him. What do you think, Mr Bauer?'

'Lieutenant, I'll tell you exactly what I think. Most of the German people are fed up with Hitl ...' He paused for a moment to take in breath as a fit of coughing overcame him. The old man spat out some red phlegm, wiped his mouth and continued, 'We're sick of the war and sick of all the restrictions. We want it all to end and to get back to a normal life again. My family and I are really pacifists. We were glad to hear that the Fuehrer is dead and that Eva Braun is dead with him. Good riddance, I say! Bring the boy up here and we'll look after him. He must be about the same age as my son, though I expect he's seen a lot more of the world than my Rolf. Anyway, I know a retired doctor in the next valley who could probably patch him up for you.'

'Thanks a bunch, Mr Bauer,' the grateful lieutenant replied, shaking his hand vigorously.

'I'll get him driven up here right away with the medicine cabinet from one of our tanks. I'll also write out an exemption notice for the curfew so you can fetch the doctor at your convenience. Just to be safe too, I'll leave you a rifle and a few rounds. The French Resistance in this area is plundering a lot of the farms. Sir, you really should keep your daughter out of sight for a few days. Things are pretty dodgy right now.'

'What's that again about the French Resistance?'

'Apparently there has been a fairly large contingent working underground in this area for a few weeks. We've been told that now they know the war is over, they're taking revenge on soldiers and civilians alike.'

'So, how long do you think it will be before it is safe?'

'Oh, about a week or so, I expect. We've got hundreds of troops moving into Berchtesgaden right now, but we must enforce the curfew until as civil order is restored.' The lieutenant paused for a moment, then went on, 'On second thought, I'll leave you two pistols as well as the rifle, just in case.'

Joachim nodded in agreement and the lieutenant got back on the radio once more. The frail old man shuffled inside and told his family about his decision to take the young soldier for a few days.

They all agreed it was the right thing to do, although Marianne was a bit put out at this sudden invasion of their privacy. Nevertheless, Brigitte and her daughter discussed where in the house they could set up some extra sleeping quarters. They decided to put a bed in the front lounge room near the window, so the injured man could take full advantage of the fresh air and see the mountains outside.

Meanwhile, Rolf went out to the Jeeps and asked, 'Lieutenant, what's the name of the wounded man?'

'He's a young Irishman,' Briggs replied. 'Name of Gleeson—Sean Gleeson.'

Chapter 2

The Irishman

Brigitte and Marianne set about preparing a bed for their unexpected guest. Joachim put on his reading glasses and studied the curfew exemption. Meanwhile, Rolf hurried down the hill to bring Kaiser to the safety of the barn. They agreed it was best to keep him out of sight for a few days.

By the time Rolf had moved the white stallion into his winter quarters again, the Jeep with the wounded soldier had made its way slowly up the hill. The injured man was strapped horizontally on a canvas stretcher across the back.

Joachim and Rolf went to meet the vehicle. They could see immediately that the young man was in considerable pain from his short journey.

Sean Gleeson was a good-looking young man, with black hair and the beginnings of a goatee beard. He wasn't as strongly built as Rolf. Sean was tall and slim—more of a wiry type. His army greens' left leg was saturated in blood from the hip to the knee. He looked forlorn, lying helplessly on the stretcher.

'Take it easy, young man,' Joachim said, touching him on the shoulder. 'We'll take good care of you. My name is Joachim, and this is my son Rolf.'

The wounded man muttered a polite greeting, took a couple of deep breaths and said, 'I'm Sean Gleeson, and, I thank you both for your charity in taking me in. Probably only be for just a couple of days.'

'Is the bullet still in your leg, Sean?' Rolf said, anxious to start some conversation and put the young soldier at ease.

'Sure is, right here in my left hip and it hurts like hell,' he replied.

Rolf turned to the driver and asked, 'Did you bring any medical supplies up with you?'

The driver quickly pulled three canvas bags from the Jeep and said, 'Yeah, pal! We have lots of bandages and some ointments in this bag. The other smaller pouch contains basic surgical instruments. That's all we have, I'm afraid.'

Brigitte emerged from the house and strode purposefully towards the Jeep. 'Let's get that boy inside,' she said, taking control. She wasn't bothered with introductions. They carried the stretcher carefully into the house.

Joachim and Rolf stayed to say their goodbyes to the other soldiers.

Brigitte said, 'The first thing we need to do is to examine your wound and clean it up. Get the bottle of schnapps down, Mari, and give this young man a drink to settle him down.'

Marianne grabbed the bottle and lifted Sean's head a little, so he could sip. She liked the look of the handsome young stranger.

Without delay, Brigitte tied her long hair back in a bun, donned an apron and filled a bowl with warm water. She inspected the ointments the driver had left, took a quick look at the medical instruments and opened up the third bag. To their surprise, it contained seven large blocks of American chocolate and two jars of coffee. Real chocolate and real coffee! The soldiers must have appreciated the goulash.

Brigitte thought for a moment about how to proceed. She was a no-nonsense farmwoman, who, at 42, was 15 years younger than her spouse.

As a teenager, she had been a voracious reader and a brilliant student. Brigitte had spent five years in Florence while her father was employed there, during which time she learned to speak Italian and to cook pasta. Returning to Germany, she had studied civil engineering for three years at the University of Munich. Unlike her husband, she was in excellent health. She did all the milking on the farm. She also did some part-time teaching in the convent school where Marianne had been educated.

Although she loved Joachim dearly, Brigitte felt a bit unfulfilled by farm life, and repressed by the isolation. She missed the challenge of study and the joy of learning. Although rural life in Bavaria was pleasant enough, it was rarely satisfying and never stimulating. The lot of a farmer's wife involved work and more work; little of it required any mental effort. However, loyalty and love for her family kept her going.

She rolled up her sleeves for the task ahead. First of all, she and Marianne turned the wounded man slowly onto his right side, so they could get better access to his wound. Marianne took a pair of large scissors and cut away Sean's trousers, while Brigitte used cotton wool dipped in antiseptic solution to clean the injury. The young soldier gritted his teeth and winced occasionally with the pain. He didn't say anything.

Observing that Sean was still in pain, Marianne asked, 'Would you like another sip of schnapps, Sir?'

'Call me Sean,' he replied with an engaging smile. He went on, 'To be honest, I'd prefer a cup of hot coffee or chocolate, if you don't mind. That schnapps is just too strong, and me an Irish whisky man from way back!'

'I'll get you one, if you call me Marianne,' she replied cheekily.

'Deal!' He shook her warm hand lightly, then watched her disappear into the kitchen.

Marianne put the kettle on and went straight into her bedroom. She brushed her long, blonde hair and put on a little lipstick. She was a tall, attractive fraulein with ice blue eyes and a fair complexion. A few freckles bridged her nose and her face glowed with good health. The fresh mountain air had treated her kindly. She had a cheerful, gentle disposition. Marianne was by far the most religious member of the family. During her final days at the convent she had delighted in teaching catechism to the younger children. She enjoyed a special relationship with the nuns, who relied upon her for all kinds of support—especially when one of them was ill.

As she tied a ribbon in her hair, Marianne noticed that her embroidered white blouse was stained with blood. She decided to leave it on anyway, and returned to the kitchen.

Joachim re-entered the house, coughing a little as he walked through the door. He asked, 'What's the damage, Brigitte?'

'It's a nasty wound. The bullet is still in there and it must have been soft because it spread out and shattered when it hit the bone. The bleeding seems to have stopped, thank goodness! But I think the fragments must come out before infection sets in.'

'Can't you just get it out with those instruments from the tank? I can take the pain,' the young man said bravely.

'I'm a farmer's wife, not a doctor, young man. It's not just the shell itself; there are loose bits of metal around it. If I take them all out, you might start bleeding again and I wouldn't know how to stop the flow. Joachim, we'll have to fetch Doctor Steifler or the poor boy might get gangrene.'

'I'll ask Rolf to go,' he replied. 'But he'd better head out right away so they can return before dark.'

Without delay, Joachim grabbed one of the canvas medicine bags and put in it the curfew exemption document, a flask of water and one of the pistols, with a handful of bullets. He went outside to give Rolf his instructions.

Taking the hot coffee from Marianne, Brigitte put it on the table next to Sean. She said, 'Don't worry, lad, we will have the doctor here in a couple of hours and he'll have that bullet out in a flash. But you must keep still. We don't mind getting the doctor, but I wouldn't like to send for the priest.'

'Thank you again,' Sean said, not sure whether she was making a joke or not. He felt weary. The shock and strain of it was starting to catch up with him. 'I'll have my coffee and see if I can get a bit of sleep. I'm so very tired. Thank you both!'

They covered him with a light blanket and retreated to the kitchen to give him some peace.

'Rolf, you'd better go by foot to Steifler's place instead of taking Kaiser. That way you'll be less conspicuous,' Joachim instructed.

'Sure, Father. I'll follow the trees along the stream and stay out of the open as much as I can, then bring the good doctor straight back.'

'Okay, take this pouch. It has some water, the curfew paper and a revolver. Son, if you have to use the gun, don't hesitate. I don't want to lose you now that the war is over. Kiss your mother goodbye before you go and make sure you convince Steifler to come back with you today.'

Soon Rolf was on his way, jogging steadily through the trees along the stream. Every now and then he ducked to avoid low branches. It was shady and cool. He made good progress. Occasionally, he stopped to have a quick sip from his flask.

Suddenly, he noticed smoke ahead. He slowed down to a walk. Quietly, he crept forward. He could see a small clearing ahead. Peering through the bushes, he was relieved to see it was only a family of gipsies. They were setting up camp for the night. There was a man with an eye-patch, and his wife and three young girls. They were dressed in rags and huddled close to the fire. One of the children had a dirty plaster cast on her arm. The other two had no shoes. Rolf took a slight detour so that he would not disturb them, and so they would not hinder his progress.

Within a few minutes he approached the ridge leading to the house of the retired Doctor Steifler and his kindly wife, Greta. She had worked as his nurse for many years and knew as much about medicine as the doctor himself.

Rolf's heart sank as he crested the ridge and saw the house emerge beyond. There was an appalling sight before him. The colour drained from his face as he recoiled in horror. Looking down, he could see the corpses of the doctor and his wife, in the front garden. They were spreadeagled on the grass— bloodied and lifeless. Sprawled nearby were the bodies of their St Bernard dog and two milking cows. One of the hind legs of the cows had been hacked off. The whole area was buzzing with flies. A flock of crows flew down from the roof and started picking at the cow carcases.

Death was all around him, thought Rolf, and he could smell it!

Who could do such a horrible thing, he thought? His presence of mind returned and he ducked for cover. A sinister silence hung in the air.

For a full 10 minutes Rolf crouched, hard up against some rocks. He watched the house and surrounding area for any activity. He trembled. His mind was racing and he felt sick to his stomach. He had never seen such a sight. Should I bury them, he pondered? Eventually, after hearing some gun shots in the distance, he decided it was too risky. He thought about making a dash into the house to get more medical supplies, but abandoned that idea, too, because of the danger.

He realised he must warn the others. After peering around in all directions, he pulled out the pistol and loaded the cylinder. Slowly, he retraced his steps to the cover of the trees along the stream.

Running at full speed, he soon came to the gipsy camp he had previously skirted.

'What do you know about the killings over the hill?' he demanded of the pitiful group clustered near the fire.

'What killings?' the leader replied, more fearful than indignant. He was a bedraggled individual with a faded red eye-patch. 'We've only been here for an hour or so. We noticed you pass by a while back, going in the other direction.'

Thinking about it, Rolf realised they couldn't have been responsible. They had no guns and certainly no fresh meat. Quickly, he told them what he'd found.

They immediately decided to put out the fire and retreat further under the cover of the trees.

Observing the three small children, Rolf asked, 'Do you have any weapons? How can you possibly defend yourselves?'

'We only have some knives,' the man responded. 'We were robbed yesterday and we have nowhere to stay. Can you help us? I'm frightened for my young girls.'

'No, I must be on my way. Stay under cover and you'll be safe.'

The man's wife sank to her knees and implored him, 'Please, Sir. Surely you can help us?'

Rolf was surprised to see that she had lipstick on. Here they were, a destitute family, desperately trying to survive in a war zone ... and she had lipstick on. He shook his head and blurted, 'Look, take this pistol. I've got to go. I'll return later if I can.'

Turning his back on them, he threw caution to the wind and ran all the way back to the farmhouse.

Joachim was waiting near the front door for the doctor's arrival.

Rolf was exhausted on reaching the house. He had to pause for a moment before he could even speak. His sides heaved as he struggled for breath. He swallowed a big mouthful of water from his flask, then motioned for his father to go inside.

Sean was asleep. Brigitte and Marianne looked up anxiously, puzzled by the fact that Rolf had not brought the doctor with him.

'They're both dead,' he gasped, as he flopped into a chair. He buried his head in his hands.

'What do you mean, son? Are you saying Steifler and Greta are dead?' Joachim said.

'Yes, shot, I think. There was blood everywhere. The St Bernard was killed too. A couple of cows as well. It was just terrible.'

Joachim and Brigitte both sat down in shock and put their arms around each other as Rolf explained further.

Marianne went to the window and hunched silently over the sill—her shoulders heaving. Quietly, she wept. For a few moments no-one said anything.

'Who would have done such a thing?' Brigitte said. 'They were such kind souls. What's the world coming to? Greta was your godmother, Mari. They've been our friends for 20 years.'

'It could have been anyone, Mother,' Rolf said. 'There are German soldiers on the run, and some of them are half-mad.

The French Resistance is apparently taking vengeance. American troops are all over the place. Who knows! The point is that it's very dangerous out there. Father, let's load the rifle and pistol and have them ready—just in case.'

'All right, Rolf, we'll load the guns and keep a watch for any strangers. By the way, where's the other pistol?'

'Oh, I gave it away to some gipsies down by the stream. They looked like they needed protection.'

'What! You gave it away! Don't you realise how dangerous things are, right now? We needed that gun. How foolish of you, Rolf!'

'Father, settle down! The gipsy man had a wife and three young girls. He didn't have a house, like us, for shelter. He needed the gun. We've still got the rifle and one pistol.'

Joachim grunted and loaded both weapons. He knew Rolf had made the right decision. Since darkness was quickly approaching, they decided to close the shutters and do a quick check on the animals before they settled down for the night. All was quiet outside.

Sean slept fitfully for a couple of hours. When he awoke, Marianne gave him the bad news about the doctor and tried to console him. The pain in his hip worsened. Perspiration broke out all over his body. His fever raged.

Marianne cradled his head and helped him sip two mugs of hot coffee. It was laced with schnapps to help get him through the night. Some of the coffee spilled onto his beard. She wiped it away with a napkin and kissed him on the forehead.

As dawn broke the next morning, Joachim started coughing again. To avoid disturbing the others, he slipped quietly outside. He checked the livestock in the barn, then went across to the machinery shed to start the old tractor and charge the battery.

When he entered the building he was shocked to be confronted by two SS soldiers. They were in tattered Nazi uniforms.

One of the men was huge, around 200 centimetres tall, with a face disfigured by an ugly scar right across the whole of one cheek. The wound was shocking. It looked as if the injury had occurred some months ago. Joachim thought that the man would be stuck with his disfigurement for the rest of his life. The other stranger was much smaller, with a badly injured foot.

Both were distressed. They each had rifles and tried to force Joachim into letting them hide out in the shed for a week or two.

The old man would not have a bar of it. He insisted, 'You can't stay here, I want no part of this. I spent a long time in Dachau—courtesy of the Nazi regime. You'll have to go. Besides, you need hospital attention.'

The two men flatly refused to leave. They told Joachim they must hide out and rest up for at least a couple of days. He decided not to argue, but to retreat gracefully and think the matter through. He walked back to the house, shouting, 'Well at least stay in the shed and keep out of sight.'

Hearing a rumble in the distance, Joachim looked down into the valley. Snaking along the perimeter road was a long convoy of armoured personnel carriers and Jeeps moving slowly past his property.

He watched them rather absently for a while and then he noticed it. About halfway along the column there was an enclosed truck marked clearly with the international Red Cross. He rushed back to the house just as Rolf was emerging.

'Rolf, there're some medics in that convoy down there. Go down and see if you can get some help for that boy.' Joachim thought he would keep quiet about the SS men, for the moment.

Without a word, Rolf fetched his bicycle and went down the hill at full speed.

Joachim watched anxiously. He decided not to wake the others. He was still unsure about how to handle the SS men, but one thing was for certain: he wanted them out of his shed and off his property, as they were so agitated they might harm his family.

He was pleased to see, after some delay, some of the soldiers below put Rolf's bicycle into the back of the medical-support truck.

They headed towards the farmhouse, accompanied by two escort Jeeps.

Sean was already awake, and moaning in discomfort, when Joachim gave him the good news.

The family stood discreetly in the background as the Army doctor and his aide came inside and went to work with military efficiency. Within about half an hour, they had removed the bullet and all the fragments—a process which caused the young Irishman so much pain that he perspired more than ever.

While the doctor inserted some stitches to close the wound, Marianne stepped forward with a bowl of cold water. Gently, she wiped Sean's face with a cloth. He received a quick penicillin shot to one of his pale buttocks and the job was over.

'We can't take him with us you know,' said the doctor. 'There's no sense taking a wounded man into another battle zone. You'll have to care for him for a few days yet, I'm afraid. I've given him a tranquilliser, so he'll sleep most of the day. Please have him take one of these blue tablets every four hours to fight off any infection—that's the big danger now. I'm sorry, but we must go now and join the others.'

Joachim interrupted. 'Before you leave, Doctor, can you please ask the other soldiers to come inside?'

'What for?'

'Please.' Joachim insisted. The tone of his voice clearly indicated that something was wrong.

The doctor went to the doorway and beckoned for the others to enter. As soon as all were inside, Joachim told them about the SS fugitives in the machinery shed, and his concern for his family's safety.

One of them ordered, 'All of you stay in the house.'

The soldiers quietly slipped outside. Remaining under cover, they fired two teargas rounds through the shed windows. It was only a minute or so before both SS men staggered out, unarmed, with their hands clutching at their eyes.

Rolf went over to watch as the two were roughly bundled into the back of a Jeep.

The taller man, the one with the disfigured face, looked Rolf squarely in the face. In a slow, menacing voice, he said, 'One day, sooner or later, I'll get you back for this.'

Rolf was taken aback by this sudden threat. He didn't reply. He didn't know how to respond. As he moved away, the soldier's voice kept ringing in his ears: *I'll get you back for this.*

The doctor put some splints on the other man's injured foot, then returned to the house. He packed up his surgical gear and prepared to depart. As he was leaving, he turned to Brigitte and said quietly, 'I know it's not my business, but you really should get your husband to have a checkup. That cough of his sounds pretty serious to me.'

She nodded in silence, knowing herself that Joachim's health was on the decline. Over the past month she had seen the telltale spots of blood on his handkerchief. She knew something must be done sooner rather than later.

Rolf looked again at the two German soldiers in the back of the Jeep. The one with the injured foot sat in silence. He held his head in his hands and kept his injured leg extended on the floor. The taller man stood up glaring at them all. He would not sit. As the driver let out the clutch and the Jeep lurched forward, the scar-faced man reached over to grab a metal bar on the Jeep to keep his balance. His sleeve stretched back to reveal a gold watch with a plaited leather band. Rolf knew he had seen it somewhere before. The Jeep had gone about 100 metres before it dawned on him. *My God. That was Steifler's watch.*

Rolf felt sick. The chances were they'd done it, he thought. What animals! Just as well they were going off to a POW camp. He decided to tell his father, but not the others.

The rest of the day passed uneventfully. The next morning Rolf and Marianne decided to find out more about their guest, Sean Gleeson.

'Sean, where exactly are you from in America?' Marianne inquired.

'I live near a town called Ephrata, in Lancaster County, Pennsylvania,' Sean replied. 'Right smack in the middle of Amish country. Bet you don't know what that means.'

'Certainly do!' Marianne retorted. 'I've got a book on religions and civilisations around the world. It has a whole chapter on the Amish people. They originally came from Switzerland, where they were known as Anabaptists. I think they moved to Pennsylvania about 300 years ago. They've a nasty habit of "shunning" anyone who doesn't toe the line. What else! Oh yes, they are farmers who use horses for everything and their wives make those nice patchwork quilts. I've seen pictures of them.'

'Not bad,' Sean responded. He was impressed.

'Do you know exactly why they make those quilts?' Marianne challenged.

'Well, for their own use, I guess. To sell them, too, I suppose.'

'Not exactly,' said Marianne. 'They make quilts mainly because it's very much a group activity that brings all the ladies together in a work situation. Just like the men share the farming chores.'

'Sean, tell us about the farming,' Rolf interrupted, who wasn't overly keen to hear any more about quilts—patchwork or otherwise.

For the next two or three hours Sean told them all about the Amish, and Lancaster, Pennsylvania and the East Coast. He regaled them with tales about his one and only trip to New York, about visiting the sad fields of Gettysburg and about the growing pollution in parts of New Jersey. He told of his family's anguish about whether or not to sell the farm. The Amish community was making attractive offers to buy their land. Most of all, he told them that, now the war was over, America was a land of wonderful opportunity.

Although Rolf and Marianne were Bavarians through and through, the picture Sean painted was not without some attraction—given all they had been through, and the fact that Germany was now on its knees, destined for years of slow recovery.

'How did you get involved in the army in the first place?' Marianne asked.

'Actually, it was through the Civil War,' replied Sean. He went on, 'When I was still at school I got a job over summer as a pilot's lookout on one of those big barges that ply the Mississippi between Baton Rouge and New Orleans.

'I worked on the deck with an old mechanic. Great guy! He was a former history teacher who specialised in the Civil War. The old fellow told me everything I ever wanted to know, and then some, about the war. I found his stories and his ideas fascinating. He told me things that the average Joe in the street would never know. His view was that the war dragged on for two years too long; that Jefferson Davis, the West Pointer who led the South, should have surrendered once Lincoln gave emancipation to the blacks. But he kept the war going against all odds and thousands more lost their lives for no purpose. The Union had blood on its hands too. The old man told me how they came up the river in gunboats and just blasted all the plantation houses along the Mississippi, killing hundreds of innocent civilians.'

'Couldn't the Confederates just blockade their passage up the river?' Rolf asked.

'No. The South didn't have a navy. They were powerless against the gunboats. It was slaughter!'

'I would have thought all those stories would turn you off a military career,' Marianne said.

'I'm afraid not. I just got more and more interested in guns and artillery. Eventually, I joined up and did my boot camp down at Biloxi on the Gulf. Didn't think I would finish up getting shot over here in Germany, though.'

'Well, they'll send you home pretty soon to recuperate,' Rolf said.

Sean stole a glance at Marianne, but she looked away.

In the afternoon, Rolf and Sean talked more about farming. They yarned for hours about crop rotation, animal husbandry, hay baling and all sorts of agricultural matters. Inevitably, their discussion led back to the war. Rolf confided that he hated the whole damn business.

They agreed that soon the fields across Europe would be dotted with the same stone memorials and sad wooden crosses that were scattered around Gettysburg, and lined up in pitiful, symmetric rows on the sweeping lawns at Arlington.

The next day began like many others, with Joachim waking the whole house as he tried to suppress the coughing fits that racked his frail body.

Brigitte decided that she would get him to a clinic in Salzburg before the end of the month, even if they had to travel by horse and cart.

Marianne lightened up the day by asking Sean, 'How's our patient today? Has the Irishman turned green yet?'

'No, I'm just fine,' Sean replied. He smiled warmly back at Marianne, though he didn't much care for the reference to gangrene.

Sean and Marianne continued to chat and exchange thoughts on many subjects over the next couple of days. Their friendship blossomed. Marianne spent as much time as she could with the handsome young soldier. Sean thought to himself that when he returned home he would like to find an American girl with such ice blue eyes, a ready smile and a quirky sense of humour to boot.

Early on the morning of the third day, as Rolf was enjoying an early breakfast, he thought something was amiss. The cattle were shuffling around too much in the barn. He grabbed the pistol. Cautiously he ventured downstairs and opened the door a fraction. Before him crouched the gipsy with the red eye-patch. In one hand, the poor man cradled an old beret full of eggs. In the other he held a pistol—the very one that Rolf had given him earlier.

For a few tense seconds they both stood still and eyed each other in the semi-darkness. Neither said a word. At length, Rolf gestured for the man to stay exactly where he was. Then he got a small sack and put in a few potatoes and onions from a nearby storage bin. He passed them over to the gipsy. The man bowed in mute gratitude and beat a hasty retreat.

As he watched the one-eyed man disappear into the trees, Rolf noticed that a Jeep was winding its way up the hill towards him. The same doctor who had patched up Sean was on board. The medic advised Rolf that they had come to collect the Irishman. He would be driven down to the airport in Salzburg for evacuation back to the United States.

All the family was sorry to hear that Sean would be leaving them, but Marianne was distraught. When she realised that her new friend would be gone from their lives in a few minutes, she felt sick in the stomach and nauseous. Abruptly, the happiness of the past few days had come to an end.

There was so much she still wanted to tell Sean: about Ludwig's beautiful castle of Neuschwanstein she had visited as a child, about her trip to the opera in Vienna, the boat ride to Herrenchiemsee, the time the snow had been three metres deep, the wonderful day when her father had surprised her with Kaiser for her birthday. There was just so much she would like to have shared with him.

Quickly, she rushed to her room. Her heart was thumping. *Oh Jesus! Why can't he stay a few days longer?* Gathering her composure, she returned with an envelope. It contained their mailing address, a gold St Christopher medal from her first communion and a small passport-size photograph for him to remember her.

As they said goodbye, Sean slipped off his dog-tags and pressed them into her hands with the quiet promise, 'I'll see you again one day, Marianne Bauer.'

'I hope so!' she replied, confused that everything was moving so quickly.

She kissed him on both cheeks and backed away with her head bowed.

Rolf gave Sean a firm handshake. He wished him bon voyage, a quick recovery and prosperity back on the farm in Pennsylvania.

When the Jeep departed, they all waved a fond farewell. Marianne tried desperately to hold back the tears that welled in her eyes. She couldn't.

Chapter 3

Joachim's passing

Everyone in the Bauer household was overjoyed that the war was finally over. Their long journey of recovery could begin. During the summer months of June and July, Rolf and Joachim worked on repairing their fences, badly damaged during the endless years of conflict. Marianne and her mother worked most days in the vegetable garden, taking full advantage of the sunshine.

In the north of Germany, the Potsdam conference took place on the 17th of July 1945, on the outskirts of Berlin. The main participants were President Truman, for the United States, Mr Attlee, for Britain and Marshal Stalin, who represented the USSR. As a direct result of this conference, war reparations were established and Germany was split into two parts—West Germany, or the Federal Republic, and East Germany, to be later called the Democratic Republic, or the DDR.

However, the partitioning of a defeated Germany wasn't the only major event unfolding in July of 1945. While peace was coming to Europe, on the other side of the world, high drama with apocalyptic potential was being played out in the searing heat of the New Mexico desert.

It was all the direct result of an earlier letter from the eminent scientist Albert Einstein to the president of the United States. Einstein had pointed out that Nazi scientists were conducting research on uranium, heavy water and nuclear fission. This warning led to the establishment of the massive, yet clandestine, Manhattan Project. Dozens of universities and laboratories collaborated on this wartime project, culminating in the July explosion of an atomic bomb. The small, obscure airbase at Alamorgordo in New Mexico—just two hours' drive south from Albuquerque, would be etched in people's minds and find its place in history as the location of the very first atomic blast.

In August, the conflict still raging in the Pacific arena came to a horrifying conclusion. The densely populated Japanese cities of Hiroshima and Nagasaki were razed by successive blasts of atomic bombs. Emperor Hirohito had no option other than to surrender unconditionally

For Germany itself, the months of autumn were remarkably peaceful now that fighter planes and Lancaster bombers no longer occupied the skies. Trucks and tractors replaced tanks and Jeeps. Law and order was slowly re-established by the occupation forces. The process of cleaning up and rebuilding began. Bavaria hummed with activity as massive amounts of debris were cleared. Roads and bridges were inspected and public safety again got some attention. A few buildings were rebuilt, but the bricks and mortar were the easy part.

There was human debris as well. Millions of people throughout Europe had to come to terms with life after the war. They had to take stock of their situation, with loved ones gone and armies of occupation in control. For most, there was not much to live for, with no money, no housing and no work. Many committed suicide and many went mad.

In September the curfew regulations were relaxed in Germany. People could move about freely in their local area—provided they carried identification papers at all times. Nevertheless, things remained tough for the majority. Europe had undergone years of turmoil, the extent of which had not been seen since the Thirty Years War over three centuries earlier.

Families had been split and fortunes lost. Thousands of businesses had been destroyed. Recovery would take years. It would be a slow and painful process. There was the massive problem of refugees. Displaced persons moved across Germany, seeking a new start to their shattered lives. Many came from the cities of Dresden, Kassel and Leipzig as thousands fled the Russian Occupation zone of East Germany.

The country was divided into strict zones of occupation. The Bavarians felt fortunate that the Americans were assigned there. For the most part, the Americans established good working relationships with local officials, so basic infrastructures were slowly re-established. However, such was the level of hunger in the cities that people moved in droves to the country every day, wanting to barter their possessions for food. The farmers had to contend with both a regular influx of city folk and the pleas of transient refugees seeking food or shelter.

Poverty was everywhere. None of the farmers had any money, but at least they still had their land and some livestock.

It was important for those on the land to do as much as possible in the autumn, before the grip of winter closed in again. Winters were sudden, harsh and unforgiving. After the first blanket of snow, domestic animals would not survive outdoors.

Within a few weeks, Rolf and Joachim had repaired all their damaged fences. They also managed to store plenty of fodder and grain in the barn.

No relatives had come forward to claim the house and possessions of the Steifler couple, so Rolf took their three surviving cows, six starving hens and some spare lumber.

Joachim's health did not improve. He refused to travel to Salzburg to see a specialist. Instead he chose to rely on a general practitioner who lived nearby and had occasionally acted as a locum for Doctor Steifler. The GP gave him a full examination and wrote up a history of his deteriorating health through the war years.

Joachim came clean about the blood spots when he coughed, but the doctor had no access to X-ray services. They both agreed to confine treatment to medication. Joachim began taking his doses exactly as prescribed. The warmer weather seemed to give his lungs some respite, but he remained a sick man.

Joachim loved most of all to be out in the bright sunshine, doing what little he could to assist his son. As the two of them toiled in the fields, they were amazed at just how much artillery was being brought down from the mountains—huge anti-aircraft guns for the most part. They were pleased to see such armaments being removed from their beautiful countryside. Such things didn't belong in these mountains.

Brigitte gave up teaching to spend more time caring for Joachim. Meanwhile, Marianne started to take full-time kindergarten classes at the convent.

Some of the nuns had been relocated by their order to urgent relief work in the pitiful city of Warsaw, so the convent was in dire need of substitute teachers.

As she went about her duties, Marianne couldn't get Sean out of her mind. Every night at her bedside she said a little prayer for him, hopeful that one-day by some miracle their paths might cross again. She longed to see his face again, with his cute little goatee beard; to see his smile and hear his voice. She didn't even have a photograph—just the dog tags and her precious memories.

The first flurries of winter came in October. By the end of November the farm was blanketed in the white cloak of winter. The whole area took on a new face as drifts of fresh snow piled up and the trees sagged under their winter burdens. Roads became slushy and dangerous. The days grew dark and the nights longer.

Rolf was well prepared for winter. He knew that if he ran short of feed for the extra stock, there was some grain over at Steifler's place he could fetch in an emergency. They had plenty of wood stored away because some old trees had fallen during a storm in the autumn and Rolf was able to cut up dry logs.

When Christmas in 1945 approached, many people in Germany took some comfort from the fact that the war crimes trials had commenced in Nuremberg.

For Joachim, there was no comfort. His health had started to deteriorate again. He began to lose even more weight and suffer night sweats. The coughing returned with a vengeance. To make matters worse, his condition was exacerbated by a bout of influenza. His breathing became more and more laboured. His frailty was such that Brigitte decided they must take him to the hospital in Salzburg.

Marianne spoke to the Mother Superior at the convent and they were able to borrow the rusty, but reliable, convent bus for the journey. They left early on a Saturday morning, with Rolf driving.

On the outskirts of Salzburg, road repairs held them up as maintenance crew filled in yet another bomb crater. Rolf spoke to the works supervisor and explained the situation. The foreman guided him through the area and they were able to reach the hospital just before noon.

When they pulled up in front of the austere building, marked Salzburg Krankenhaus, Rolf overheard his father say, 'Brigitte, my dear, I don't think I will ever come out of here alive.'

'Nonsense,' she replied firmly, determined not to break down herself. 'You'll be just fine, once they figure out the right treatment.'

They entered the hospital and were appalled at the sight before them. Every room, every passageway and every corridor was packed with patients. Many were amputees and most appeared to be soldiers. This was the human debris of battle, still seeking treatment some six months after the conflict ended, their frightful injuries a telling reminder that the cost of war is a lingering one.

They had all kinds of afflictions. Many wore bandages concealing yet unhealed wounds and some had the same raucous cough as Joachim. Others were talking to themselves and seemed mad.

After a long delay, Joachim was eventually processed by the reception staff and escorted away for tests. They settled down to wait, standing in a corner together. It was freezing in the hospital, so Rolf and Marianne paced up and down the main hallway to keep warm. After a while, they found a vacant chair for Brigitte. She sat silently and patiently. Absently, she fingered her rosary. She feared the worst. An hour passed, then two, and still there was no word. Late in the afternoon, they had a cup of coffee, but none of them wanted to eat. They felt empty and filled with despair!

Finally, after what seemed an eternity, a doctor appeared and came directly towards them. Approaching Brigitte, he said, 'Frau Bauer, I'm afraid I have bad news for you. Your husband has tuberculosis and his condition is now complicated by pneumonia. Unfortunately, TB is a bacterial disease. It seems to have attacked his lungs as well as his kidneys and lymph nodes. If we can stabilise the pneumonia over the next 48 hours, he may pull through. But I have to tell you that he's in a critical condition at the moment. I'm sorry.'

Marianne put her arms around her mother. They both started to cry.

Rolf said to the doctor, 'Can we see him for a few minutes?'

'Of course you can, my boy. He won't know you are there because he's heavily sedated. Follow me.'

As they entered the ward, Brigitte cried out in surprise at just how much her Joachim had deteriorated in the past few hours. His eyes seemed hollow and his face was white and drawn. Joachim's breathing was very shallow. She eased herself onto a chair and kissed him gently on the forehead, unable to control her tears.

Quietly, Rolf and Marianne also pulled up chairs and joined the vigil beside their father. They sat in silence most of the time, occasionally offering words of comfort to each other. At one point, Joachim moved a little, but then he settled down again, his breathing ever shallower.

Around eight o'clock that evening, Joachim's condition worsened. The attending physician arranged for the two other patients in the ward to be transferred to another room. Marianne started to cry again. She was inconsolable. They all realised that Joachim was fading.

The doctor approached Brigitte quietly and said, 'Mrs Bauer, Father Vogel, the priest from Berchtesgaden, is nearby in the hospital chapel. Shall I get him to come?'

Brigitte nodded without hesitation. A growing awareness was creeping over her that her partner of the past 25 years was slipping away. Joachim's breathing was barely perceptible now. She thought how well he had been just a couple of weeks ago and couldn't understand why he had gone downhill so quickly.

After just a few minutes, the kindly Father Vogel silently entered the room, accompanied by two nuns. The two sisters placed a crucifix on the bedside table and lit a small wax candle on either side. Then they kneeled beside the bed with the distraught Marianne between them.

Father Vogel gently embraced Brigitte, whom he had known for many years. Without seeking her approval, he immediately started to administer the last rites of the Catholic Church. Just as baptism at the start of life is a fairly short ceremony, extreme unction at life's end is also a sacrament that only takes minutes to deliver.

However brief, it was a task that was all too familiar to this man of God. He had seen more than enough suffering and grief over the past few years. The priest opened a small satchel, kissed his violet stole and placed it on his shoulders. He commenced with the familiar words, '*In nomine Patris, et Filii, et Spiritu Sancto.*'

A minute or so later, the priest reached over and started to anoint Joachim's forehead with the sign of the cross. The old man suddenly opened his eyes and inclined his head slowly towards Brigitte.

'Water!' he gasped impatiently.

Brigitte picked up the glass on the dresser and gently put her arm behind Joachim's head. She helped him to take a small sip. He tried to speak but was unable to do so.

Brigitte kissed him lightly.

His stern face slowly relaxed into a weak smile as he gazed up at Brigitte. His eyes were glazed. A single tear ran down his cheek. Leaning close to his face, she heard him whisper, '*Brigitte, ich liebe dich*! [Brigitte, I love you!]'

And then he died.

The journey back home that night was a torturous trip for the rest of the family. Brigitte cried most of the way. She felt an overwhelming sense of loss and insecurity now that her man had been taken from her. She was not prepared for this. She worried for her children and chastised herself with feelings of guilt. She could have done more for her Joachim. Why hadn't she taken him to hospital earlier? Why had she let him work outside in the cold? When was the last time she'd told Joachim she loved him? She knew he had changed. The war had made him bad-tempered and grouchy. But she had still loved him. Oh! How much she'd loved him. But never again could she hold him.

For her part, Marianne felt enormous sadness at the loss of her dear father. She crouched in her seat, silent and still—not wanting to move or speak. Every now and then she would wipe the tears from her eyes and blow her nose. She vowed that every night, for the rest of her life, she would say a prayer for her father.

Rolf was different. He felt anger, a blind and furious anger: at the Germany that had first interred his father, and then ruined his health by forced labour and malnutrition; at Hitler, who had caused so much grief to his people; at the industrialists who had made fortunes manufacturing guns; and anger that his father had died before his time. They had planned to expand the farm after the war—to try some new crops, buy more pigs and build a new machinery shed. And Rolf felt sorrow. A deep, gut-wrenching sorrow that this man whom he had so loved and respected was gone from his life forever.

They arrived back at the farmhouse just before dawn. Each of them knew that their home would never be the same again. Rolf thought to himself that it would be a long time before laughter was again heard in this household.

The funeral was at 2 pm the following Monday.

Brigitte entered the church with Rolf and Marianne at her side. She noticed that the nuns had decorated the altar with pure white chrysanthemums—a stark contrast to the black linen draping the altar. Brigitte wondered for a moment where they could have got such blooms in the middle of winter. Then her eyes fell on the coffin and she went to pieces. She pictured Joachim's lifeless body lying pale and cold in the shiny wooden box. The thought that never again would she talk to him made the tears well up in her red eyes. Then she imagined his body lying under the cold ground. She wept.

The church was packed. Joachim's kindly nature had endeared him to so many throughout his life. The Requiem Mass began. Although they could each hear Father Vogel's monotone voice in the background, none of the Bauer family was listening. They were buried in their own thoughts. As the priest climbed the creaky pulpit stairs, they looked up.

'My dear brethren,' he began, 'Life is bitter sweet. The Lord sends us many trials. The last few years have been a time of great suffering in Germany. Those with courage have suffered the most. Joachim Bauer was a man who chose to speak up. He paid dearly for that bravery. First in prison and then ultimately with his life. Let there be no doubt that Joachim would be alive today were it not for Adolf Hitler.' He paused a moment to let his words sink in. Father Vogel was acutely aware that there would have been a few who had been diehard Nazi sympathisers in his congregation. He wanted them to squirm, and squirm they did.

The priest went on with his homily. He spoke at length of Joachim's kindness, his love for his family and his gentle nature. After the Mass, the funeral procession travelled about 800 metres along a narrow, paved road to the town cemetery.

It was a sorrowful journey, made worse by freezing rain and blustery winds. What a dreadful, damp day to put my Joachim into the frosty soil, thought Brigitte.

She walked tall and bravely for the sake of her children. It was now her duty to look after them; to console them, care for them and protect them. At the gravesite, Brigitte kept her composure. She had no tears left. Calmness came over her. She thought of the good times before the war: climbing the mountains in summer with Joachim at her side, building up the farm, their joy when Rolf and Marianne had been born, the day they had bought Kaiser. There was so much for which she was thankful. She wrapped her arms around Rolf and Marianne; *I'll look after them now.*

Soon it was all over and the body was laid to rest on a gently sloping mound, next to a rose garden. The rain had stopped. There wasn't a dry eye in the crowd. The priest said his final, '*Requiescat in pace*'. The mourners drifted away.

That evening, in her room, Marianne sat down by her lamp and wrote a long letter to Sean. She told him the whole story. She described the depth of her own sadness. How she yearned to see him again. She told him that her mother would not cry in front of them any more. She told him of the anger and bitterness that Rolf felt towards Germany. She discovered that the process of putting her feelings into words helped a little.

In the morning, she decided to go to the convent and straight back to teaching. No sense in staying home, because she would only spend all day crying.

Brigitte was going to spend the day with friends. They were due to pick her up at about 11 and take her down into Berchtesgaden for a quiet lunch.

Before she left, Marianne said, 'Mother, would you post this letter to Sean for me when you go?'

'Of course, child,' she said, putting it into her handbag.

At exactly 11 her friends arrived and Brigitte embraced them warmly, grateful for the companionship. When they got to the restaurant she had two glasses of sherry before her meal to steady herself. Surprisingly, her appetite had returned. She ate a portion of sausages and sauerkraut, as well as a little apple strudel. It seemed safe and cosy in the dining room, with a wood fire crackling away in the background. Her friends consoled her.

Brigitte had two glasses of red wine after the meal. She decided that she would never again cry for Joachim in front of her children. Moreover, she resolved to provide strength and guidance to Rolf and Marianne. Also, she would do more to help Rolf on the farm. She might try to go back to teaching. Things would work out somehow!

After a while, she took Marianne's letter from her handbag. She agonised over what to do with it. If she posted the letter, she knew that the friendship of the young couple would almost certainly develop further. One day the two could marry and Sean Gleeson would almost certainly take his bride back to

America. It was a painful decision that tore at her heartstrings. She loved her Mari so. The very thought of losing her only daughter was too painful to contemplate. With a troubled conscience and a heavy heart, Brigitte eventually tore the letter to shreds.

She confided to her hosts. 'God forgive me! I've just lost my dear Joachim to Germany. I'm not going to lose my Mari to America.'

Chapter 4

A wealthy industrialist

B rigitte was racked with guilt over the following months. She knew that she had betrayed her daughter, but she didn't have the courage to admit her sin to Mari. Every day was a wrestle with her conscience. Although the problem gnawed at her constantly, she couldn't take the fateful step of coming clean on the whole matter. Her anguish was exacerbated by a continuing lack of fulfilment in her own life. She wanted to study, to read, and to get involved in something new. Farming just wasn't enough for her. Life was so subdued and sad now that Joachim was gone. A cloak of melancholy hung over the household. Rolf was broody and quiet. Marianne was a picture of sadness.

Things did not improve throughout Germany in 1946. The country, with so much of its production capacity and infrastructure destroyed, could not support a population boosted by refugees. The Americans, who controlled Bavaria, were more interested in rebuilding their zone than the Soviet Union, for example, which took over East Germany, or indeed Britain, which had the northern part of the country and the Ruhr.

A major impediment to recovery was the post-war strategy of the Allies. The four Occupation Forces initially took a very harsh and punitive approach toward their defeated enemy. Of the four powers, America, Britain, Russia and France, America clearly led the way in promoting a widespread rehabilitation approach. However, while the US enjoyed worldwide acclaim for her enlightened approach to reform and rebuilding, the American Army did have problems in maintaining order among its own serving ranks. Hardened soldiers, away from home and still intoxicated with victory, often over-stepped the mark with their drinking and behaviour towards the defeated populace. This lack of discipline severely affected world opinion; the problem of control was made worse by the fact that there were just too many American troops stationed in Germany immediately after the war. The total population of US forces in Europe numbered around three million in 1946. A significant number wanted to go home because there wasn't enough for all of them to do, the war over and won.

Fortunately, by the middle of 1947 the number of Allied personnel throughout Europe had declined and most of those who wanted to return home were allowed to do so. However, the economic situation was still desperate for the people of Germany. The winter of 1947 was one of the most severe on record and many perished from cold, hunger and disease. Tuberculosis was in epidemic proportions in Europe. Millions remained under-nourished.

Rolf had to keep the livestock in the barn for three weeks longer than usual because the winter snow persisted. He still had plenty of grain in a storage cellar beneath the barn, safe from refugees and vagrants. Rolf made inquiries about getting fertiliser for the spring, but there was none. He would have to make do with manure again. There was so much to do on the farm, now that Joachim was gone. The labour occupied his mind and eased the bitterness in his heart.

At the end of May, when sunny skies returned, Rolf started work on an extension to the barn, using some old beams salvaged from Doctor Steifler's place. He planned to increase his holding of pigs from four to 10 and to build additional roosting perches for the poultry. Now that his father had gone, Rolf felt a compelling desire to make his own mark on the farm. He wanted to build something for himself. Perhaps one day he would be able to buy another property and extend the farm. Rolf also decided to expand their small orchard so that they would have more fresh fruit, with some to spare for preserving. For the first time, too, he planned to put in a crop of asparagus. Demand for this vegetable was steadily growing throughout Europe.

The war and Joachim's passing had changed his outlook. Becoming more independent, he was determined to make the farm as self-sufficient as possible.

Marianne continued teaching at the convent. In July of 1947 she was promoted to the important role of assistant principal— a position normally reserved for one of the clergy. She threw herself into her work with a driving sense of commitment and determination. Her duties extended from normal classes to religious education and sports sessions. Marianne particularly liked the physical-education classes in the school gymnasium during winter. They kept her fit and she always enjoyed a laugh with her students. The older children were allowed to take skiing lessons once every two weeks and Marianne conducted these sessions also. The work was fulfilling. It occupied her mind and gave her some satisfaction that she was playing her part to rebuild the country. During the week she stayed at the convent overnight, returning home every Friday evening to spend the weekends at the farmhouse.

Despite her busy life, Marianne never forgot about Sean Gleeson. Every single day she thought about him and every night she prayed for him. Please God they would meet again. Although they spoke of Sean Gleeson only occasionally, Marianne got the impression that Brigitte wasn't pleased with her continuing interest in the soldier. Once, Marianne brought home some American magazines she thought her mother might like to read. Brigitte didn't read a page of them.

Soon after that, the Mother Superior surprised Marianne by asking, 'Marianne Bauer, have you ever thought about joining our order and becoming a nun? I'm sure you would be a very worthy candidate.'

'Oh! No, Reverend Mother. I couldn't leave my mother and Rolf alone. Who'd wash Rolf's dirty overalls on the weekend?'

She withdrew quickly. Marianne preferred not to get into a discussion on this subject that had started to occupy her mind and was causing her some consternation. Besides, she wanted to have a chat to Father Vogel about her future before she decided anything.

On October 1st, the Nuremberg trials eventually came to an end. The result was that 12 senior Nazis were condemned to death. Another seven were handed prison terms and three were acquitted. The Bauers considered this result a pitiful level of retribution for the millions who had perished.

Meanwhile, Brigitte was becoming resigned to life after Joachim. She still felt paranoid about the possibility of losing her Mari to that American.

Two letters and a postcard had arrived from Sean. Brigitte kept each of them in her bag for a while, pondering what to do. Each time she destroyed them, begging her Maker's forgiveness as she did so. As best she could, she helped Rolf on the farm and warmly welcomed her daughter back home with a hearty meal every Friday evening. They talked away the whole weekend. But it wasn't enough for Brigitte. She felt unfulfilled and a little envious of her daughter, who was so gainfully employed. There was a void in her life. She started to apply for part time work in the area. Brigitte would have been happy to take up a position in a shop or restaurant, but paying jobs were scarce.

Eventually, in early 1948, she was delighted when a position as a language translator came her way. It involved the written translation into English of building contracts for a new and successful company based in Munich, called Europa Constructions.

The firm had been established specifically to capitalise on the post-war demand for rebuilding industrial premises in central Europe. The company also engaged in bridge-repair contracts and the supply of heavy-duty steel girders, trusses and lintels to other construction companies. There were two subsidiary organisations—Europa Machinery and Europa Trucking.

The machinery arm concentrated on the short-term supply of pile drivers for building sites, while the transport company hired out dump trucks for the clearing of construction and war debris.

Brigitte put on her best outfit for her job interview at the office of Europa Constructions in Salzburg. She arrived at 9:45 am for her 10 o'clock meeting and waited nervously on a wooden chair in the austere loneliness of an empty reception room. The clock on the wall ticked loudly as the minutes dragged by.

At precisely 10 am she was ushered into the office of Wolfgang Schmidt, the managing director for the company's operations in Germany, Austria and Italy. Herr Schmidt was a solidly built, professional man, dressed in a navy-blue suit, white shirt and a bow tie.

Brigitte figured he was about her age or maybe a year or two older. His hair was slicked back neatly. He smiled warmly and invited her to sit. At a side table, he poured them both a cup of coffee and thanked her for arriving promptly.

After glancing at her documents for a moment, he told Brigitte that he too had been a schoolteacher, in the beautiful city of Passau on the Danube. When she was at ease, he got down to business. First, he told her that most of the work would be for the parent company, Europa Constructions. This firm was enjoying vigorous growth, while business for each of the two subsidiaries was falling off. The job involved taking construction contracts drawn up in German or Italian and translating them into English so that his English-speaking colleagues could appraise them properly before signing.

'Mrs Bauer, I must emphasise that this is not an easy position,' he said. 'Nor is it just a technical translation job. We would want the successful candidate to gradually build up some real expertise in construction contracts, to help us identify the risks and liabilities we would face, and to recommend ways that we might re-word agreements so that our commercial exposure is limited. And to liaise with our legal people on any contentious points and generally help us to be more successful by avoiding bad contracts. Is this something you would be prepared to do?'

'Let me be frank, Mr Schmidt,' she replied without hesitation. 'I've lost my husband and both my children are grown up. Quite honestly, I get bored and depressed at the farm all day and I am looking for a challenge. Something in my life to get enthusiastic about. I am fed up with feeling sorry for myself and I'd like to get back to doing something a little more academic than feeding pigs and planting potatoes. Mr Schmidt, I have the language skills and I have studied civil engineering. Let me prove my worth to you. Give me a trial for a couple of months, and if you're not entirely satisfied, I'll resign.'

'Sounds a reasonable proposition. You do have good credentials, Mrs Bauer, but unfortunately I have two other candidates to see today. To be fair, I can't make a decision until I have interviewed them as well. But I'll make my selection tonight and have my assistant send letters out tomorrow. Would you like to have another coffee with me before you leave?'

'Certainly,' she replied, and took the opportunity to talk more with Mr Schmidt about the challenges of being a schoolteacher. They conversed idly for almost an hour before she left. Brigitte found that she liked this very polite gentleman from Europa Constructions.

For his part, Wolfgang Schmidt had already made up his mind who was going to be the successful applicant. At one point he lowered his guard and mentioned to Brigitte that if she got a typewriter she could do some of the translation work at home. He knew this would save her the long bus journey down into Salzburg every day.

That evening Brigitte told Rolf she was quietly optimistic of being successful. But she dared not reveal to her son that after only a couple of hours she felt a certain warmness towards the confident, well-dressed businessman she had met only that morning.

Rolf was delighted for his mother. It was the first time she had seemed enthusiastic about anything since Joachim had passed away.

Meanwhile, Marianne had made an appointment to see Father Vogel. She walked slowly and thoughtfully towards the church, wondering just how to begin. The old priest met her at the door to his office at the side of the presbytery and took the initiative.

'What's troubling you, my child?'

'Father, I don't know what to do with my life. I'm so confused. On the one hand I love teaching children. That is my biggest joy. But what about the rest of it? Sometimes I feel that I'd like to enter the convent and become a nun. And then there's Sean.'

'Who's Sean?'

'Oh, he's a young American soldier. He was wounded and stayed with us for a few days at the end of the war. I really liked him, Father. It was good just to be with him. The pleasure of his company, as they say, I could happily marry a man like Sean and raise a family.'

'Well, have you seen him since? Does he write to you?'

'No, he's back in Pennsylvania somewhere and I've never had a letter from him, but I know he felt something for me, too.'

'How old are you now Marianne?'

'I am 20, Father, almost 21 in fact.'

'Well, young lady, you have plenty of time. I wouldn't rush into anything. The world has many options and we need to be careful in the choosing. I'll get you some information about other convents in Europe. You've only seen the teaching side. There are nuns who do missionary and charity work. Others who care for the sick and some convents, as you know, are contemplative. So I'll get you some documents to read, but it'll probably take a month or two. You know how mail delivery is these days.'

'Thanks, Father!'

'Now, I suggest you write a note to this American to find out whether he has the same feelings for you. Don't be too obvious about it. Just tell him what's been happening lately and ask how he's getting along. If he doesn't reply or show any interest, you may as well put that behind you.'

'Father, you always give such sensible advice. I'll write to him again tomorrow. Thanks again and good night.'

The next day Brigitte was delighted to receive a formal letter of confirmation from Europa Constructions. The offer invited her to start work in two weeks at the Salzburg office. She prepared a thank-you letter to Mr Schmidt and decided that she would visit the library to see if she could borrow some books—specifically on the building industry and contract law.

Meanwhile, Marianne carefully worded her letter to Sean. She chided him on the one hand for not responding to her previous correspondence, but at the same time wrote that she often thought about him and would like to keep in touch. In the envelope she included a class picture taken a few weeks earlier in the school gymnasium. The photograph showed her standing proudly behind her a class of beaming young students sitting on a vaulting horse.

Marianne asked her mother Brigitte to post the letter on her way to the library. Yet again Brigitte agonised. She felt more secure now that she had nailed down a job for herself. Still, she couldn't bear the thought of her only daughter leaving the country. At length she tore the envelope to shreds—again persuading herself it was the right thing to do. At the library, she was able to get two recent books on contract law and a useful reference manual on building regulations.

Brigitte threw herself into her new job with the passion of someone starved of mental challenges. In the first month she caught the bus into the office every day, instead of attempting any work from home. Brigitte had her hair cut shorter. She brushed it back to give herself a more professional look. To further her change of look, she bought two lightweight linen suits and two smart woollen outfits as well as three smart skirts. In order to lose a few kilograms, she started to forfeit lunch and take a brisk forty-minute walk instead. She gave up sugar in her coffee and watched her diet. In the office, she built good relationships with the other staff, impressing them with her industrious and cooperative approach. Brigitte developed a feel for the Europa Constructions business surprisingly quickly, for a schoolteacher-cum farm-woman. Soon she could discuss the issues of prime contracting, limitations of liability, penalty payments, subcontractor agreements and so forth. Her technical translation work was first class. Wolfgang normally worked from the Munich office. Though she occasionally glimpsed him on his flying visits to their Salzburg premises, the two did not speak again until four months after she had started.

He called on her at about 10 am one morning and asked her to go to lunch with him in a nearby restaurant. Something about extra responsibilities, he intimated. She gladly accepted the invitation, but was concerned about more work because she was already taking some home on the weekends. Wolfgang explained first of all that he had received glowing reports on her progress.

He said he had personally reviewed much of her work and thanked her for her efforts with his customary politeness. He went on to explain that he wanted to extend her role from backroom contract administration work into the operational side of the business. Specifically, he wanted her to undertake a short trouble-shooting assignment. The problem, he explained, was that his company was losing profit.

Europa Constructions could win big contracts, but often lost money in their execution. There were just too many things going wrong: subcontractors not meeting their obligations on time, deficient materials, labour disputes, industrial accidents, pilferage and so on. He wanted her to review all their big projects over the past two years, to compile a list of the problems encountered, and to assess them in order of impact and suggest remedies.

'Brigitte, I realise this all may seem a bit daunting, but it is largely an information gathering and analysis exercise. I believe you can do it. You would be assigned a full-time assistant in the Salzburg, Munich and Milan offices. I would need you to start on this undertaking immediately and give me a report in three months' time. What do you say?'

Brigitte took a moment to absorb the impact of it all. She relaxed her anxious frown and replied, 'Mr Schmidt, I'd be delighted to take on the assignment, but what about my regular translation work?'

'Talk to Karl back in the office about that. I'll authorise him to put on a part-time translator for a few months. And, by the way, please call me Wolfgang.'

'Very well, Wolfgang, you'll have my report on time, in three months. Thank you for showing such confidence in me.'

They each smiled and shook hands on the deal. Brigitte thought he held onto her hand for a little too long. She didn't mind.

Later that day, as she was talking to Karl Becke, the office supervisor, she asked quietly, 'Karl, is Wolfgang just the managing director or does he own shares in Europa Constructions as well?'

'Goodness, Brigitte, don't you know? Wolfgang Schmidt owns the whole lot. He's a millionaire. Several times over, I dare say.'

In the following month, Brigitte again threw herself into her work, determined to meet the three-month deadline they had agreed.

Rolf was also fully occupied and forever busy on the farm. He wanted to increase productivity and consolidate their household position for the future.

Marianne remained unsettled. She read the brochures from Father Vogel, but wasn't really interested in starting off somewhere else. Still dismayed at not receiving any response from Sean, she became more melancholy than ever. After a few depressive months, she eventually made the decision to enter the local convent as a probationary novice.

The Mother Superior was delighted with her decision. She looked forward to welcoming Marianne to her cloistered community. In January of 1949, Marianne Bauer took her vows of poverty, chastity and obedience for three years.

Brigitte and Rolf watched the ceremony with mixed feelings of pride and sadness. Neither really wanted to see Marianne leave their family home. Brigitte shed a few tears when she saw her Mari adorned in her black, novice's habit.

Marianne's room in the convent was plain and austere. It was absurdly small. More than that, it was always cold. The few pieces of furniture had suffered the ravages of time. Only a small mat, threadbare in the centre and frayed at the edges, covered the wooden floor. A narrow, leadlight window provided the only source of natural light.

On the ledge beneath the window, Marianne nurtured three pelargonium cuttings in clay pots. Even these plants refused to flourish in the cold confines of her room.

As it happened, Marianne did not warm to convent life so much as tolerate it. Most of all, she felt the convent's rules on the matters of vanity and pride were silly. The notion of having to walk against the wall down a corridor to show humility, rather than charging straight down the centre, seemed extreme. Equally, she was perplexed by the ruling that when going to chapel one had always to kneel next to someone who was there already. Even the general discipline of keeping one's eyes downcast did not sit well with this vibrant and fun-loving Bavarian. Yet, she tolerated it. There just didn't seem to be many opportunities in her life. The convent gave her some sense of security and purpose.

Compliance with convent regulations wasn't the only problem. Soon after Marianne joined the cloistered community, another novice from the previous year's intake began to take an unhealthy interest in her. This novice was a frail and timid girl from Switzerland named Karin Zuller, who could often be seen standing alone, talking to herself. Even her nun's habit could not hide the skeletal features of this emaciated creature, who took every opportunity to sit or stand next to Marianne.

Marianne quite liked Karin, but she thought she needed psychiatric help. She did nothing to encourage her friendship. Indeed, Marianne firmly pushed Karin away whenever she approached too closely or touched her. Bodily contact was absolutely forbidden in the convent.

Marianne felt sorry for Karin. She was a troubled and pitiful soul, desperately searching for someone to love in the coldness of her convent world. Marianne couldn't understand why the Mother Superior had not organised some help for the disturbed young woman. It wasn't just her gaunt appearance; Karin was clearly suffering some kind of mental breakdown.

One day, Marianne asked two of the other Sisters about Karin. She was told in whispers that the girl was the only daughter of a wealthy Swiss real-estate tycoon. Further, that he paid the convent very handsomely to keep his girl, rather than have her committed to an asylum.

Brigitte missed her Mari, who did not come home on weekends any more. They met for only a short time at Mass on Sundays now.

The three months didn't take long to pass, and Brigitte managed to finish her work assignment on time. She asked Karl Becke at the office to arrange a meeting, so she could review her findings with Wolfgang Schmidt.

Word came back the next day that Wolfgang was busy, personally overseeing four important projects in Venice. She would have to travel down there for a couple of days to meet him. He would send a car.

On the picturesque journey to Innsbruck, then up over the Brenner Pass into Italy, Brigitte was anxious that her analysis and recommendations would be up to her employer's expectations. At the same time, she looked forward to meeting Wolfgang again.

When she arrived, she was taken directly to his hotel on the Rio San Caterina canal, where there was a message from Wolfgang, The note indicated he would be occupied all day, but that they would meet over dinner that evening at 7 pm. He had arranged a private room where they could eat at one table and work at another larger one nearby.

With a couple of hours to kill before their meeting, Brigitte asked at reception for advice on how to see some of the city quickly. Leaving the hotel, she walked briskly towards the

Grand Canal. She was surprised that there was no soil anywhere—just cobblestones. Brigitte took a gondola as far as the Rialto Bridge, then made her way by foot through the streets and alleys towards the square of San Marco. She couldn't help noticing how the dirty canals contrasted with the crystal clear streams of her native Bavaria. Nevertheless, she admired the beauty of the old buildings, especially the grandeur of St Mark's Basilica and the towering clock tower nearby. The huge square, covered entirely in paving slabs of grey trachyte stone, seemed incongruous in a city so pressed for space. The rich Byzantine and Renaissance architecture of the buildings reminded Brigitte of the lovely Baroque churches which dotted her native Bavaria. Looking up at the four magnificent metal horses above the main facade of the Basilica, she remembered reading a history book that mentioned these four treasures. Apparently, there was no information available anywhere on their origin or even the composition of the metal alloy. Speculation was that they had probably been brought from the hippodrome of Constantinople in about the 13th century. The only fact quoted in the book was that Napoleon had taken them to Paris after he conquered Venice, and that they had been subsequently returned to the canal city during the Austrian regime.

Her thoughts returned to the present. Brigitte got her bearings and made her way back to the hotel, where she eased herself into a luxuriously warm bath to prepare herself physically and mentally for the meeting ahead.

The dinner itself was a fairly quiet affair—both of them were a little nervous. Immediately afterwards, they got down to work.

Brigitte reviewed the projects she had analysed. Altogether, she had assessed the performance of 37 construction jobs.

Brigitte showed Wolfgang how she had grouped all the problems encountered into specific categories—contractual problems, weather problems, problems with local regulations and so forth.

Finally, she outlined how she had listed each category in terms of its financial impact on the profitability of Europa Constructions. This exercise showed clearly that about 70 percent of Wolfgang's margin erosion on profits was directly attributable to poor supervision, safety observance and labour control by the site foremen he employed. She noticed that he was impressed by her insight, and pressed on to discuss her plan. Her recommendations included an immediate performance review with all site foremen, the sacking of those who didn't shape up, and after-hours training for the remainder.

The education Brigitte proposed would be targeted towards resolving the most recent trends in poor construction results, so that a continuous improvement cycle was established.

The only recommendation Wolfgang did not immediately accept was her final suggestion: that he should pay every site foreman a confidential bonus for those jobs brought in on time and within 5 percent of the original budget. He said that he would have to think about that one!

When they finished, Wolfgang thanked her profusely for her efforts and walked her to a small wine bar at a nearby hotel for drinks. He explained that he had had to get personally involved in the four jobs in Venice because there was the possibility of a great deal of flow-on business. The projects were all similar, but at the same time all different. He told her that buildings in the city were subject to progressive subsidence, as the ebb and flow of the tides weakened their foundations.

Each job involved the construction of a new lower floor above the existing, which was subject to periodic flooding. But the works had to be designed and executed with great precision so that the overall stability of the old buildings did not suffer. The difference was in the additional modifications to be carried out on each, in conjunction with the flooring works. In two of the buildings, a complete refurbishment of the fascia was required, with repainting and re-glazing. One of the others required an entirely new roof and the final building had to be remodelled for opening as a new hotel. Wolfgang considered he might even start a new company just to concentrate on refurbishment work in Venice. However, he did not confide to Brigitte that a great part of his personal involvement had to do with greasing the palms of local authorities to avoid costly bureaucratic delays.

They talked on until about 2 am, about all sorts of things, including Wolfgang's childhood in the beautiful city of Passau to the north. He told her proudly of his time as an altar boy at St Stephen's Cathedral—one of the most famous baroque churches in all of Europe. And how he had often acted as tour guide for parishioners and visitors who wished to know more about the massive church organ. He still remembered the statistics—largest church organ in the world, 17,000 pipes, and the longest, over 11 metres, with five sets of pipes in the nave of the church. Yes, he remembered it all.

He told her, too, how he loved to look down from the bell towers at the delightful confluence of the Danube, Inn and Ilz rivers. Brigitte sensed that Wolfgang really missed the beautiful city. While she had never visited Passau herself, she had seen it described in a book with the flattering epithet of 'the Bavarian Venice'.

For her part, she spoke fondly about her troubled daughter and her industrious farmer son. All the while, she felt a growing affection for this man who had come into her life so suddenly. After their short walk in the bracing evening air back to the hotel, Wolfgang gently kissed her on the cheek.

He was surprised somewhat by his own boldness. 'Thank you for a lovely evening, Brigitte. I'll be busy all day tomorrow with my architects. Please explore the city some more and let us meet again at seven in the lobby for dinner.'

For the next three nights they went out together, choosing a different restaurant. Each time they grew closer, feeling more and more comfortable with each other. On their fourth and final night in Venice, Wolfgang took her to an intimate little seafood restaurant on the nearby island of Muranto.

When their meal was finished, they each had three glasses of chianti and some exquisite cheese that was a house specialty. Reluctantly, at about midnight, they caught a gondola back to the hotel.

On the way, as he held Brigitte in his arms, Wolfgang remarked, 'Brigitte, we seem to be getting on just splendidly. Do you think that one day you and I will be married?'

Without a moment's hesitation, she replied, 'I certainly hope so!'

Chapter 5

A family apart

Wolfgang appointed Brigitte as his executive assistant in the summer of 1949. He gave her sign-off authority and a wide range of responsibilities. Soon she had about 20 staff, reporting directly to her. Brigitte responded well to her new role and demonstrated a wide range of untapped business skills, surprising even herself with how much she enjoyed the new challenges.

She and Wolfgang grew even closer as she spent more and more time in his company. Often the two of them worked alone, burning the midnight oil. Eventually Wolfgang plucked up the courage to ask her to relocate to Munich. He wanted her near him all the time—to have her by his side at the headquarters of Europa Constructions.

'But where would I stay?' she asked.

'Well, I've got an empty apartment next to mine on Richard Strauss Strasse in Bogenhausen. It's lovely there right next to the Isar.'

'Wolfgang, my dear, I'd like to move in next to you, but I couldn't do so in good conscience. What would Rolf and Mari think, for goodness sake?'

'Why don't we get married, then, Brigitte? You know how I feel about you.'

'Give me a week to discuss it with Rolf and Mari, then I'll let you know. I'd love to become your wife, Wolfgang, but my children must be comfortable with it all. You do understand, don't you?'

'Of course, Brigitte, take your time. I appreciate your position.'

Two days later she spoke to both Rolf and Marianne.

To her surprise, neither was upset that she wanted to marry again, even though they had each loved Joachim so dearly.

Marianne hugged her mother. She told her she and Rolf had already discussed the prospect. They were both happy to see her take the plunge. Each of them had met Wolfgang several times and they could sense that he really cared for their mother.

They decided to have the wedding as soon as possible. It was set for six weeks later, at the end of August in the small church at Berchtesgaden. The nuns at Marianne's convent insisted on preparing all the flowers and the altar. Rolf decided he would cater for an outdoor reception up at the farmhouse.

On the day, the church was jam-packed with invited guests. Many well-wishers crowded the pathway outside. It was a glorious summer day for the wedding at 2 pm. Brigitte and Wolfgang beamed with joy. Many in the congregation shed a tear for them. Happiness had been fairly hard to come by lately. The highlight of the ceremony was a solo rendition of *Ave Maria* by Marianne—unaccompanied. From a microphone high on the choir balcony, her clear soprano voice permeated every part of the church and floated outside. Perfect pitch and perfect diction! She captivated the congregation. They listened to her every note in absolute silence.

Brigitte was surprised by the improvement in Mari's singing. She felt so proud of her daughter.

As Rolf watched from the front row, he noticed how the past few years had taken a heavy toll on Father Vogel.

After a few photographs, the whole congregation piled into all sorts of vehicles and made their way up to the farmhouse. Marianne was glad to see that some of the nuns from the convent had kept their promise and were going to attend also.

Rolf handled the reception very well. He had laid out trestles in front of the house, with some long wooden benches he had made up especially for the occasion. Everyone was relaxed. They had a great time. There was plenty of food and perhaps a little too much beer. As the afternoon wore on, Rolf gave all the young children a ride on Kaiser, sometimes with three or four on his back. The white stallion was slower and more docile than in his younger days.

At one point, Marianne surprised everyone as she kicked off her shoes and jumped on Kaiser for a quick gallop—her habit flying about in the wind. Father Vogel looked up at the strange spectacle. He stole a little smile to himself. He had seen far too much misery lately to be overly concerned with such an outburst of spontaneous fun.

Around eight o'clock, as darkness set in, everyone packed up and headed for home. Brigitte and Wolfgang thanked them all warmly for their company, good wishes and gifts.

One man, a distant relative of Brigitte's, who seemed a bit dishevelled, took the liberty of asking Wolfgang about giving him a job. Brigitte protested, but Wolfgang insisted on writing down the man's name and address. He wanted to impress his bride on this—their special day.

After the happy couple had departed for their honeymoon in Italy, Rolf and Marianne both felt a bit low now that the euphoria of it all was over. Maybe life was passing them by!

By the end of September, Brigitte and Wolfgang had combined the two apartments in Richard Strauss Strasse, making one their living quarters and the other a work area for Europa Constructions. The company was going from success to success. They worked about 12 hours a day, six days a week, resting only on Sundays.

Brigitte's involvement in the firm and in her married life was such that she had time to visit Marianne only every couple of months. She didn't manage to see Rolf once between September and Christmas, though she did drop him a postcard from Milan and one from Venice.

Rolf kept in touch with Marianne every month. He had an agreement to supply the convent with firewood during the winter. Each month he delivered a load with his old truck and spent an hour or so with his sister. She enjoyed his regular visits. When he came with his January load, she gave him a thick polo-neck jumper she had knitted in cashmere wool over Christmas.

By April, the weather had started to warm up and a few trees were covered in blossom. About halfway along the garden path, between the church and the convent, there was a paved square, entirely surrounded by a bed of colourful pansies. On one side there were picnic chairs and tables; on the other, a small grotto dominated by a carved wooden crucifix. As the weather warmed, any relatives of the nuns who attended Mass would usually walk to the square and have a chat at the tables before going their separate ways. Typically, those nuns who were alone at the service usually stopped for a quick prayer at the grotto, then moved on quickly to the convent to help prepare for their communal lunch.

On the third Sunday of April, Marianne knew that Rolf would not be at Mass, so she left the church promptly and headed down the familiar path. Like a good novice, she kept her eyes downcast. Because the sun was shining through the low cloud and it wasn't too cold, she decided to stop at the grotto and say a quick prayer for Joachim.

In front of the crucifix, there was a small step to kneel on, and a rail to rest one's elbows. Because the step was narrow, with bushes at either side, it was customary to wait until someone had finished praying, instead of squeezing in alongside.

Marianne saw there was no-one else at the grotto, so she kneeled and closed her eyes in prayer. A shuffling movement by her side distracted her. She sensed that someone had knelt down right next to her. Opening her eyes, she looked discreetly to her side and saw it was a man wearing some kind of uniform. She felt like saying some words of protest at his intrusion, but he jumped in before her and said, 'Hello, Marianne!'

She jumped up in surprise. In a flash, she realised that the man standing only an arm's length from her was Sean Gleeson.

'Sean! Oh my God! It's really you!' She threw herself at him and buried her head in his shoulder. Passers-by looked on in wonder. Tears trickled down her cheeks. At length she said, 'Sean, it's wonderful to see you. I thought we'd never meet again.'

He kissed her gently on the forehead and replied, 'Well, I've just been assigned to the base at Augsburg. I got here last week and found out from Rolf last night that you were here. He told me about your father. I'm so sorry, Marianne. He was a good man, brave and kind—a man of conviction. I liked and respected him. Last night I stayed at the farmhouse. Rolf and I had a few beers and talked non-stop until two in the morning. I couldn't wait to see you today. I must say I was devastated to hear that you'd entered a convent.'

'Well, you should have replied to my letters,' she retorted quickly. 'Was that too much to ask? Just a letter or postcard in reply!'

'Say, wait a minute, Marianne. First of all, I've never received any letters from you. Secondly, I did write to you at least three times. I used exactly the address you gave me.'

'Well, that's odd,' she replied, puzzled by what could have happened.

Then she stood back from him and said, 'Let me take a good look at you now. Yes, you've put on a few kilos but you do look a handsome devil in that uniform, Sean. Still got that little beard, I see. How's the hip?'

'It's just fine, thanks to your help,' he laughed. And then seriously, 'Marianne, you look just lovely, even in that monkey suit. It's the first time I've seen a nun with freckles across her nose. Are you happy in the convent? Do you really want to spend the rest of your life cloistered away like that?'

'Sean, I'm just a novice at the moment. The novitiate is a kind of probationary thing. You know—to see whether you're really prepared to take the lifetime vows. Frankly, I'm not sure what I want to do. I must say that I'm very pleased to see you again, though.'

'Could we spend some time together, then? You told me once you wanted to show me that castle Neuschwanstein. Well, it's not far from Augsburg, and I can borrow a Jeep. What do you say?'

'I'll have to discuss things with the Mother Superior. Her name is Mother Magdalene. I can raise it with her straight after lunch, but I don't think she'll agree. In any case, it will take some time to get an answer. Can you go somewhere local here and get yourself a meal, then ring the bell at the convent, say, at two o'clock? By then I might have some indication.'

'No problem. I'll get a bite, then have a look around.'

'All right. See you at two then,' Marianne said with a big smile. She turned and hurried down the garden path.

Sean had a bowl of broth and a few white sausages for lunch, washed down with apple juice. He longed for a beer, but thought he shouldn't have liquor on his breath when he got to the convent. His stomach churned in anxious anticipation when he rang the brass bell in front of the nunnery.

Marianne answered the door and told Sean that the Mother Superior had insisted that she discuss her request during the week with Father Vogel, before she made any decision. As phone calls to novices were discouraged, Marianne said she would get a note to Sean as soon as she had any news. He wrote down his Augsburg address and held her hands briefly for a couple of precious moments. Marianne had to return to her duties, so they said a fond goodbye.

Sean felt so happy to have seen Marianne again, but disappointed not knowing when next they would meet.

On the following Wednesday, the Mother Superior met Father Vogel. She explained Marianne's situation and the circumstances surrounding her extraordinary request to spend a weekend off in the company of a male acquaintance. The priest did not respond immediately. She went on to say the request should be refused outright, as an unacceptable risk to Marianne's vocation. To her surprise, Father Vogel took a different point of view. He contended that Marianne had probably entered the convent seeking refuge rather than fulfilment, and that for months now she had clearly been despondent, He added that they had no right to play God and deny the couple an opportunity to test their relationship.

The elderly priest and the protective nun continued to debate the issue. At times their discussions became heated. Father

Vogel emphasised that Marianne had not fully come to terms with the loss of her father. Eventually, he insisted that the Mother Superior go along with Marianne's request.

Mother Magdalene wasn't at all happy with this outcome. However, she knew that the priest outranked her. They agreed that things should proceed quickly, so that the whole matter was resolved one way or the other.

On Thursday morning, at the Army base, Sean Gleeson received a telegram which read, 'Come to convent at ten Saturday morning for decision.'

Sean left the Augsburg base at 7 am and drove east along the autobahn as the early-morning fog lifted. He arrived at three minutes to 10, feeling hopeful but apprehensive.

A stern-looking nun opened the door and took charge immediately. 'Good morning,' she said. 'My name is Mother Magdalene. Please come into the front room.'

On entering, he could see Marianne was already seated. Before he could say a word, the Mother Superior continued, 'Mr Gleeson, Marianne has told me all about your situation. What are your intentions, exactly?'

'Well, Mother, I'm not sure. It's over four years now since we've seen each other. I'd just like to be with her for a little while.'

'And what of her vocation?' Mother Magdalene said firmly.

'Mother, I'm still a novice and—'

'Sister, let me handle this please. Now, are you a Catholic, Mr Gleeson?'

'Absolutely, Mother,' Sean replied quickly. 'My parents are both from County Cork in the old country.'

Mother Magdalene paused for a moment and looked out the window. At length, she turned back and said, 'I've had a long discussion with Father Vogel about this matter. We don't exactly see eye to eye on this. However, here's what we propose. This matter must be resolved quickly. I don't want one of my novices distracted from her vocation and responsibilities. Sister, against my better judgment you may spend next Saturday and Sunday with Mr Gleeson, provided you are chaperoned at all times. I suggest your brother, Rolf. You must not wear your habit at all on the weekend. Get a beret or something to cover your head. I want you back in this convent by 10 o'clock on the Sunday night. At that time you should either re-affirm your desire to continue in this community, or pack your bags and leave. Now, how does that sound?'

Marianne and Sean glanced at each other for a moment, then nodded in unison. Each of them was very satisfied with the arrangement.

'All right, one final matter. Sister, you will not discuss this matter with any of the other nuns, and you must say goodbye to this young man now and go back to your duties.'

At that point, another nun entered the room and whispered something to the Mother Superior. Mother Magdalene turned to Sean and said, 'I have a small emergency and I need to leave you now, Mr Gleeson. It was nice to meet you. God bless!'

Realising that they were alone at last, Sean gave Marianne a big hug and said, 'I'll pick Rolf up at seven next Saturday, then call for you at about nine. Is that okay?'

'It's more than okay, Sean, it's just wonderful. I'll be waiting. Don't get accidentally shot in the hip, or I'll have to cut your pants off again.'

He turned to leave, but she called him back.

'Sean, there's something I hadn't thought of. It's a bit embarrassing really.'

He grasped her hands and said reassuringly, 'Come on, Marianne, out with it!'

'Well, I'd like to get a couple of things in town during the week, but it's this poverty thing, you know. We're not allowed to keep even one pfennig in our rooms and I won't see Rolf at all this week.'

He laughed at her awkwardness, and replied, 'Is that all? You had me worried there for a minute.'

He pulled a wallet from his hip pocket and put two hundred marks into her hand, then closed her fingers over the notes.

Sean left the convent smiling to himself—happy with the day's results.

During the week, Marianne took Mother Magdalene's advice and bought herself a maroon beret to cover her hair. It had been trimmed severely to accommodate a nun's veil. She also got a new black skirt, a pink sweater, a pair of high heels and some make-up to camouflage her freckles. Finally, she bought a small, but expensive, bottle of perfume.

In compliance with Mother Superior's wishes, she carried her new things back into the convent discreetly. However, she did confide in her two closest friends about the weekend arrangements.

The next Saturday morning, Marianne ate her breakfast quickly and jumped into the communal shower at about 6:30. The water was only lukewarm, so she didn't turn on the cold tap. A cold draught coming into the room interrupted her thoughts about the day ahead. She sensed the door had been opened. Quickly, she grabbed a towel to cover herself. She slid back the shower door and saw a tearful Karin before her.

'You're leaving,' Karin whimpered, 'You're leaving. You can't go Marianne, I love you. Don't leave me here. I'll kill myself.'

Marianne embraced her and said, 'Karin, I'm not sure what I'm going to be doing. I do know that you need some help. My advice is for you to get out of here. Go home for a while and be with your family. You need support. I can't talk to you right now. Dry your eyes and go back to your room.'

Unfortunately for Marianne, Karin would not be put off so easily. Abruptly, she threw herself on the floor and wrapped both arms around Marianne's ankles in a desperate attempt to keep her from leaving. Marianne was nonplussed by this sudden gesture. She grabbed at a nearby cupboard to keep her balance.

At that point the door opened again and Mother Magdalene peered in. 'What's going on here?' she demanded.

'Someone told Karin I might be leaving and she's a bit upset,' Marianne replied defensively.

'Is that any reason for such undignified behaviour?'

'Mother, please don't you try to blame me for this. Karin obviously needs help. You know it and I know it. You should send her home. Send her anywhere in fact. She's slowly going crazy in here. Now, if you'll excuse me, I have to get dressed.'

With that she unceremoniously pushed Karin out of the shower room into the passage next to the Mother Superior, and slammed the door behind them.

Sean and Rolf arrived in the Jeep a little early at 8:45. Marianne was in the foyer ready to leave. She was desperate to get going, but decided not to tell the two men about her disturbing encounter.

Sean thought she looked just beautiful in her new black skirt and high heels, topped off with the bright pink sweater and maroon beret. Soon they were on their way.

On Rolf's advice they drove directly to the Salzburg-Munich autobahn and then headed towards Rosenheim.

The sun shone brightly overhead in a cloudless blue sky. Sean told them all about his life over the past four years; how he had hated the desk job he was saddled with while he recovered; that he had also disliked the postings he'd had in Washington and North Carolina before he'd been moved back to Germany. He chose not to reveal how much pressure he'd applied to get a transfer back to Europe.

When they came to the scenic lake called Chiemsee, they stopped for half an hour and had some coffee from a flask Rolf had packed. Marianne surprised them by producing a tin of gingerbread biscuits from her overnight bag. She told Rolf all about Ludwig's unfinished castle on an island in the middle of the lake that could only be reached by boat.

Sean wondered just how many castles this King Ludwig the Second had built.

Soon they were on their way again, thoroughly enjoying each other's company. Just after Rosenheim, Marianne suggested they turn left and head down through Bad Tolz.

'No, Marianne, it will slow us down too much,' Rolf said. 'It's quicker to follow the autobahn right through Munich, and go down the other side past Landsberg.'

'Oh, please, Rolf. Let's go my way so that we can see Oberammergau. I've never been there and we could stop quickly at Linderhof while we're there. Sean, you'd like to see Oberammergau, wouldn't you? You know! It's the place where they have the passion play every 10 years. People even come from America to see it. It's booked out for years ahead!'

'I don't mind,' Sean replied. 'Whatever you guys want to do.'

'All right, we'll take the next exit,' said Rolf. He went on, 'Maybe we should stay in Garmisch overnight. Sean, you be careful, she's got you under her thumb already.'

They drove more slowly now, taking in the beauty of the Bavarian countryside. Arriving at Oberammergau at noon, they spent two hours walking the streets, admiring the wooden carvings for which the old town was renowned.

Sean bought Marianne a small-carved nativity scene of superb workmanship in different coloured woods. They had a chicken salad for lunch, together with some dark beer from the Andechs monastery. Sean made a mental note to visit that establishment one day and collect a larger supply.

In the afternoon, they travelled the small distance to Ludwig's favourite castle, Linderhof. It was an opulent building by anyone's standards, both inside and out, reflecting the King's baroque fantasies. The conducted tour took over an hour and, when the guide described the building as Ludwig's wedding castle, Marianne and Sean glanced at each other and shared a quick smile. When their visit was finished, it was too late for them to get to their original destination—the fairytale castle of Neuschwanstein.

They decided to drive on to the twin towns of Garmisch-Partenkirchen and stay there overnight. Late in the afternoon, as the cloak of dusk was descending, they checked in at a small inn right in the heart of the town and took three rooms on the first floor. The trio decided to meet in one hour.

It was a night to remember! Such fine food, all the singing and dancing, and there was the beer! Both Sean and Rolf each had four full litres of dark beer during the evening, between ample helpings of sausages and sauerkraut.

Marianne had only one litre of beer, but she more than did her share when it came to the singing and dancing. In her bright pink sweater and with radiant cheeks flushed by alcohol, she was a far cry from the demure novice Sean had met two weeks earlier.

After he had put most of the chairs up onto tables as the customary hint for closing, the innkeeper eventually had to ask them to leave. All the other patrons and most of the staff had already gone home. Marianne put an arm around each of her men and herded them step-by-step up to the first floor. She pushed Rolf into his room first, then planted a kiss fairly and squarely on Sean's lips. It brought an instant grin to his drunken face.

The next morning they slept in. No-one had much of an appetite for breakfast.

Eventually, they headed off just before 11. On arrival at the tourist town of Fussen, they had a quick cup of coffee before going on to the castle. They were delayed a little because Rolf insisted on having a large helping of apple strudel with his coffee. There weren't many tourists about. They easily found a spot in the car park below the castle.

Marianne kicked off her high heels and put on flats for the trek ahead. They set off and she soon ran ahead. Marianne yelled back that she could beat any soldier or farmer to the top. Rolf decided not to chase her, because his bad leg still made running awkward.

However, Sean took off in pursuit. After about 70 metres, he caught up. He wrapped his arms around her and lifted her off the ground. Sean swung her around and around. 'Even a man with an injured hip could catch up to you,' he gasped.

Rolf watched contentedly, in the background. He had not seen his little sister so happy since before the war. After about 10 minutes they reached the castle. Their legs were heavy and aching from the climb.

Neuschwanstein castle, like Linderhof, amazed Sean. He had never seen anything so splendid and opulent. They took the full tour and learned all about the history of the building and many of its precious artefacts. Most of the exhibits were priceless works of art, but the kitchen really fascinated them. It was fitted with special plumbing that allowed hot air from the chimney to be channelled into a turbine that automatically turned spits for roasting game and poultry. The kitchen even had a system for plates to be warmed by the heat escaping from the large stove to the chimney.

'I could build all that if I had the materials,' Rolf said.

'Sure, Rolf,' Sean replied with a smile, winking at Marianne in the process.

Time was marching on, so they headed north, planning to have their evening meal in Munich. As they drove past Starnberg Lake, Sean suddenly brought the Jeep to a screeching halt by the roadside. The vehicle sent up a cloud of dust on the shoulder of the road. Other motorists blasted their horns in protest.

'What's the matter?' said Marianne, puzzled by Sean's behaviour.

'Didn't you see it? There was a sign back there to a Benedictine monastery. It was the one they call Andechs. You know, where they make that terrific beer we had with lunch yesterday.'

'Oh! I'm not sure we have time to go there, Sean. It's four o'clock already.'

'Hey, little sister, who got their own way yesterday?' Rolf interjected. 'If Sean wants to try another drop of that monastery brew I think we should oblige him. Just to be sociable, I might have one or six glasses myself.'

Marianne shrugged in mute surrender, knowing she was outnumbered.

When they arrived, they visited the monastery chapel. It had probably the largest collection of painted wax candles in

Europe: huge candles, each almost two metres tall and about 20 centimetres in diameter—hundreds of them. Again Sean was amazed at the things one could see in Europe that were nowhere to be found in his United States.

Soon they were drinking one-litre beer mugs again. By now they were getting hungry. They bought some oven-fresh pretzels from the priory bakery.

Marianne urged Sean to take it easy on the beer, because he still had to get them home safely. They drove away as it turned to dusk, but then stopped on the banks of the Ammersee Lake to watch the brilliant red sun go down.

The evening was warm and it seemed so peaceful there. They all lay back on the grass, absorbed in their own thoughts and at peace with the world. Since Rolf knew he didn't have to drive, he had drunk much more of the monks' very agreeable produce than Sean had. Rolf snored as he was overtaken by sleep.

After a while, Marianne said, 'Are you awake, Sean?'

'Sure am! But I'll sleep like a log tonight.'

'Sean, I've something to tell you?'

'What is it?'

'I think I love you, Sean Gleeson. Me a novice and all.'

'I love you too, Marianne. I've fancied you from the first moment I saw you. Come here.'

She put her head on his arm and he cradled her to him, feeling more and more confident that this lovely girl might one day be his bride. They clung together for a while, enjoying every moment of blissful togetherness.

At length, they reluctantly woke Rolf and started the journey back towards Berchtesgaden.

Halfway back, on the autobahn, Rolf glanced at his watch and exclaimed, 'Look at the time. It's five to 10 already. You'll be nearly an hour late, Marianne! What will you tell them?'

'I'm not going to tell them anything, Rolf. You are!' she replied.

'What do you mean?' he protested.

'Rolf, I don't want to go back to the convent. I'd like to stay with you for awhile and sort myself out. I need time to think. When we get to Berchtesgaden, I want you to phone Mother Magdalene and tell her I've decided to leave for a while—maybe permanently. She'll understand. They give novices more flexibility than ordained nuns. In a few days I'll go in and have a chat to her. You'll do this small favour for me, won't you? Please Rolf, please!'

'Okay, okay, if you're sure that's what you want.'

Marianne was relieved indeed to hear Rolf agree. She knew she had successfully avoided ever having another distressing confrontation with Karin.

About an hour later, they bade a fond farewell to Sean, so he could start the long drive back to Augsburg. Rolf had invited him to come to lunch on the following Saturday; an invitation Sean had accepted in a heartbeat.

As they locked up for the night, Rolf said to Marianne, 'I know that one day you might finish up marrying Sean, and I'm very happy for you. He's a good man. But what are you going to do over the next few months if you only see him on the odd weekend?'

'Rolf, I was thinking on the way back tonight that I might try and get a teaching job in Augsburg. Would you mind?'

'No, go ahead. That's a good idea, but please visit me more often than Mother does. She doesn't seem to have any time for us now. I suppose she's always busy. You'd better get in touch and tell her you've left the convent. Let her know that Sean is back, too. I'm sure she'll be pleased, because she told me in her last letter that she didn't think you were too happy lately.'

Rolf went to bed happy for his sister. He liked the young Irishman and thought they would make a good couple.

At the same time he felt a certain sadness, with his father gone, his mother now living in Munich and Marianne moving to Augsburg. Their once tight-knit family was fast becoming a family divided.

Three days later Marianne learned that Karin Zuller had attempted suicide and was being sent to a psychiatric clinic back near her home in Switzerland.

Chapter 6

The letters

The following week Marianne phoned Brigitte. She brought her up to date with the news that she had ended her novitiate and was back at the farmhouse with Rolf.

Her mother responded, 'Well, I'm pleased for you, Mari. I never thought you were really happy there. We can see lot more of each other now. You'll be good company for Rolf.'

'But that's not all, Mama. You know that American we looked after at the end of the war—Sean Gleeson? Well, he's been in touch with me. We're getting on famously.' There was no response. Just silence. Eventually, Marianne said, 'Are you still there, Mama?'

'Yes, yes, of course, Mari. You just surprised me a bit. When you say he contacted you, do you mean he's written to you?'

'Oh, no, he's here in Germany. He was just posted to the Augsburg base. Rolf and I went out with him last weekend. He's such a nice man, Mama.'

'I'm sure he is, Mari,' Brigitte replied, her voice shaking a little. 'The question is whether or not you want to get involved with an American or not. You know that once these things start, there's often no stopping them.'

'But I really like him, Mama, and I know he's fond of me. Rolf seems to get on very well with him too. They had a few drinks together a couple of times.'

'All right, Mari, I'm sure he's a good man. Why don't I catch up with you both in a couple of weeks and we can have dinner or something?'

'That would be lovely, Mama. Whenever it suits.'

Over the next few days Brigitte was troubled and introspective.

Observing that she was quieter than usual, Wolfgang asked what was bothering her. Though initially reluctant to share her vexing situation, Brigitte told him the whole story. How she had destroyed the letters going to and coming from America. She thought Wolfgang would understand perfectly.

However, he disagreed with her well-intentioned interference. 'Imagine if it was you, instead of Marianne? How annoyed you would be that someone had tried to orchestrate your life like that,' he argued.

Talking though the matter further, Brigitte eventually agreed that she had indeed done her only daughter an injustice. Nevertheless, she resolved not to admit her fault. Rather, she would make up for it in some way over the next couple of years. She was determined to make good, without her Mari realising she was trying to redeem herself.

Just before Christmas in 1949, Brigitte spoke frankly to Wolfgang about where she fitted in to his will arrangements. She also checked the balance in her own bank account, and was pleasantly surprised. Her wages went automatically into her account, but she hardly ever withdrew anything. Wolfgang provided a generous housekeeping allowance for their apartments, and he relished buying her new clothes and gifts.

Reassured of her financial stability, she then invited Marianne, Sean and Rolf to dinner at Boettner's seafood restaurant in Theatinerstrasse. They had a sumptuous meal washed down with plenty of white wine.

Marianne was delighted that her mother seemed to be warming to Sean, who impressed them all with his Irish charm. For his part, the young soldier got on very well with Wolfgang, whom he met for the first time that evening.

Their dessert was black forest cherry cake, followed by coffee and schnapps all round. When the dishes had been cleared, Brigitte declared with a smile, 'I've got a couple of announcements to make. First, I must tell you that our business is going very, very well. One construction job alone we just finished in Frankfurt has returned a profit of three hundred thousand marks. So, times are good for Europa Constructions. Thanks to my clever husband here!'

She took Wolfgang's hand for a moment, then pulled three manilla envelopes from her handbag—one large and two smaller ones. She went on, 'My dear Wolfgang provides for all my needs. So I've signed the farm over to you, Rolf and you, Mari. Here are the deeds. You jointly own it outright now.' She gave Rolf the larger envelope.

They both murmured their thanks, not quite understanding why such a transfer was really necessary. They always had had the feeling they would inherit the property one day.

Brigitte picked up the other two envelopes. 'Now, it is my pleasure to give both my children another gift. Mari, you should think about getting yourself a car so that you can get to work when something turns up. Buy something reliable so you can drive to places like Augsburg, for example,' she said knowingly. She handed her daughter the envelope and winked at Sean in the process.

'Rolf, my boy, this back of mine knows how hard it is to crank that old tractor when it doesn't want to start. This should help you get a new one.'

Marianne and Rolf opened their envelopes to find twenty thousand marks in each. They both kissed their mother then Rolf lifted his glass and said, 'Join me, please, in a toast to the best mother in the world.'

When they left the restaurant it was snowing lightly as they headed towards the Marienplatz. They ambled around the square, taking in the Christmas lights and music. From one of the colourful stalls, they bought mugs of piping hot gluhwein.

It was a delightful evening in Munich—cold but not bitter. There was no wind and the snow was soft and light. They were all happy, enjoying the warmth and security of each other's company. Strolling along, they did some window-shopping and listened for a while to a children's choir singing carols. Instead of getting a taxi, they decided to buy some chestnuts and walk back to the apartment through the English Garden. That night, they all slept soundly, the result of good food, good wine and good exercise.

Brigitte thought that the evening had gone very well. Perhaps her Mari would never know about the letters. Who could tell her daughter anyway? Only she and Wolfgang knew about them and she trusted him implicitly. She dozed and slept the soundest of all; her conscience was appeased.

January 1950 came and went. In the first week of February, Marianne got a lucky break. The army base in Augsburg needed a language teacher for three days a week. The job was to take classes for US soldiers wishing to learn German. Sean put in a word for her, and soon the position was hers.

Marianne found an apartment on the second floor of a grand old building near the centre of the old city. Sean borrowed an army truck and with the help of his good mate, Patrick O'Connor, helped her move her own furniture from the farmhouse to Augsburg.

Patrick was a fairly short, athletic-looking man, of solid build. His short army hairdo and clean-cut appearance belied a mischievous sense of humour. Sean liked him because he was always optimistic and cheerful. However, he knew to his peril that this fellow Irishman could not be trusted when it came to practical jokes. On meeting Marianne, Patrick had said, 'So you're the one with the freckles he wouldn't stop talking about back home.'

'Shut up, Pat. We've got plenty to do today without all your damned gossip.'

They all laughed—Marianne with an indulgent smile to herself.

Rolf had helped them load the truck and yet again he was impressed by the friendliness of the Americans. Before they left, he showed them his brand new tractor, and how it started with the simple turn of a key and the touch of a starter button.

Marianne gave her horse Kaiser a big hug before she climbed up into the army truck.

Over the next few weeks she saw Sean almost every evening. Together, they explored the beer-halls, coffee shops and restaurants of Augsburg—especially in the old part of the city. They travelled to nearby towns and tourist attractions on the weekend in her new Volkswagen. Occasionally, they went to a performance at the opera house in Munich. Along the way, Marianne met many of Sean's Army pals. She liked them all and they thought he was one lucky soldier.

Their love for each other grew stronger and it wasn't long before Sean presented her with a diamond engagement ring.

Marianne was overjoyed. She had known it would happen one day. They decided to have a party to celebrate. Sean wanted his many pals at the base to share his happiness, so he arranged to hire the social club on the compound for the celebration.

Unfortunately, Wolfgang couldn't attend because he was tied up in delicate contract negotiations in Italy.

But Brigitte said she would definitely come because she now had a car and chauffeur at her disposal. The growth in their business was such that they could afford such luxuries. Europa Constructions had just branched out into building sport stadiums. The austerity of the postwar years was rapidly diminishing. Europe was richer now and Wolfgang was determined to secure even more new business by constructing soccer stadiums in central Europe.

Brigitte had her driver collect Rolf from the farmhouse and they travelled together from Munich to Augsburg.

Rolf noticed that his mother had been drinking but didn't say anything. She muttered that whenever Wolfgang was away, she always thought of Joachim. Rolf decided not to enter into that discussion. He made a mental note to keep an eye on her throughout the evening and make sure she didn't have too much more.

When they arrived at eight the party was in full swing. A band of four was playing and the room was brightly decorated with balloons and streamers. At the side there were trestles laden with wooden kegs of beer. Hot food was served from a nook at the end of the hall.

Some of the soldiers had brought their wives and girlfriends, so Marianne had a chance to make new acquaintances.

Rolf also met many new friends. The soldiers seemed to have inquisitive minds and asked him all kinds of questions about farming in Bavaria. They invited Rolf to come to an open day at the base, but he politely declined. He had seen enough of guns and didn't like to leave the farm unattended.

The evening wore on and everyone got merry. There was a toast to the happy couple, proposed by Patrick. The soldiers presented them with an exquisite 12-piece Italian dinner set, edged in gold. It was magnificent. After some not-too-subtle prompting from the audience, Sean thought he had better say a few words. He climbed onto a chair and pulled Marianne up onto one right beside him.

'My dear friends, thanks for coming tonight. Thank you also for this beautiful gift. We'll treasure it all our lives.' Putting his arm around Marianne, he went on. 'I want to tell you something about the Bauers. This family took me—an enemy soldier—into their home when I was wounded in '45. They cared for me. Since I've returned to Germany on this posting, they've given me every kindness.'

'I bet you have, Freckles,' someone in the background said.

They all laughed for a moment. Sean continued. 'The friendship, love and respect I have for this family just shows the stupidity of war. I love Marianne. I'm the best of pals with her brother Rolf over there, and with her mother Brigitte seated at the end of the table. Let's drink a toast to friendship. To the hope that none of us will see another war in our lifetime.'

Before Sean stepped down, Patrick said loudly, 'Say, Sean, the firm that put the gold on that there dinner set do a good job plating shotguns as well. Will we be needing to give them an order?'

All the soldiers laughed, so Marianne joined in, although she didn't have a clue what Patrick was talking about.

When they stepped down, Sean and Marianne thanked them individually for the gift. As they mingled she noticed that everyone was calling her 'Freckles'. She suspected that Patrick probably had a bit to do with her new nickname, but didn't mind the familiarity of it all.

Soon it was midnight. Because Army regulations required the hall be closed at 12, the guests started drifting away. Nearly all the soldiers gave Marianne a big kiss and a hug for her engagement. Sean didn't mind in the least because he was so proud of his 'Freckles'.

Rolf noticed that his mother was a bit the worse for wear. He chided himself for not watching her more closely. He prised the empty glass from her grasp and called to his sister to get on the other side. Gently, they lifted her to her feet. One either side, they walked her out to the car.

The chauffeur was ready and waiting. He held the back door wide open. As they guided Brigitte onto the back seat, she came out of her daze momentarily. She surprised Marianne by muttering, 'Mari, I'm so sorry about the letters. I'm so sorry!'

Before Marianne had a chance to respond, she fell into a stupor again. They decided Rolf should take her straight back to her apartment in Munich to sleep it off.

Preparing for bed an hour later, and mulling over her mother's words, something dawned on Marianne: on each of the three occasions she had written to Sean, she had asked her mother to post the letters. Also, her mother would have been the first one to see any letters coming in from America. She could hardly believe what she was thinking. Could her mother really have done this?

The next evening, Marianne and Sean talked over the matter at length. They agreed it was plausible that Brigitte's intervention was the reason no letters had got through over a three-year period. Moreover, they concluded that had she not been so drunk, she probably would never have acknowledged her action.

As she pondered things further, Marianne became angry and then absolutely furious with her mother. How dare she interfere in her life like that!

She phoned her mother the next morning but was told by the housekeeper that she would not be home until about six in the evening. Since Sean was off-duty that afternoon, Marianne asked him to accompany her to Munich, where she would get to the bottom of the matter.

Wolfgang came home from the main office around 4 pm at his wife's request and they discussed tactics. They agreed the only course of action was to come tell all, and to strongly make the point that Brigitte had felt insecure after Joachim's death and hadn't wanted to see her daughter finish up overseas.

Sean accompanied his fiancee up to the apartment and, after polite hellos, Marianne demanded an explanation from her mother over her drunken remark about the letters.

Brigitte was most contrite. She broke down and asked Sean and Wolfgang to give them a minute. When the men had withdrawn, she told her daughter through her tears how vulnerable she had felt after Joachim had died. She explained also, that apart from her children, she had no living relatives left in the world at the end of the war. She argued that she had desperately wanted to keep her children close to her. Now, with the wisdom of hindsight, she realised that her actions had been very selfish.

If Brigitte had expected an understanding reaction from her daughter, she was terribly mistaken. Marianne went on the attack and berated her mother fiercely. She said she loved Sean and that her mother had robbed them of three years.

Brigitte had never seen her daughter so upset. She was shocked even further when her Mari called out to Sean that they were leaving. Marianne pushed Sean before her and stormed out, slamming the door behind her.

Mother and daughter didn't speak at all over the ensuing weeks.

Marianne got on with her teaching. From the beginning of March she took classes five days a week, instead of three. She was just settling into a routine again when Sean gave her the news that he was to be posted back to the United States from the first of June. The Army needed soldiers with some exposure to Germany to run induction programs for replacement troops being sent there. Unfortunately for Sean, he fitted the profile of the instructor they wanted.

Meanwhile, Wolfgang was fast-establishing himself as a success story in the European construction industry. Word had spread over the past year or so of his new approach to labour relations. Everyone knew it was Europa Constructions policy to have all contributing parties win and be satisfied on their projects.

By the simple expedient of offering bonuses to his site foremen for on-time or early completion, Wolfgang had generated something of a paradigm shift in the way contracts were negotiated. Beyond the penalty arrangements that had prevailed for years, positive clauses were included in his contracts, providing incentive payments to Europa Constructions for early completion and cost containment. The best foremen in the industry were attracted to his company. He managed to win many competitive bids where on-time completion was a major consideration.

Wolfgang was now a leading industrialist and a millionaire several times over. However, he wasn't content. The fallout between his wife and Marianne remained unresolved. Also, he wanted to share more of his good fortune with Brigitte. She cared for him, and had come into his life at a time when he had needed a loving companion. Wolfgang thought it was time he showed some leadership. He pondered a number of ideas for a few days, then hatched a two-step plan. Step one was to orchestrate a reconciliation between Brigitte and Marianne. The second step must be something bold and imaginative that would bind the family together forever.

That evening he persuaded Brigitte that she, and she alone, must mend the rift between herself and her daughter. He urged her to phone Marianne and keep on calling her if necessary until they could have another meeting and settle their differences.

The next morning, at 7:30 am, Brigitte dialled Marianne's number, to catch her before she left for work. With a tremor in her voice she began, 'Mari, can we patch things up between ourselves? It makes me so sad that we are not talking. Maybe we could—'

Marianne interrupted her, 'Oh, Mother, I'm so glad you called. What's done is done. Let's be friends again. Life's too short to carry silly grudges. Why don't I come over by myself on Saturday? The weather is not too bad. We could walk over to the English Garden and have some bratwurst together.'

'That would be lovely, Mari,' Brigitte replied. She was barely able to hold back the tears of joy welling in her eyes.

'Mother, I'll tell you more about it on Saturday, but Sean has just been posted back to America from the start of June to run some training courses. That makes it awkward for us to make any marriage plans at the moment. Anyway, let's talk about everything, like we used to.'

When she got off the phone, Brigitte sent a telegram to Rolf, who still refused to have a telephone installed at the farmhouse.

The telegram read, 'Patched up things with Marianne stop we are meeting in Munich on Saturday stop I am so pleased.'

Brigitte then phoned Wolfgang. Excited, she told him she was talking to Marianne again. Things between them were back to normal. She also brought him up-to-date on the news that Sean was being posted back to the United States. Finally, she told him of their difficulty now in making any wedding plans. Wolfgang was delighted with this turn of events.

After he put the phone down, Wolfgang sat quietly in an armchair and looked out the window for 10 minutes or so. His mind was racing. At length he stood up and strode purposefully to his desk. It was time to put step two into action.

Chapter 7

Marriage in Manhattan

B rigitte's meeting with her daughter went well. They hugged each other warmly to start, then chatted for nearly three hours in the English Garden. Afterwards, they strolled arm-in-arm back to the apartment for dinner with Wolfgang. Marianne felt a growing affection for this man who had had brought so much happiness and fulfilment to her mother's life.

The next week, Wolfgang prepared a thorough plan for step two and instructed his secretary to check out the details. When satisfied, he went over the proposal carefully with Brigitte. He explained to her that in the past month he had made a windfall profit of nearly half a million marks on the sale of a development site purchased some years earlier. So funding was not an issue. Brigitte posed a few queries, but was generally comfortable with the whole plan. They agreed to assign one of their best coordinating staff, an astute young man called Martin Kohl, to manage the venture from start to finish.

Wolfgang knew that first of all he had to get the support of the rest of the family. He booked several rooms at a new resort hotel overlooking the beautiful Tegernsee Lake, just south of Munich, for the following weekend. When Rolf, Sean and Marianne all confirmed they could come, he asked Martin to go down with him on the Friday night to set things up.

Wolfgang had sworn Brigitte to secrecy, so the rest of the family was intrigued, to say the least, about the proposed meeting. After arriving on the Saturday, they had a leisurely lunch. Wolfgang invited them to move from the dining area into an adjacent suite that had been set up as a conference room.

He began. 'Thanks for coming at such short notice. First, I should introduce one of my right-hand men—Martin Kohl. Martin will be helping me this afternoon. Let me start by saying that your family, through my dear Brigitte, has given me great joy and a new lease of life. She has given me the spark and the energy to grow and consolidate my company. Business is good. It's very good. But that's not enough. I want to share some of my good fortune. As you know, I have no children myself. Like my dear wife, I have no brothers or sisters either.'

He hesitated for a moment and took a deep breath. 'You are my family now. The ones I care about. Please, give me the pleasure of sharing something with you since I have been so fortunate lately.'

They sat in silence on the edge of their seats, wondering what was to come next.

'Here's what I'd like to do. Marianne and Sean; we know that soon you would like to get married. But it's awkward with Sean going back to America soon. My wedding gift to you both, or rather I should say a present from both Brigitte and myself, is this. If you agree, we will arrange for you to be married in late June or any date in July in New York City.'

Marianne gasped. Sean was open-mouthed in his surprise.

'All right, let me continue. First of all, please hand out those folders, Martin. In the set of papers before you, there's a list of the possible dates. The two marked with an asterisk are the easiest to organise. This arrangement is based on the assumption that there will be up to 60 guests with 25 coming from Europe, and the remainder from within America. On the two dates with an asterisk I can book forty rooms at the Plaza Hotel. That's right, isn't it, Martin?'

'Yes, Sir. We would need to firm up on a booking fairly quickly.'

'All right, now for the church. I suggest St Patrick's on Fifth Avenue, which is close to the Plaza. Again, we can secure a wedding booking on either of those two dates. What else! Oh, then there's travel. I'll book and buy the plane tickets for everybody, so don't worry about any costs there. For photos, we can go over to Central Park, which is right opposite the Plaza. It will be lovely and green in June or July. Show them all the map, Martin.'

As the young man unfolded the large map, Brigitte said, 'You'll love St. Patrick's. It's actually modelled on our cathedral in Köln—Gothic, with double spires. Very ornate! I read all about it in a library book a few years ago.'

Wolfgang wondered for a moment if there was anything in the world his clever new wife hadn't read about.

Martin laid the map of New York City on the table. The Plaza Hotel, St Patrick's and Central Park were each highlighted. He also opened up a floor plan of the rooms at the Plaza. All the rooms were to be booked in a cluster on the fourth floor. Some had views of Central Park.

'This would be wonderful,' said Marianne, tracing her finger along Fifth Avenue. 'I see the hotel is only six or seven blocks away from St Pat's. Are you sure you can afford it all, Wolfgang?'

'The cost is not a problem, I can assure you, my dear. It would be my pleasure to spend the money. Besides, Brigitte and I haven't had a holiday since we got married. It will do us the world of good. Also, I want to spend some time in New

York and check out some opportunities over there. So I do have a couple of ulterior motives, you know.'

Sean stood up, shook Wolfgang's hand and embraced him warmly.

'Thank you, Sir, I don't know what else to say. Thank you from the bottom of my heart. And good luck with your business talks in New York. It would be simply wonderful if you started something up over there as well, so we could more easily keep in touch.'

'We'll see,' he replied. 'I have to be very careful any business in America wouldn't mess up affect the success of our operations here in Europe.'

Rolf also shook his hand and said, 'The greatest joy in life is bringing happiness to others. Wolfgang, we will remember all our lives this wonderful gift to our family. Sorry—to your family.'

Embarrassed a bit by these words, Wolfgang went on quickly, 'Martin, what else is there? What do we need to start the ball rolling?'

'Well, Sir, I'm not sure whether you mentioned that the reception would be at the Plaza also. Also, the hotel can organise the flowers, limousines, catering and so forth. They handle weddings all the time. The first thing we really must do is to settle the actual wedding date. Then we need a list of all the guests and what city they're coming from. I'll take it from there. Might I suggest that before we leave tomorrow, we get the date settled and try to get the guest lists finalised within two weeks, or three at the latest.'

'Good thinking, Martin. I think that's all for the time being. Please read through the rest of the documents and brochures today and enjoy your stay. If you have any questions at all about the arrangements, just speak to Martin. Shall we have dinner tonight, at seven in the upstairs dining room?'

They all nodded; each was absorbed in their own thoughts, but excited at the boldness and adventure of Wolfgang's plan.

Brigitte looked on in proud admiration of this man she so loved and respected.

The date was set for early July.

The next couple of weeks went by quickly as guest lists were drawn up. Sean sent all the details to his parents in Pennsylvania, asking them to invite 12 people of their own choosing.

Brigitte was very excited about this wonderful event for her daughter. However, her enthusiasm was tempered by the knowledge that Marianne would live in America from July onwards.

Martin Kohl had been promoted to be one of Wolfgang's deputies because he always got the job done. He had joined Europa Constructions about a year earlier and had immediately impressed both Wolfgang and Brigitte with his level of initiative.

Martin was a person able to focus on the task at hand. He knew the value of planning and the need for attention to detail. At the age of 25, this young man also appreciated the value of friendships, and that what one achieved in life was as much a result of personal relationships as of knowledge itself.

Martin brought all his commercial acumen to the wedding plans.

He sent the hotel some slightly exaggerated profile information on Wolfgang Schmidt to ensure they knew that their customer was a prosperous industrialist. He liaised with the hotel management to work out deals on the ground transportation, catering and flowers. When the total package was sorted out, he even arranged for a return bus trip on the Sunday down to Pier 83 to be included into the deal. This was for those guests who wanted to take the scenic Circle Line boat journey around Manhattan Island. Martin was very satisfied with the hotel, and impressed too by the professionalism of the Plaza staff.

Rolf travelled to New York with Patrick O'Connor and two of Sean's other Army mates. The rest of the family had left two days earlier.

When the plane flew over Manhattan Island, Rolf was sure he could see the Empire State Building among the skyscrapers below. They passed directly over a long rectangle of green, which Rolf assumed must be Central Park. Looking out to the right he glimpsed the unmistakable sight of the Statue of Liberty rising majestically on its stone pedestal in New York harbour. Rolf felt a real buzz of excitement as the plane veered sharply left and descended towards Queens and the massive airport complex of Idelwild.

On leaving Customs his eye was immediately caught by a uniformed driver holding a white piece of cardboard with 'Mr Rolf Bauer' boldly displayed. As he and the three soldiers followed the chauffeur outside, Rolf thought that young Martin was on the ball as usual.

After registration, Rolf phoned Sean to insist he keep his promise of going out with them that Friday evening for a final drink before he tied the knot. It was only 6 pm and still broad daylight when the five friends assembled in the lobby.

Rolf felt a little out of place because he was the only civilian in the group, but at least they were all dressed in civvies.

Before they left, they decided to watch the start of the television news in the lounge. The soldiers wanted to keep in touch with events unfolding in Korea. A couple of weeks earlier

North Korean forces had crossed the 38th parallel and stormed down towards Seoul. According to the news, the situation was now tense. The UN had authorised several Western nations to help out South Korea. When the news items on Korea finished and the station crossed to commercials, they thought it was time to get going.

They decided to try the famous subway system. Out on Fifth Avenue, the traffic noise was deafening. Impatient motorists leaned on their horns in the peak-hour congestion. Sirens wailed in the distance. Descending some grotty steps, they caught the train downtown to 34th Street. It was packed. The air-conditioning didn't seem to be working, so they were glad to come up to street level again.

Browsing through Macys, they were amazed at the size of the whole store. They started to walk uptown along the colourful, diagonal cross street called Broadway.

Soon they spied a bar that looked inviting. Patrick ordered the first round. They perched on some stools at a round table. Nearby was a group of six young men in navy uniforms. The sailors looked as if they had been there a while, because they were a rowdy bunch. Rolf insisted on getting the second round.

When he ordered from the bar, the tallest sailor stood up and pushed him in the chest saying, 'I've been listening to you. I could pick that accent anywhere. You're a Kraut aren't you? A bloody Nazi, that's what you are. Why don't you go back to Germany, where you belong?'

Rolf didn't even have time to react. What happened next took place in about three seconds flat. As soon as the sailor had finished speaking, Patrick jumped to his feet, spread his legs for balance and punched the inebriated man with all his might in the solar plexus. The sailor went down breathless to the floor, gasping for air and unable to speak. His friends didn't say a word.

Patrick asked, 'Any of you others want some action, too?'

'No, pal, he was a bit out of order there,' one of them replied. 'Too much to drink, you know.' They pulled their friend onto a chair. He struggled for air.

Sean suggested they try somewhere else. They ambled off up Broadway.

As they walked along, Rolf grabbed Patrick by the arm and said, 'Pat, there was no need to hit that guy so hard, I wasn't overly concerned about his Nazi comments.'

'Listen, Rolf, you're a visitor to this country. We don't treat guests like that in America. This is supposed to be the land of the free, for God's sake. It will be a good while before that guy has another go at a foreigner.'

Rolf just nodded, intrigued that an Irishman, who had been living in the United States for only three years, would defend his adopted country so stoutly.

Sean spotted another bar with a green shamrock illuminated in leadlight above the doorway. They entered the small Irish establishment at about 8:30 and didn't emerge until the wrong side of midnight.

By this time, neither walking any distance nor navigating the route back to the hotel seemed possible. Instead, they all squeezed into the one cab for the short journey back to the Plaza.

July in New York is always hot. The wedding Saturday in July of 1950 proved the rule. By 1 pm, still an hour before the service, the temperature was touching 32 degrees. The humidity was stifling. Despite the oppressive heat, it was a bustling, exciting time at the Plaza, as the wedding guests introduced themselves to one another in the hallways or in the lobby.

Unbeknown to Sean, 10 of his army mates had driven up to New York that morning with their uniforms freshly pressed to form an honour guard.

He was lost for words for a moment, as he walked up the front steps of St Patrick's with Rolf.

'Thanks guys, thanks very much!' he said in a breaking voice. He walked through the two rows of uniformed soldiers standing ramrod straight at attention in the summer heat. Sean chatted to his mates for a couple of minutes then moved inside.

Rolf stayed out the front, because he would give Marianne away, in place of Joachim. A small crowd had gathered to watch the proceedings, most of them huddled close to the church walls in the precious shade.

When Marianne, resplendent in her guipure lace wedding dress, alighted from her limousine, the crowd burst into spontaneous applause. The bride-to-be was indeed radiant; her freckled face was a picture of happiness as she took Rolf's arm for the short walk to a new life.

The young priest who conducted the service was a cheerful fellow who obviously warmed to the task of conducting weddings. His smiling face and relaxed manner appeared to have a calming effect on the congregation and everyone enjoyed the event.

Sean thought Marianne was more beautiful than he had ever seen her before. How lucky he was that she now wore a wedding dress instead of a nun's habit. He would indeed love, cherish and obey his freckle-face for the rest of their days.

When they emerged from the church, the honour guard had dress swords in the air, forming an archway for the married couple. All the 10 young men in attendance thought Sean was a very lucky man.

'I love you, Mrs Gleeson,' Sean whispered, before the well wishers descended upon them both.

Brigitte met Sean's parents; telling them she was delighted that her daughter was finally marrying their son. She confided to Mrs Gleeson that the day the two had first met, at the end of the war, she had sensed that there was something between them. Brigitte had expunged all lingering guilt about the sorry episode of the letters from her mind by now.

Meanwhile, Wolfgang strolled around the side of the church, to where the impromptu honour guard was assembled in the shade. Some lit up smokes.

'Where are you lads off to now?' he asked.

'Oh, we'll start back to Pennsylvania soon,' one replied. 'Best to get as far as we can before it gets dark. Lots of road works on the pike, you know.'

'When do you go back on duty?'

'Not until Monday morning, Sir. Why do you ask?'

'Gentlemen, what you have done today was a very generous thing. To travel all the way up here when you weren't even invited to the reception is a gesture I think should be rewarded. If you can stay, I would like you to attend the reception and stay overnight at the Plaza, as my guests. I know they have spare rooms available tonight and I will pick up the tab. What do you think?'

'Thank you, Sir, sounds like an offer too good to refuse. We have four cars in the side street down there. We'll need to find somewhere to leave them overnight.'

'Leave all those details to me,' Wolfgang said. 'I'll be back in a moment.'

He found Martin Kohl nearby, talking to one of the bridesmaids, and gave him instructions regarding the honour guard.

Martin approached the group, who were chatting away excitedly about their unexpected night in New York.

'Hi guys!' he said. 'My name is Martin Kohl. I am Mr Schmidt's executive assistant. Give me an hour to organise everything, then drive to the car park entrance at the Plaza. I'll arrange four parking spaces for you—just mention my name to the attendant. When you go up to the lobby, also mention my name and there will be 10 rooms ready for you. The wedding reception is in the Edwardian Room. I'll wait around near the entrance to show you to your seats. Mr Schmidt has also asked me to give you fifty bucks each in case you need to get shaving gear, underwear or anything.'

He handed them each a 50-dollar note from a thick envelope of bills that was his contingency fund for the wedding.

'Now, any questions?'

'Well, thanks, Martin. We'd like to thank Mr Schmidt also. Is he still about?'

'No, he's had to go down to Central Park for the photographs. Why not catch him after the reception is over?'

They nodded.

Martin started to walk away, then turned back suddenly.

'One more thing,' he said with a grin. 'You guys keep away from the black-haired bridesmaid. I saw her first.'

They laughed. Most of them were more concerned with how best to spend their 50-dollar windfall.

Meanwhile, back at the Plaza, all was in readiness for the wedding reception in the elegant Edwardian Room.

Designed along the lines of a traditional French chateau, the Plaza seemed an ideal place for a wedding reception, more so than most other hotels in New York. The Edwardian Room was exquisite. It had views of both Central Park and Fifth

Avenue and had magnificent beamed ceilings and original, handcrafted light fixtures.

The reception was an overwhelming success.

When she heard the full story of the soldiers sitting at the extra table, Brigitte felt so proud of her husband's generosity. She made a point of introducing herself to the young men and encouraged them to mingle with the other guests.

Rolf spent a lot of time talking to Joseph Gleeson, Sean's father. Joseph had originated from County Kerry in Ireland 20 years earlier and made his farm successful. The older man told him that they were almost certain to sell the farm by the end of 1950. His acreage was fully surrounded by Amish farms now, and the price they were offering was too good to refuse. Besides, his wife, Carmel, suffered terribly from rheumatism in the winter months. They were both keen to move to Sarasota on the Florida coast, where Joseph's two brothers both lived. Joseph explained to Rolf that Carmel's sister lived just outside the nearby town of Clearwater, so there were family benefits for both of them in moving south.

'What about Sean?' Rolf said. 'He doesn't mind if you sell the farm?'

'No, we've discussed it with Sean. He'd like to go on the land one day, but probably not onto my farm. It's a bit claustrophobic, you know, being surrounded by people of another culture. The Amish don't mix with the rest of us. It's an unusual existence; at times almost bizarre. We can be out ploughing fields next to one another, yet they never seem inclined to chat or even wave. Anyway, Sean has told us he would prefer investing in a bigger acreage in a warmer state, further south. We'll give him some of the proceeds to help him get started.'

'How can the Amish afford to buy new properties, anyway?' asked Rolf.

'Basically it's because they don't spend much money. They pour all that they earn back into their farms, on fertiliser and improvements. They spend nothing on cars, holidays, electrical goods and things like that. If you don't spend, you gradually accumulate.'

Rolf hoped that one day he would get a chance to visit Lancaster County, and see for himself these Amish farms. He remembered Sean telling him how they were experts in contour ploughing. Also, how they used a team of six horses to do the heavy ploughing. He'd like to see that.

As the night wore on, Martin made good progress in getting to know the dark-haired bridesmaid, Renate. She was Renate Becke, the second daughter of Mr Karl Becke, who worked in the Salzburg office of Europa Constructions.

Martin's efforts were somewhat constrained by the fact that Rolf also had two dances and a couple of chats with Renate. The two laughed a lot together, as if they were getting along famously.

Undeterred, Martin persevered and later in the evening he scored a long and fruitful talk with the attractive girl. He discovered she had been a childhood friend of Marianne and that she worked in the company's Salzburg office. Martin made a mental note to visit Europa Constructions in Austria at the first opportunity, and to check which flight Renate would be using to return to Europe.

Sean and Marianne were filled with joy on their special day. When Sean heard what Wolfgang had done for the honour guard, he rushed over to his new father-in-law and gave him a bear hug.

Wolfgang himself was delighted with the wedding. All had gone without a hitch—testimony to Martin's preparation and attention to detail. As he sipped his fourth glass of cold water for the evening, Wolfgang wondered why on earth he always felt so tired and thirsty lately.

Too soon, the enchanting evening was over. Marianne and Sean had received some lovely presents, which they unwrapped for all to see. They asked Martin to arrange storage of their gifts for a few days at the hotel until they returned from Niagara Falls.

The bridal couple walked to every table to say thank you and goodbye. Then they retired for the evening, exhausted after such a hectic day.

As they rode up in the elevator to the bridal suite, Marianne wrapped her arms around her new spouse and whispered in his ear, 'By the way, I love you too, Mr Gleeson.'

Chapter 8

The fire

As summer turned to fall in 1950, the Bauer family started to go their own ways again. The newlyweds were back in Lancaster after their honeymoon in upstate New York. It had been a wonderful trip. Sean took some memorable photos of Marianne squealing in girlish glee at Niagara Falls. She enjoyed the thrill as the *Maid of the Mist* churned against the current, pushing the sturdy tourist boat ever deeper into the cascading spray below the falls. This was an exhilarating experience the couple would remember to the end of their days. They also visited Buffalo and Syracuse. On the way back to Lancaster they broke their journey by staying one night at Binghamton and one evening in the Wilkes Barre area.

No sooner had Sean reported again for duty than he was assigned to Washington DC. His original role of conducting induction courses for soldiers embarking on a European tour of duty was extended to include those headed for the Korean peninsula.

Fortunately, a lot of information had already been prepared on Korea, and he was able to glean further first-hand accounts from wounded soldiers returning from that country. However, he did need help, because his workload was steadily growing. He put in a requisition to have one Patrick O'Connor, presently serving in Augsburg, relocated to DC as his assistant. Sean figured he could have Patrick take over most of the German courses, while he concentrated on improving the quality of the training material for Korea.

Unfortunately for Marianne, there was no military accommodation available in Washington, so she was obliged to stay in Lancaster. She filled her days looking for work, and looking also for furniture to fill their small, but empty and desperately lonely apartment.

After a couple of weeks she got a surprise visit from the Gleesons to say they had sold their farm. An offer from an elder of the local Amish community had been just too good to turn down. The Amish wanted to use the whole property for vegetable farming and had made a bid close to twice the market value.

The old couple seemed relieved that finally the matter was over. They talked excitedly about their move down to Sarasota on the Florida coast. Marianne offered to help with the packing and they said she and Sean could keep a few pieces of furniture they no longer needed. Finally, Joseph told Marianne that as soon as the sale settlement was completed, the young couple would be getting a sizeable cheque, as Sean's entitlement to some of the proceeds.

Marianne couldn't wait for Sean's bus to get in from Washington that Friday night. She wanted to share his joy at their forthcoming wealth, but also to tell him about the loneliness of a newly wed living alone.

They did a lot of talking that weekend. Sean said he was hopeful that accommodation for the two of them would be available soon. He also gave her the good news that Patrick O'Connor had just been assigned to Washington.

Sean surprised his bride somewhat by saying he wanted to get out of the Army soon. 'Marianne, I've been a soldier now for seven years. I don't want to be in uniform forever. Let us wait and see how much money we get from my father. I'd really like to buy into a farm down south somewhere, and build a future for us on the land.'

'Whatever you think, Sean. I was brought up on the land, so I've got farming in my blood, too. It's a good life for children. All helping out with chores on the farm.'

'What's this *all helping out* business, just how many kids do you propose to have, Mrs Gleeson?'

'As many as you want to give me,' she giggled, giving him a peck.

Meanwhile, in Munich, things were taking a turn for the worse. Wolfgang had just returned home after an appointment with his doctor in Prinzregentenstrasse. Two weeks earlier he had given blood and urine samples, as he did every year without fail—part of his annual health checkup procedure. His face was still pale as he walked into their apartment.

'What is it, Wolfgang?' Brigitte asked, sensing something was wrong.

'My blood sugar has gone through the roof. The doctor can't understand why it has gone up so far in just one year. It was all right at my last checkup. Blood pressure is up a bit too, but he seemed more concerned about the glucose count. Apparently it's approaching the danger level.'

'Did he say you were diabetic?' Brigitte asked with genuine concern.

'No, not exactly. He said I might be. He asked me lots of questions and I told him how thirsty I've been lately. Even for a doctor he seemed a bit guarded. He said an inflamed pancreas or just stress could cause a high reading. I think he may have been holding something back. Told me I'm overweight as well, of course! Said the more your body weighs the more insulin it has to produce. Oh, Brigitte, just as things were going really well for us, this has to happen.'

'Well, now, let's not get too worried until we know the full story. What's the next step? Do you have to do more tests?'

'No, not right now. For three weeks he wants me to go on a strict diet—mainly carbohydrates with definitely no sweet or fatty foods. No alcohol either. Here's the diet sheet he gave me. The other thing he said I must do is exercise. Walk at least three kilometres a day.'

Brigitte looked over the diet plan and said reassuringly, 'Wolfgang, it'll be easy for us to stick to this plan. I will help you all the way. Let's do even better with the exercise and double it. We could walk three kilometres each morning and evening in the English Garden. I'll exercise and follow the diet too. It seems a very healthy mix. Heaven knows, I should lose some weight as well.'

'What about the meeting in Berlin next week with those new contractors?' said Wolfgang.

'Let Martin handle it. He has proved himself time and time again. The young man loves a challenge. He'll be all right.'

'I suppose you're right,' replied Wolfgang, momentarily encouraged by the support of his faithful wife.

'What happens after three weeks? More tests, I presume?'

'Yes, he said I would need a blood check again and maybe some kind of glucose tests as well.'

'All right, it's 4:30 now. I'll make some pasta for dinner, then let us have our first walk after that. Tomorrow, I'll go to the shops and stock up on the diet stuff. You'll be fine, my dear. We'll get through this together.'

Wolfgang nodded. He knew Brigitte would be positive and help him through this trial. The problem was that he had not told his wife or the doctor the whole story. He hadn't told either of them that he occasionally had blurred vision and suffered some numbness in both feet.

At the farmhouse, Rolf was preparing for yet another winter. Things had been quiet since he got back from New York, although the local police had just visited all farms in the area. They called to advise that there had been a major prison outbreak recently and asked each farmer to be vigilant for any escapees.

Rolf loaded his rifle and kept it close at hand near the front door. As was his custom, he had ample dry wood stacked away for winter together with a good supply of hay. He had traded some asparagus, potatoes and onions for five sacks of barley from a farmer about four kilometres down the main boundary road. His old truck needed repairs to the gearbox, so he decided to collect the barley using a small trailer behind the tractor.

Rolf set off in the morning at 10 and stayed at his friend's farm for lunch, before heading back at about 2:30. He towed the grain, with a few large pumpkins his neighbour had thrown in perched on top.

About halfway home, he glanced around to check his load and noticed that one of the pumpkins had fallen off about 50 metres back. He stopped the tractor and strolled back. The pumpkin wasn't damaged. As he carried it back to the tractor he saw a cloud of dust over the rise ahead. A motorbike came into view. It was travelling at high speed. Rolf noticed that the rider was very big; so big, in fact, that he seemed to dwarf the bike beneath him. He put the pumpkin back on the sacks, then decided to let the bike pass, before he moved back up into the driver's seat.

As the rider slowed down a little to pass, Rolf noticed something that made his blood run cold. On the side of the big man's face there was an enormous scar! He knew who it was in an instant. Could it be just a coincidence? Perhaps it was just by chance that the giant ex-SS soldier was coming from the direction of his farm. Quickly, he slipped the tractor out of neutral and took off.

Gathering speed, he moved the vehicle right up to top gear. Even before he crested the rise, his heart sank. Billows of white smoke rose in the sky ahead. His worst fears were confirmed. The whole farmhouse was ablaze and burning fiercely from one end to the other. There was absolutely nothing Rolf could do except watch it burn. His only consolation was that all the animals were outside the barn. Mercifully, they had been spared from the conflagration.

Slowly, he got down from the tractor and surveyed the devastation. The whole upper floor was burned out and collapsing onto the barn area below. It sent up further clouds of smoke and sparks. He knew there would be nothing left. Cattle in a nearby pasture were running up and down against the far fence, bellowing in distress.

Sparks were flying everywhere. The fire was so fierce that everything inside would be destroyed. He was thankful that the title documents and his savings passbooks were in a safety-deposit box at the bank. The big machinery shed and the hay-storage barn had also escaped the fire.

He watched a little longer and then tried to approach the building. Heat radiation forced him back. He looked on helplessly. After a while, Rolf sank to his knees in despair. He thought, why me? After all my years of toil on this farm, why did I have to lose everything?

Still on his knees, he buried his face in his hands and cried as he had never done before. He was still weeping 10 minutes later when some of his neighbours started to arrive. The billowing smoke, now visible for kilometres around, attracted them. His friends tried to console him, but Rolf was still in shock.

Not for the first time, his despair turned to bitterness and anger. His first thoughts were of vengeance, but then commonsense prevailed. He realised the perpetrator would be many kilometres away by now—possibly across the Austrian border. Soon a police car arrived. They didn't bother to radio for the fire brigade because the damage was already done.

Rolf told them about the motorbike and the scar-faced man whom he had first encountered at the end of the war. The police advised him that this man was the only escapee still at large following the recent prison break-out. Further, that he was a suspect in two rapes and a murder that had recently occurred. Rolf felt nauseous. He knew he should have told the authorities earlier about Doctor Steifler's watchband. The police took a few more notes, but sped off as soon as Rolf had indicated the direction the motorbike had taken.

A while later, Rolf's nearest neighbour, Boris Mueller, approached him and asked, 'What are you going to do for the next few days, Rolf? You can stay with us if you like. We could take some of your stock over winter too, but I don't have room for them all.'

'Thanks, Boris, but I think I will stay with my mother in Munich for a couple of days. The hay shed survived and I have some grain in there. I'll feed the stock before I leave and use your phone if I may. I'm sure my mother will send a car to pick me up.'

'Sure, Rolf, of course. Stay in Munich for a week, if you need to. I can keep an eye on the cattle, pigs and Kaiser for you. What about the hens? Did they get caught in the fire?'

'Yes, unfortunately. I let them out for a run this morning, then locked them up again under the house before I left. They all burned. Thanks very much for your help.' He shook the hand of his good friend Boris and left to collect a few bales of hay.

As he gave some hay to Kaiser, Rolf put his arm around the neck of the old horse that had been his companion on the farm for so many years.

Suddenly, he felt an enormous love for this animal. They had been through so much together. Now all his family had left the farm, the main building was in ashes and yet Kaiser was still there. A faithful friend through it all!

Later that evening, Rolf told the whole story to Brigitte and Wolfgang.

They immediately offered him accommodation in either one of two spare apartments they had in Munich and Salzburg. Also, they told Rolf about Wolfgang's new diet and offered him the use of the car and chauffeur for a couple of weeks. They planned to cut right back on their level of business activities for a while and walk everywhere they needed to in Munich.

Rolf decided to take the Salzburg apartment, so he was closer to the farm, but to stay the night in Munich and head out in the morning.

Before they retired, Brigitte asked, 'Rolf, aren't you going to ring Mari and tell her what's happened?'

'No, mother, not just yet. Let me think about it for a while. When I've decided what I'm going to do, I'll give her a ring. I'll call you, too, of course and let you know my plans.'

For the next two days Rolf reflected about what course of action to take. He was 25 years old now and didn't really want to spend more time alone on the farm. Besides, rebuilding would take at least a year and couldn't begin until after winter, which was fast approaching. He was also a little envious of

Marianne and thought that he, too, would like to find a partner. Basically, he wanted to leave everything in Germany for a while and travel around while he was still young; to see other parts of the world, especially the United States, which held a strong fascination for him after his unforgettable trip to New York.

In Salzburg, he made arrangements for all his livestock to be sold as soon as possible and for the farmland to be put up for lease on an annual renewal basis. He also had negotiated with a nearby orphanage, which had plenty of land, and persuaded them to take Kaiser as a pet for the children. He knew Marianne would be happy with this arrangement, because she knew many of the teaching staff there very well.

Eventually, Rolf phoned Marianne and told her all that had taken place. She started to cry over the phone, but Rolf said, 'Hold your tears, Marianne. Things could have been worse. That madman might have killed me if I was home at the time. All the cattle and pigs survived because they were outside. Kaiser seems to like all the attention the kids are giving him at the orphanage. Yes, the farmhouse is gone, but someone might re-build it one day. Now, as I've told you, the land is up for lease. It's strictly on a one-year basis, in case we change our minds. When the stock is sold, I'll give you half the proceeds. I wouldn't mind coming to America for a while. Could I stay with you and Sean for a few weeks?'

'That would be wonderful, Rolf. Sean is working in Washington at the moment and gets home only on weekends. You would be good company for me. I'm a really good driver now and my Volks never lets me down. Starts every time! I could show you right around this area. Please come over as soon as you can.'

'All right, all right, give me a week or so to finalise things over here and say my goodbyes to Mother. Did you know Wolfgang has a minor medical problem at the moment? Too much sugar in his blood, or something like that.'

'Rolf, I'm no medical expert, but even I know that high blood sugar is not a trivial problem. Find out what the situation is and let me know. I hope things work out all right. Mama has had enough grief in her life already.'

It took Rolf about 10 days to finalise the sale of the stock and machinery, sign the leasing papers and pack what meagre belongings had survived the fire. He would catch the plane to the US from Munich, but would spend a couple of days with Brigitte and Wolfgang before he left.

When Rolf arrived at their apartment, he saw that his mother's eyes were very red. He knew something was wrong.

'It's Wolfgang,' Brigitte explained as she held her son's hand. 'He went for more tests two days ago and they have confirmed that his body can't produce insulin any more. That's why his blood glucose reading was so high.'

'So what about the diet? Didn't that improve things at all?'

'No, apparently his pancreas has given up all together, so his body doesn't produce any insulin at all. He'll have to have injections every day from now on,' Brigitte replied.

'It won't be too bad, Rolf,' Wolfgang interjected.

'We're going to hire a live-in nurse as soon as we can, to look after my diet, tests and injections, so your mother doesn't have to worry about that. We'll get through this together. It's just a matter of coming to terms with the fact that I'm a diabetic and adjusting our lives accordingly. It's not a death sentence. Just a matter of sensible management, the doctor said.'

'What about your business?' said Rolf.

'Well, it's time I started to delegate more to others. Besides, I think I may sell off two of my smaller companies and invest a bit for retirement. I can do that without putting Europa Constructions itself at risk. Maybe travel a bit more, as well. We can take the nurse with us. What about you, Rolf? What will you do now?'

'I had planned to go to America for a while and spend some time with Marianne and Sean. But maybe I should stay here. Sounds like you might need some help from time to time.'

'Nonsense, Rolf,' Brigitte said. 'You do whatever you want, my son. Wolfgang and I can work through this little challenge ourselves. You have your own life to lead. Visit Mari if you want to. Travel around America and get it out of your system. Whenever you come back to Germany, we'll welcome you with open arms and help you get started again.'

'I agree,' said Wolfgang. 'You're only young, Rolf. See the world while you can and, when you come back, maybe I can talk you into working with me. I'm going to need a couple of reliable men to help me run the business in future. Do you need any money, my boy?'

'No, I'm all right. I've been saving for a couple of years now and I've just got some money from selling the stock, the truck and tractor, which I'll share with Marianne.'

'Well, good luck to you, Rolf. Call us or write if you need anything at all,' Wolfgang said. Warmly, he shook the hand of the young man he had grown to love and respect.

Chapter 9

A waitress in Pennsylvania

Rolf arrived in Philadelphia on a chilly Wednesday morning in November 1950. His sister Marianne waited at the airport. She kissed him on both cheeks and hugged him warmly.

As they left the city in her trusty Volkswagen and headed west to Lancaster, Marianne said, 'Rolf, I've got so much to tell you. But first I must say again how sorry I was to hear about the farmhouse. You put so much work into that place. It must have broken your heart to see it burn down.'

'Yes, it was sad, but life goes on, you know. Sometimes such things are the catalysts for the start of something new. To be honest, Marianne, I have to admit that I was in a bit of a rut. If it weren't for the fire, I probably would've spent the next 10 years of my life vegetating alone on the farm. Look at me now. I've got a few thousand dollars to burn. I want to see some of America before I go back and settle down again. By the way, you know I have the farmland on lease? How would you feel if I sold it one day and we just went fifty-fifty on the proceeds? I'm not sure that I ever want to rebuild there. It reminds me too much of Father.'

'It's up to you, Rolf. I think I'll be spending the rest of my life in America. Sean wants to get out of the Army soon and buy a place down south—maybe in the Carolinas. His folks sold their place a while back, and Sean just got a cheque for 40,000 dollars from that deal. I think he'll resign as soon as this Korea business is over. By the way, I haven't told you the best news. One of Sean's pals runs a road-transport business and is looking for a truck jockey for a month or so. Apparently his driver had a car accident and broke his leg. The route is a picturesque one, from a couple of pick-up points here in Pennsylvania into New Jersey and back. Sean said it was just four days a week and that the pay was very good. What do you think?'

'Well, it sounds good, Marianne, but what's a truck jockey?'

'Oh, he's the one who helps with loading and unloading. Normally he doesn't do any of the driving.'

'Well, I hadn't expected to work, because I'm not short of money. But I suppose that if the job is there and I can sort out whatever red tape is involved, it would be a good way to see the country and not eat into my savings. Let's find out more about it from Sean on the weekend.'

The next day, Marianne took Rolf for a drive around some of the properties in Lancaster County. They had all day, so first they headed south to have a look at Strasburg, then back up to Route 30 to Paradise. At one of the tourist restaurants in Paradise they tried an Amish-style lunch of shoofly pie, various cheeses and relish. Rolf topped his meal off with a big helping of hot apple pie.

In the afternoon it began to rain, off and on. They pressed on and drove north across 340 then headed west towards Ephrata to see the Gleesons' old place. The land seemed fertile and the farms prosperous. Rolf thought they were every bit as neat and well maintained as the rural holdings in his native Bavaria. He saw many Amish working the land, oblivious to the rain showers. Others he saw travelling along in their small black buggies with noisy steel-rimmed wheels. What a curious people, he thought—no electricity, no cars, and not even any tractors. Theirs was a Spartan existence, apparently with hard labour at its core. While he didn't understand their ways, he admired this simple, unpretentious community for pursuing a traditional lifestyle in an increasingly materialistic world.

On the Friday they also went for a drive. Starting early, they drove down across the Susquehanna River to the old town of York. After a coffee and some window shopping, they went on to the historic area of Gettysburg. They toured the memorial fields dotted with remembrance stones, plaques and signs of all kinds. Marianne noticed that her brother seemed unusually quiet. Sensing his discomfort, she suggested they have a quick lunch in Hanover, then head back across the Susquehanna.

When Sean arrived home that evening, he and Rolf went through a fearful number of beers after dinner. Fortunately, the apartment had a wood fire and the atmosphere was warm and cosy as the three friends sat around chatting and drinking by the glowing embers. At about ten o'clock, Marianne made up some hamburgers with bread rolls toasted on the coals. She and Sean had one each and Rolf demolished two without any trouble at all. Sean told Rolf all about his work at the Pentagon. There were some 10,000 military personnel and another 20,000 civilians working in or attached to the huge, purpose-built defence headquarters.

Marianne listened intently to every word and remarked, 'You know, guys, this reminds me of that time we sat by the lake near the monastery. Though I fancy the pair of you have had even more to drink tonight.'

'Well,' Rolf replied. 'The beer may not be as good as the monks' brew, but it's quite an agreeable drop, wouldn't you say, Mr Gleeson?'

'Indeed, Mr Bauer, a most agreeable brew. As they say in the old country, the good things of life should be enjoyed while they can and never be wasted. Would you not agree, Mrs Gleeson?'

'I would, Sean. But I'm not sure that you need to have quite so much. Anyway, tell Rolf about that job that's going on the truck.'

'Okay, Rolf, here's the deal. One of my pals does the transportation for this clothing company called Children's Clobber. They import raw yarn, weave it into cotton or whatever, dye up the fabric and make children's clothes. The problem is the whole operation is scattered over a few locations and they need quick transfer of goods between each. The driver can't handle the whole run by himself in a day, so they use a jockey to help load and unload each consignment as quickly as possible. You with me so far?'

'Yes, keep going.'

'Well, it's only for a month or so until the regular guy gets fit again. I know it pays well though, because it's often a 10-hour day with overtime after the first eight. Only four days a week too. There's no run on Fridays.'

'Thanks, Sean, that sounds like it would be good fun for a few weeks. It'll keep me fit and I can see some of the countryside. How can we settle it?'

'The driver lives just a half an hour or so up the road, in Reading. I've met him a few times. Nice old bloke, but his language is a bit rich. Why don't we all take a drive up there on Sunday? If the driver says okay, you could probably start on Monday, if you like.'

On Sunday they set off a little early so Sean could take one last nostalgic look at his old farmhouse on the way. His parents had already moved down to Florida. They had sent back a postcard saying how happy they were to finally escape the Pennsylvania winters.

On their arrival in Reading, the old driver, Jim Masterton, took one look at the size of Rolf and was immediately keen to have him on board. They sorted out the pay rate and agreed not to bother about filling out any forms. It would be a handshake agreement, strictly on a cash basis for hours worked, with one week's notice on either side. The expected duration was five weeks, and Rolf could start on the Monday.

When they got back to Lancaster, Rolf said he would go for a run because he hadn't had any real exercise for weeks. In fact he just wanted to get out of the house for a while, so Marianne could have some time alone with Sean.

Before he went to bed that night, Rolf gave Marianne and Sean a bank draft he had brought with him from Germany. It was for Marianne's half of the proceeds from the sale of stock and machinery. He thanked Sean again for fixing him up with the job and wished him well for the week. An army buddy of Sean's, who lived in nearby Marietta, and also worked in Washington, would pick Sean up at 6 am in the morning, for the return trip to DC.

After Sean had left early the next day, Marianne fixed a couple of sandwiches for Rolf then drove him up to the driver's home in Reading. It was a frosty morning, but the trusty little Volkswagen kicked into life right on cue at the third attempt.

Old Jim seemed very happy indeed to see Rolf again. When he climbed in, Rolf was pleased too that the van was a modern, enclosed vehicle with a good heater. As they drove to the factory on the other side of the town, Jim explained more about the daily routine.

'Look, follow this map, Rolf. We start each day here in Reading at the packaging plant and take finished goods straight up along Route 78 right into Paramus, New Jersey. In Jersey, the company has a combined raw material store and a distribution centre for their packaged products. They have a Weaving Mill and Dyehouse in Scranton as well as a cut-and-sew plant in Wilkes Barre. Each day, we do the same trip. Reading to Paramus via Route 78, then back west on 80 to Scranton, south a little ways to Wilkes Barre, then further south to the Reading, drop off and that's it. Any questions?'

'Two actually, Jim. Why is the company so scattered about? And how come it takes 10 hours or so? Looking at the map, I would have thought the whole trip should take only about six or seven.'

Jim laughed and responded, 'Good questions, Rolf. On the first one about locations, who gives a shit? This company employs people in four separate locations. You'll see that the cut-and-sew plant alone in Wilkes Barre has about 300 employees. Don't sweat it, Rolf. If they want to have a dozen locations, more power to them. It has kept me in a good job for years now. Now for your second point, about the time it takes. Aside from the loading and unloading time there are three problems we'll encounter. The first is roadworks. Every bloody trip you have to put up with road repairs, especially on Route 80. Even in the winter months, they keep at it. Then there's the damned snow. It's been pretty good so far, but we'll get a decent fall or two before Christmas. Last hassle is car wrecks. There's just so much traffic nowadays that any crash on the interstate tends to cause a backup. Especially at this time of year, when the roads are so goddamn wet.'

'So, I guess we need to load and unload as quickly as we can to offset these other delays,' Rolf said.

'Dead right, son. Here we are at the packaging plant. The cartons will all be ready behind the roller door on the dock.

Use that hand trolley in the back. You truck them out as quickly as you can, and I'll stack. Okay?'

'Sure,' Rolf said, anxious to get stuck into some hard work again and keen to impress his new friend.

Fifteen minutes later Rolf said, 'That's the lot, Jim, and they gave me this paperwork too.'

'Good work, Rolf. We've got some room left, so let's have those customer returns stacked up on that pallet over there as well. They have to go back to Paramus for inspection.'

'If they inspect them in Paramus, why don't they get the customers to send them directly to Paramus?' asked Rolf.

'Same answer as before, son. Who gives a shit! Load the damned returns.'

The old man grinned to himself. He liked Rolf's inquisitive nature and knew the trips would be more interesting with this young German than they had been with his regular jockey, who never talked at all. He usually carried a portable radio in the cabin and would turn the volume right up and listen to music every kilometre of the way.

It was a fairly uneventful journey across to New Jersey, though Rolf did spot a few white-tail deer through the trees. Old Jim said that every year in the hunting season he went after white tail with his mates.

Rolf responded that he could never kill such a beautiful animal.

Jim said, 'Rolf, I can respect your point of view on that. Most people either love or hate hunting. But in this country, it certainly pays to know how to use a firearm. Especially if you travel on the interstates a lot.'

With that he reached under the driver's seat and pulled out a lever action 44/40 repeater. 'I always keep this little baby in the truck. Chances are I'll never have to use it. But think about it, Rolf. Say I was driving on my own at night and had a tyre blow-out. I'd have to protect myself and the load from anybody who might be interested in helping themselves to whatever is in the back.'

He handed the rifle to Rolf and went on, 'You see, the point is that highway troopers rarely cross state lines around here, so it's common for crooks to pull a hold-up, then hightail it over the nearest border and disappear. By the way, that's a lever action obviously. There's nothing up the spout right now. You have to work the action to put a new shell in the chamber each time.'

'Yes, I follow, and I guess you're right. Better to be safe than sorry,' Rolf replied. He pushed the rifle back under the driver's seat.

As they travelled north on the New Jersey Turnpike to Paramus, Rolf noticed how chemical plants polluted the air, belching smoke of all colours into the grey sky. He thought for a moment how greatly this industrial part of New Jersey differed from the clean mountain air of Bavaria.

At the warehouse in Paramus, they loaded two batches of yarn that had been spun onto cones for direct loading onto weaving machines. The first few cartons were to go straight to the looms in Scranton for weaving into a tight-knit fabric, for boy's shorts. The other batch was destined directly for the dyehouse section of the Scranton plant, for colouring up in pressure vessels while still on the cones. Finally, they top-loaded some small cartons of new buttons and zippers for the cut-and-sew machine room in Wilkes Barre. They closed up the doors and Jim guided the heavily laden truck, groaning in protest, out onto 17 South to pick up Route 80 West and head back to Pennsylvania.

Despite its load, the truck made good progress. But, as Jim had predicted, they were slowed down a lot approaching the Delaware Water Gap because of roadworks. Joining the slow queue of traffic converging into a single lane going west, Jim said. 'Every day it's very slow along here, because they're doing bridge work up ahead. When we cross the river and come to Stroudsburg, I'll introduce you to Roxy. That'll lighten up your day!'

'It's okay. I can appreciate the scenery more when we slow down like this.'

He wondered to himself what Jim meant by that last remark. Was Roxy a person, a dog or what?

Soon they pulled into a trucker's roadhouse in Stroudsburg. Jim indicated that they might as well have lunch there, since it was after noon already. They chose a table near the window so they could keep an eye on the truck, and Jim beckoned to the waitress to come over.

Rolf looked up as she approached. Before him stood the most attractive woman he had laid eyes on in his life. Tall and statuesque, with shining black hair, the waitress sported a long ponytail. She gave them both a flashing smile from a mouthful of perfectly white, slightly protruding teeth. Her skin was an olive brown and it was clear from her tan that she had spent considerable time outdoors.

She gave Rolf a second glance, then turned to Jim and said, 'Hi, Jim, what can I get you two guys today?'

Rolf was puzzled by the strange accent. Before he could say a word, Jim stood up and said, 'Roxy, let me introduce my new friend first. This young man is Rolf Bauer. He's just come out from Germany. Be working with me for a few weeks. Rolf, this is Roxanne Regan. All the way from Australia.'

Rolf jumped to his feet and put out his hand. 'I'm delighted to meet you, Roxanne.'

That was about all he could say because he was so bowled over by this lovely young woman before him. She looked just perfect. He figured she was probably about his own age or maybe a year younger. Most of her hair was tied back with a big rubber band. Loose strands at the front still cascaded down her forehead. Her uniform was stained and rumpled from the day's work, and she looked a little tired. Yet she was a beauty. No question of that—green eyes, sparkling teeth and that intriguing accent to boot.

'Good to meet you, Rolf, You can call me Roxy, too, if you like. Matter of fact, you can call me Roxy, if you don't like, as well,' she laughed.

They both ordered a steak for lunch. Rolf decided to have some pecan pie so that he could see more of this Australian with the good looks and unfamiliar accent. Too soon, it was time to be off again.

After they paid, Rolf said to Roxy, 'Will you be here again tomorrow, Roxy?'

'Sure will,' she replied. 'I'm working five days a week here for the next month, then I fly back home. Been in America for 12 months now. Kind of a working holiday, you know. I'll see you tomorrow, Rolf. Take care!'

As they continued their journey, Rolf unpacked the sandwiches Marianne had made and threw them out the window for the birds. He thought about Roxy all the way back.

Marianne was reading a book in the Volkswagen, in front of the Reading facility, when he finished for the day. He decided not to tell her about Roxy, yet.

However, Marianne did notice that her brother seemed extraordinarily cheerful after his first day's work.

True to form, the next morning the Volkswagen kicked into life at the third attempt. As they drove again towards Reading, Marianne noticed, for the first time in her life, the unmistakable smell of after-shave on her brother.

Just after noon, Jim and Rolf pulled in again to the truckstop. This time, Roxy looked decidedly different. Her rumpled and soiled uniform of yesterday was replaced with a perfectly clean one that seemed crisp and starched. Her pony tail hairdo was tied back with a pink ribbon, matching her pale pink lipstick. Instead of the jeans she had had under her uniform yesterday, she wore a smart, black, tailored skirt.

Rolf was delighted to see her again. He thought she looked a real knockout. When they finished their meal, Jim excused himself to talk to one of his mates at a nearby table. Rolf took the opportunity to chat a bit more to Roxy, but it was awkward with the diner being so busy.

As they pulled out onto the highway and headed west again, Rolf said to Jim, 'Hey, Jim, that was a bit odd back there. Today Roxy looked a lot more dressed up than yesterday, don't you think?'

'That was for your benefit you big ox,' replied Jim. 'I've been going to that particular truckstop for three months now and Roxy has never been dolled up like that before. You should ask her out.'

'Maybe on Friday. Sorry, Thursday. I'll do just that, Jim. I forgot for a moment we don't work on Fridays.' Rolf wondered if Marianne would lend him the Volkswagen for a day on the weekend.

Thursday came around soon enough and again Jim discreetly left Rolf alone for a few minutes on the pretence of making a phone call. Seizing the opportunity, Rolf popped the question and was very pleased, to say the least, to get an affirmative response. He arranged to call for Roxy at 10:30 on the Saturday morning. They would drive to Allentown for lunch and catch a movie afterwards.

When they approached Reading towards the end of the day, Jim seemed to be deep in thought and then he made Rolf a surprising offer.

'Look, Rolf, there's an old pick-up in my backyard that I only use occasionally because I've got a car as well as this truck. You can borrow it for the next few weeks, while you're working with me. As I say, it's a few years old now, but it goes well and the heater works okay. It'll save your sister driving up to Reading every day. You'll have to buy the gas, of course, but I'll be giving you a pay packet today. What do you say?'

'That's fantastic, Jim. How generous of you! Thanks very much indeed. Should I give you a few dollars for the wear and tear?'

'Oh, gimme a break. Of course not. I've said you can have it. Just make sure you don't lose the tarp and ropes I keep in the back. Put them on the floor in the front if you're leaving the vehicle for any length of time. In fact, it's probably best to lock it up as well whenever you leave it, because there's a rifle under the seat of the pick-up, too.'

'Okay, Jim,' Rolf replied, relieved that he wouldn't have to ask Marianne and Sean about borrowing the Volks.

On that Thursday evening, Rolf told Marianne all about the sun-tanned Australian he had met only on the Monday. She was delighted for her brother. Sean was also pleased to hear the news when he arrived home late the next night.

On the Friday, Rolf went into Lancaster and bought himself a brown corduroy shirt and camel-coloured sweater to match. He got a new can of tan polish for his shoes, filled the pick-up with gas and checked oil, tyres and water. Finally, he bought a fold-out map of the State of Pennsylvania.

At 10:30 exactly on Saturday morning, Rolf pulled up in front of Roxy's apartment building near Stroudsburg. She must have been waiting, because she quickly emerged from a second-floor door and made her way down the stairs. Roxy was dressed in a red topcoat over jeans and a pair of black boots with chunky heels. She had a blue clasp in her ponytail and wore a pair of ruby earrings. Rolf thought she looked simply splendid. He held the car door open and she jumped in quickly to escape the cold.

As they drove to Allentown, she told Rolf her life story. Born in the small town of Maffra, in the State of Victoria, Australia, she was an only child who had lived most of her life in the country. She had been a real tomboy in her early years and thoroughly enjoyed the freedom of living on farms, with her own array of pets. Her parents had originally been involved with dairy farming in Gippsland, but later moved into wool. Dairy farming had involved too many early starts for their liking.

Roxy was pleased with the move towards sheep, because it broke her heart whenever the older cows were sold off to an abattoir as their production waned.

During Roxy's childhood, her parents had bought and sold several properties. She moved about a lot and had never stayed at the one school for more than a year or so. Her school reports described her as a 'tomboy' with an assertive and very headstrong personality. Roxy had been popular with other students because of her friendly nature. She loved school sports and, for the most part, ignored her homework. When she was 17, her parents had purchased a large property in southern New South Wales, and they still lived there.

Roxy told Sean she'd gone to boarding school for a year and hated every minute of it. She'd found the whole school environment too disciplined, prescriptive and claustrophobic, also fairly pretentious. The only thing she liked was the sports activities. She'd excelled in basketball, athletics and swimming.

After boarding school she had worked in a geriatric hospital as a trainee nurse, for over two years. During that period, she told Rolf, she had changed a lot. She'd become more compassionate. She came to realise that life was short and that every moment should be treasured, because illness and old age caught up with everybody, all too quickly.

Eventually, she'd tired of nursing and wanted a change in her life. She found that she got easily bored with the daily grind of work and had drifted from job to job, all the while getting itchy feet.

Following a stint as a waitress, she found that this occupation enabled her to easily move around from place to place. This had led to her decision to head off to America for one last fling, before settling down back in Australia.

When she had finished her story, Rolf said, 'Well, I'm certainly glad you came to Stroudsburg, Roxy Regan.'

'So am I,' she beamed in reply.

In Allentown, they ate lunch at a quaint Italian restaurant. The atmosphere was cosy and warm, with a wood fire burning under a polished copper chimney in the centre of the room.

Rolf began to talk about his life. As he did so, Roxy found herself feeling sorry for the sad times that had befallen him. Rolf described how hard it had been for his family during the war years; how his father had suffered so much; about the hopes and despair of the German people. She listened intently. Occasionally, her brow creased into a frown. Rolf completed his tale on a positive note. He told Roxy all about Marianne's wedding in New York, and explained that he, too, was glad to experience the culture of the United States.

After lunch, they went to the movies to see two new Western adventures screening at a theatre just around the corner from the restaurant.

One featured a stony-faced Randolph Scott and the other an equally uninspiring Gary Cooper in the title role. Neither film could be described as a cinematic masterpiece, but the Indian chases were exciting. Besides, the company was good.

After the movies they did some window-shopping for a while. Rolf was delighted when Roxy put her arm through his and kept close by him as they walked along. Soon it was time to start back to Stroudsburg. Roxy's girlfriend in the apartment was travelling on to Canada the next day, so she didn't want to be out too late. They got a hamburger and Coke each, to eat in the pick-up. Rolf bought a handful of Hershey bars for the glove box. They arrived back in Stroudsburg, just as some snow flurries began to fall. Rolf showed Roxy to the door and, in a most polite fashion, thanked her for her company.

Roxy grabbed him by the jumper, pulled his face down a bit and planted one on his cheek. 'It was great, Rolf. We could go out again next weekend, if you like. In the meantime, I'll see you again on Monday. Take care, won't you; it looks like you'll have snow all the way back.'

Rolf didn't mind the snow in the slightest on his return journey to Lancaster. He was on top of the world. Although Roxy was more headstrong, he thought she was a bit like Marianne. They were both tall and cheerful. And each was blessed with a good sense of humour. How lucky he was. More and more, he liked the United States of America.

When he arrived back at Lancaster, Sean and Marianne were watching a late news bulletin on television. Apparently China had just entered the Korean War—on the side of the North.

They watched the whole segment and then had a coffee by the fire.

Sean said he was worried Patrick might be sent off to the front line in Korea. He considered his own position was probably safe, because they would select single men ahead of the married ones.

'Anyway, Rolf, tell us about your day,' Sean said. 'How did you get on with that girl, what's her name again? Roxy, isn't it?'

Rolf told them about their lunch together, and the movies. Also about eating sloppy hamburgers in the car as they drove along.

Marianne was pleased when he mentioned that they planned to go out somewhere again the next weekend.

'Listen, I've got an idea,' Sean said. 'Why don't the four of us go for a picnic or something, before the weather gets too cold?'

'Good idea, Sean, but where?' Rolf replied.

'I've got it. There's an old fishing spot I used to visit down on the Susquehanna. If we took both vehicles, we could bring some firewood back in the pick-up. There's plenty of dry wood near the bank. It kind of builds up along there every time the river floods. In fact, why don't we light a fire while we're down there and cook some steaks for lunch? That would be fun!'

'Okay, sounds good to me,' Rolf replied

'I'll ask Roxy on Monday if she'll come along. I'm sure she'll want to join us'

'Great,' Marianne said. 'That's all set then.' She was anxious to experience something new in America, and to meet Rolf's new friend.

Chapter 10

Incident on the river

At noon on Monday, when Jim and Rolf called in again at the diner, Roxy said she would love to join in the cookout by the river. She insisted on bringing all the steaks, and explained to Rolf that she and the other diner staff could get them cheaply from the truck-stop refrigerator. Also, that she would be sure to select some of the best cuts for their outing.

'That's great,' said Rolf. 'You'll really like my sister, Marianne, and her husband, Sean, when you meet them. We'll have a great time. I'll buy some nice red wine during the week to go with the steaks.'

'Rolf, I don't really want to wait until the weekend before I see you again. How about coming to my apartment for dinner on Wednesday night? That is, if it's not too far for you to drive back after your day's work.'

'Hell, no!' replied Rolf. 'Most of the day, I'm just sitting in the truck. The loading and unloading doesn't take long at all. Let's say eight o'clock on Wednesday evening.'

Roxy nodded. She thought that some spaghetti with salad and bread rolls might be the ticket.

On Wednesday, Rolf brought a change of clothes in his pick-up so that when he finished work he could go directly to Roxy's place from Reading. He had a quick wash-up and shave after work, in the men's room at the plant, then set off for Stroudsburg.

The traffic was light and the night was clear. He arrived in Stroudsburg about 25 minutes early. Thinking it would be impolite to barge in early, he waited until just before eight before driving up to the apartment.

Roxy welcomed him with her flashing smile and gave him another little peck on the cheek. The table was laid out beautifully, with a lace cloth, candles and even a bunch of winter pansies in a small vase. Her apartment was small, but tidy and warm. She was dressed in a short, black evening frock and wore high-heeled black shoes. Again she wore the ruby earrings, but this time with a matching ruby brooch. It was the first time Rolf had seen her decked out in high heels. He liked what he saw.

They ate and talked, had some beer then ate and talked some more.

Roxy knew that she was rapidly falling in love with this big German farmer. Rolf was equally aware that Roxy was becoming more than just a friend. They moved to the sofa and had a couple of glasses of bourbon.

Rolf said, 'I mustn't have any more to drink now. I have a fairly long drive back to Lancaster. I'll get too drowsy.'

'Sure, Rolf, I'll make us some coffee.'

As Roxy stood at the stove waiting for the jug to boil, Rolf came up behind her. He put his big arms around her waist and kissed her on the back of her neck. She smelled so sweet and felt so warm and soft. Roxy turned around slowly and they kissed each other fiercely on the lips. It was a long, enduring embrace, leaving no doubt that this was more than friendship.

Looking into her eyes, Rolf said, 'I never dreamed that I'd fall in love with an Australian Fraülein.'

Roxy took Rolf by the hand and led him towards the bedroom door. 'Let's leave the coffee a minute, Rolf.'

It was after 2 am when Rolf turned off the pick-up the next morning, back in Lancaster. Marianne heard him come in. She allowed herself a knowing smile.

The following Saturday, Rolf left early to collect Roxy. The couple returned to Sean's place at about 10:30 in the morning. After introductions all round, they set off for the Susquehanna.

Marianne had packed a large flask with hot coffee and some bread rolls, ketch-up and beer. As she and Sean travelled along in the Volkswagen, she remarked to Sean that Roxy seemed to be a really good match for Rolf.

'I agree, Marianne. They seem to be good together. What a funny accent she has. Kind of an English sound, but nicer. It's good to see Rolf so happy.'

In the pick-up, Roxy had her arm entwined in Rolf's. She sat close to him on the bench seat. An icebox bouncing around in the back had an ample supply of steaks, plus extra beers. Roxy was feeling more than a kinship with Rolf; it was more a kind of belonging.

The weather was kind to them that day. The sun shone briefly for a while, and, though it was cold, there was no wind at all.

They reached the river and Sean drove along the road near the bank for several kilometres. The trees along the river had all lost their leaves. Occasionally, an abandoned bird's nest broke the monotony of the bare branches. The Susquehanna itself was an awe-inspiring sight. This was a mean river. It became all the more dangerous over the winter and spring. Rising in New York, in the area known as Otsego County, the river wound its way over 600 kilometres to Chesapeake Bay, in Maryland. The water flow had once been recorded at a million cubic feet a second. The Susquehanna was a waterway that demanded respect.

At length, they pulled off onto an old track leading down to a clearing just beside the water. The area was so overgrown with bushes that they would have to back right out. There simply wasn't enough room to turn the vehicles. It was an excellent spot—small, but private and sheltered from the wind.

Rolf and Sean gathered enough dry bark and firewood to get a good fire going.

Sean said, 'Rolf, before we leave, let's load the pick-up with some of those logs over there. Most of them are so short we won't even have to cut them. They're pretty dry. Should be perfect for the fireplace.'

'Yes, good idea, Sean. There's a tarp in the back. We can cover them and tie the load down in case it rains on the way back.'

Sean produced a couple of large Army fry pans from the boot of the Volkswagen. It wasn't long before they had the steaks cooking over hot coals.

'Well, we've gathered the wood and lit the fire, Mr Bauer. I think we deserve some light refreshment, don't you?' Sean said.

'If you insist, Mr Gleeson,' Rolf replied. He pulled two bottles from the icebox and threw one to Sean. They made their way through the bushes to the riverbank to share a couple of beers, while Marianne and Roxy had a good chat next to the fire. The Susquehanna was about a 400 metres wide at this point. Both men could feel the chill coming off the surface of the icy water. Back at the fire, the two young women developed an immediate liking for each other and sensed they would be good friends for a long time.

As she would be leaving for Australia at the end of December, Marianne invited Roxy to have Christmas dinner with them in Lancaster. It was an offer Roxy immediately accepted.

Lunch that day was a delightful meal between four friends relishing each other's company by a warm fire in the land of the free. Sean and Rolf were getting stuck into the beer, so the girls had some as well. As the afternoon wore on, they got the tarpaulin out of the pick-up, spread it out and all settled down next to the fire.

It was cosy and luxurious just to relax in the warmth; their senses were already lulled by full bellies and American beer.

Eventually, Rolf found it a bit too hot by the fire, so he and Roxy went for a walk along the river. In fact they didn't go too far at all. In the bushes, they stopped and kissed with a passion born out of desire and fuelled by Budweiser.

Rolf said, 'Roxy, I wish you weren't going away at the end of the month. I'll really miss you. You mean so much to me.'

'I know, Rolf. I'm falling in love with you too. Let's just take it a week at a time and see how we feel about each other around Christmas time.'

He kissed her again and held her tight. They made their way back to the others.

Sean was fast asleep and Marianne was cleaning up. She put everything back in the car and poured some coffee for them.

It was now about four in the afternoon and getting colder, so Rolf put another log on the fire. While the girls drank their coffee and Sean snored, Rolf spent about half an hour throwing small logs into the back of the pick-up. At one point, he thought he heard the sound of a motorbike through the trees, but paid it no mind.

Dark storm clouds passed across the sun and the light started to fade. They decided it was time to get moving. Marianne said she would take Roxy in the Volkswagen so they could have a bit of a gossip on the way back. They pulled the logs out of the fire and spread them out so it would die down more quickly. Marianne and Roxy had some fun spraying beer over the glowing embers. The red coals hissed back in angry protest. The girls jumped in the Volkswagen to escape the cold.

Sean was fully refreshed after his nap. He told Rolf he would drive the pick-up because he hadn't helped with any of the loading. They spread the tarp across the logs and tied it down. Some of the coals still glowed a little, so they both turned their backs on the ladies and pissed on the dying embers. Rolf opened the door of the pick-up and jumped in the passenger side. He yelled out to Sean, 'Come on, driver, let's go. It'll be dark before we know it.'

As Sean grasped the handle of the driver's side door, he sensed a rustle in the bushes. A dirty, bearded man in a leather jacket jumped out from the shrubbery behind him. Slightly taller than Sean, and powerfully built with massive shoulders, he was a balding hulk of a man with tattooed arms and decaying, yellow teeth.

In the space of only about 10 seconds, he king-hit Sean on the side of the head with his closed fist, slapped a handcuff on his wrist, bundled him forward and manacled his arm to a bracket on the front bumper. Rolf couldn't believe his eyes. The whole thing was bizarre. It had all happened so quickly without a word being spoken.

As he gathered his wits, Rolf flew out the passenger side. He was determined to wreak swift vengeance on Sean's attacker. Unfortunately for him, there was a second man, an unkempt thug with a crewcut, wearing an old army jacket. He had been concealed in a crouched position on the passenger side, with a short tree branch in his hand. As soon as Rolf tore past, he rose up and lashed out with a fearful blow at head height. It knocked Rolf unconscious on the spot.

Seeing the unprovoked attack from behind on Rolf, Sean became distraught and angry, 'You bastards, you cowardly bastards, what do you want? We haven't got any money!' he yelled.

By now Marianne and Roxy had realised something was amiss. The pair got out of the Volkswagen and approached the pick-up—their mouths agape in surprise.

'Run!' shouted Sean, sensing the real purpose of the attack. 'Get away. Run for your lives!'

Before the frightened pair even had a chance to absorb it all the vagrants were upon them. The crew-cut one jumped on Roxy's back. His sheer weight forced her to the ground He sat astride her back, grabbed her by her ponytail and laughed as she struggled beneath him.

'Get off me you fat, stinking bastard,' Roxy yelled in vain.

The other, bigger, man had tackled Marianne to the grass also and straddled her by sitting on her stomach. His enormous weight alone caused her great discomfort and she struggled for breath and squirmed in anguish. Sean was beside himself with rage. The big man ignored Marianne's distress, seemingly gratified by her pain. He grabbed both her wrists and forced them back onto the ground behind her head. His foul breath made her wince in disgust. Callously, he ripped open the blouse beneath her sweater. Sean wrenched at the handcuffs frantically, but it was useless.

Fortunately, the blow that had struck Rolf didn't keep him out for long. As he came out of his daze, he could see beneath the pick-up what was happening ahead of the vehicle. His eyes darted around for any weapon he might use. He quietly dragged himself up, thinking he would carefully pull a piece of wood from the back. Then he remembered! Old Jim Masterton had told him there was a 44/40 under the seat of the pick-up as well. Thankfully, the passenger door was ajar. Rolf ever so quietly moved his arm under the seat. His hand closed around the cold steel of the barrel.

Shutting out the screams, he tried to concentrate on what he had to do. He crouched down and looked under the pick-up again. Clearly, Marianne was the one who needed immediate help. The man on top of her was now holding her bra aloft; brandishing it like some kind of trophy.

Slowly and quietly, Rolf crawled around the back of the pick-up. The grass at the roadside was thick and lush and helped dull the noise. He could see that the man on top of Marianne now had his huge, grubby hands around her throat and was choking her. Rolf worked the lever action to put a bullet in the chamber. The ruffian heard the unmistakable sound. He glanced up to see Rolf with the gun aimed at his head.

'Let her go now, or you die!' Rolf said in a very deliberate tone.

'Not fucking likely!' was the only response.

'For the last time, let her go now!' Rolf barked.

'Drop the gun first!' the bearded man shouted, making no attempt to release his hold.

They were the last words he spoke. A shot rang out and summary justice was unleashed. The heavy 44/40 slug pushed him right off Marianne. He was dead in a heartbeat.

Without a moment's hesitation, Rolf turned his attention to the other man, who had both hands on the back of Roxy's head.

He had been pushing her face mercilessly into the grass. Although she wasn't really injured, her face was white as she frantically gasped for breath.

'Kill him too!' screamed Sean.

'Move away from her now!' Rolf demanded, as he nonchalantly aimed the rifle at the man's temple.

The crewcut man moved his hands quickly from Roxy's ponytail and slowly got to his feet. He backed away a couple of feet and pleaded, 'You don't need to shoot me. I could have snapped the neck of that bitch if I'd wanted. I'm outta here! Don't try and stop me!'

'Stay exactly where you are!' Rolf barked.

To emphasise the point, he tried to fire a shot in the grass just ahead of the assailant.

When he pulled the trigger, nothing happened.

The attacker looked surprised, then a hideous grin spread across his face.

'Work the lever!' Sean screamed.

The man lunged back towards Roxy. Before he reached her, his spinal cord was shattered as a soft-nosed 44/40 slug splattered his neck. His body twitched for a moment and then it was still.

The girls struggled to their feet and the four friends stood silent for a while. Their minds were trying to absorb the horrifying events that had unfolded in only minutes. It was as much the shock of the encounter as anything. Fifteen minutes earlier they had all been happy and on top of the world. Now their whole world was falling apart.

Sean broke the silence by pleading, 'Get me out of these things, for God's sake.'

Rolf searched through the pockets of the dead men until he found a set of keys. He released Sean, whose wrist was bloodied from his futile struggles.

Roxy went first to Marianne. She was as white as a sheet and still trembling. She helped her button her torn sweater. Marianne's neck was already darkened from the bruising, but she was soon breathing freely again. The two embraced. Marianne wiped some of the dirt and grass stains from Roxy's face.

Rolf was physically upset. He was shaking with the full realisation that he had just taken the lives of two human beings.

Roxy put her arms around him. She held him close with her cheek against his and said, 'Rolf, you did what you had to do. You had no choice. If you hadn't shot the bastards, Marianne and I would be dead by now.'

For the next 10 minutes confusion reigned. They tried frantically to collect their thoughts and decide what to do next. Sean was the exception. He remained fairly calm and seemed deep in thought. The others agreed that they must call the police and come clean on what had taken place.

Rolf said, 'Sean, we're going to call the cops and tell them the whole story. Are you okay? You look pretty damn pale.'

'Gimme about 10 minutes before we do anything,' he said firmly.

Sean examined both bodies, and checked the men's wallets and clothes. He then inspected the forearms of each attacker. Next, he walked further back along the track and around a bend, looking for another vehicle. Instead, he found two Harley Davidsons parked by the side of the road.

Meanwhile, Rolf went up to Roxy, who was giving Marianne a drink of cold coffee to help her breathing.

'Roxy,' he said. 'You could walk away from me now and I would understand. I guess I'll probably be tied up in court for ages over this and I know you want to go back to Australia. I'd understand if you wanted to move on and put this whole business behind you.'

Roxy was livid with indignation at Rolf's suggestion. 'Don't talk to me like that, Rolf Bauer. Just who the bloody hell do you think I am? Some floozie who's going to walk off as soon as you get into strife. I want to marry you—to share the rest of my life with you. So let's have no more of this "walk away" bullshit.'

With that, Marianne and Rolf both put their arms around their dear Roxy. No words were necessary. Her loyalty to the Bauers had been severely tested this day. She had not been found wanting.

Sean was deep in thought. His military mind was doing a situation analysis of the events that had transpired. Carefully, he weighed up all the factors involved.

As he approached, Rolf said, 'Okay, let's get this over with. How about we go straight to the police and tell them everything?'

In a slow and measured voice, Sean replied, 'No-one is going to the police.'

Chapter 11

Concealing the evidence

The trio were taken aback by Sean's words. Anxiously, they waited for him to explain. He took a deep breath, paused for a second and said, 'Look, it's important to understand the full implications of what has happened here. First of all, these two are both ex-service men from the United States Navy. Their bikes are registered in California and from documents in their wallets I'd say they are both from San Diego. They've probably been drifting about for a couple of years now, because all their stuff is worn and dirty. One problem we have is that the guy with the crewcut is no ordinary seaman. He's got more decorations than a Christmas tree. Even carried a wad of newspaper clippings about his achievements in the Pacific. One article is about his leadership in a battle against the Japs. The other cites his bravery in single-handedly putting out an engine room fire at great risk to his own life. The man's a goddamn war hero.'

'But, Sean, surely it was self-defence,' interrupted Marianne.

'Absolutely! Self-defence would stand up in the case of the one who was trying to strangle you, Marianne. The problem is the other guy. Think about it! He had no weapon. We all know he'd have broken Roxy's neck if he'd got hold of her. The question is whether or not that justifies shooting him dead.

Personally, I think it was the only thing to do at the time. Hey, I yelled at Rolf to pull the trigger. But if we go to the cops, others will make their own judgment. A smart DA, for example, might argue that Rolf had time to shoot him in the leg, and lobby for a manslaughter charge at least. Then there's the Press. They'd have a field day over this. I can just see the headline. "German visitor to the US, working illegally in our country, shoots dead one of our war heroes".'

'Hang on a minute,' said Rolf. He was more than a little dismayed and defensive at Sean's cold assessment of the situation. 'I shot them both, so I can face the music. There's no need for the rest of you to be drawn into this.'

'Not so, my friend,' Sean replied. He put a re-assuring hand on Rolf's shoulder. 'I'm an accomplice in this as well, Rolf. I yelled at you to shoot him. Remember! Anyway, the big problem we still face is the use of deadly force when they had no weapons. Precedent comes into the whole equation too. This isn't Europe, where civil law applies. In America we have common law, where precedent is king. Some smart lawyer would only need to dig up a similar incident where lethal force was judged to be an over-reaction and we would be in big trouble.'

Roxy intervened. 'Sean, okay, you've told us what the situation is. There's no way I want to see Rolf spend a day in jail over this pair of scum. If we're not going to the cops, just what do you propose?'

'Well, we can't bring them back and I'm damned if I want my military career and discharge benefits screwed up by this pair. I say we get rid of everything—the bodies, the gun and the bikes. Everything. We remove every single trace.'

Sean waited for a reply from the others. When none was forthcoming, he went on, 'Here's my plan. First of all, we'll all go back to work on Monday if possible as though nothing has happened. I'll cover up these gashes on my wrist and, Roxy, you'll need to put make-up over those scratches on your chin. Rolf and I will have to get rid of everything here by end-of-day tomorrow. It won't be easy, but it can be done. Once we've concealed all the physical evidence, it'll be easier for us to put this whole bloody mess behind us. We'll hide the rifle, the bodies, their clothes and the bikes all in different locations. Now, are we all agreed on this as the best course of action?'

The other three nodded in silent assent. They didn't have any better ideas, nor did they have any pity for the assailants whose lifeless bodies were only a metre away in the gathering darkness.

Sean went on. 'Okay, let's do it, then. The first thing is to get the girls on their way home. Rolf, drive the pick-up off to the left there a bit, so that Marianne can back the Volkswagen past it. Roxy, maybe you should drive instead of Marianne.'

'Sorry, Sean, I've never driven on the right before. It's left-hand drive in Australia. Probably better if Marianne can drive. I might draw attention to us.'

'I'll be fine,' Marianne said. 'I just want to get out of here. Is there anything you want us to do when we get back, Sean?'

'No, just act normally. We'll be home about an hour after you.'

When the Volkswagen had gone, Sean said, 'Rolf, don't worry, my friend. We'll get through this. I'll stand by you all the way. Just help me with everything for the next 24 hours or so.'

'All right, Sean, I'll go along with your judgment on this. But before we do anything, tell me exactly what your plans are. I've got a pretty big stake in all this.'

'Fair enough, buddy. Here's the deal. I've worked half of it out anyway. First thing we should do is wipe the rifle clean of fingerprints and throw it in the river on the way back, a few miles further along. Then tomorrow morning, we'll bury the bodies in a land-fill site I know on a new section of the interstate. They don't work on the weekend and the spot I have in mind is not visible from the existing highway. We must get rid of the bodies first. That's our top priority. After that we'll figure out what to do with the Harleys.'

'A couple of comments,' Rolf replied. 'First of all, let's take the rifle apart and throw the three sections—the lever action, the barrel and the stock all in different parts of the river a mile or two apart. Secondly, let's strip the bodies right now of any identification—documents, marked clothing, rings and so forth so that we don't have to worry about that in the morning. Also, let's lay these vermin out straight before rigour mortis sets in so they'll be easier to handle tomorrow. There's a tool box in the back of the pick-up, so I'll take the rifle apart straight away in the light of the headlights.'

Sean nodded in silent approval and moved over to strip the bodies of any identification. The more he got to know Rolf, the more he respected the intelligence and commonsense of his farmer friend.

Soon they were ready to leave and backed the pick-up out onto the river road. They had concealed the bodies and the bikes in the bushes at the roadside and drove off with very mixed emotions. At suitable intervals, they hurled the gun components out into the Susquehanna and then made their way back to Lancaster.

The pair arrived home at about seven and all four stayed up until after midnight.

The girls didn't cook an evening meal, since no-one felt hungry. Sean and Rolf went over their plans for concealing the bodies in great detail. Then they turned their attention to the motorbikes. How could they make both machines disappear? For two hours they racked their brains and couldn't come up with any plausible solution. They considered burying the bikes, burning them, putting them into the river—all sorts of options. But none of them seemed foolproof. Eventually, they decided to leave the bikes in the bush where they were for the time being, until they could find a satisfactory answer.

The two men went over their plans to dispose of the bodies over and over again.

Roxy went to bed about 2:30 am in Rolf's room, while he settled himself down on the sofa an hour later. A dull fire still burned in the hearth. When Marianne got up around 4:30 am for a glass of water and an aspirin, the sofa was empty. If ever there was a time that two souls needed to cling together, this was it, she thought.

Sean and Rolf set out at first light in the morning. They arrived at the riverbank by 8:30 and were relieved to see the area undisturbed. There were no fishermen or hunters around. Quickly they lifted the bodies onto the pick-up and then covered them with the tarpaulin. As they roped the load down, Rolf remarked how clear their tyre prints appeared in the roadway.

'Don't sweat it, Rolf,' Sean said. 'The forecast is for thunderstorms and hail tomorrow. Those tracks will soon be gone.'

They pushed the two motorbikes even further into the dense bush and wiped their fingerprints from the handlebars.

Without delay, they backed out and proceeded to drive the 50 kilometres to the road-construction site. As they approached the track leading off to the new road works, they noticed a trooper's car parked on the shoulder. Rolf decided to continue past without slowing down. They went on another eight kilometres until they came to an overpass, then decided to chance it and make their way back again. After only a kilometre or so, they saw the patrol car speeding off in the other direction with its lights flashing.

Both men breathed a sigh of relief as they drove on to the track leading from the highway. Within minutes they came to the new section. It was a deep valley being progressively filled by rocks, building material, soil and all kinds of dry fill, so that the new section of interstate could remain reasonably level at this point. Huge earth-moving equipment surrounded the perimeter. The contractors wanted to complete the fill during winter, in time for compacting works in the spring.

Carefully, they looked around and could see that there was no other person or other vehicles in sight.

'This is just perfect,' said Rolf. 'How did you know about this place?'

'Oh, it was entirely by chance. I was hitching a ride home one Friday afternoon and the truck that picked me up made a diversion to this spot to drop off some rubble. The driver said they take in about 70 truck loads a day, so it won't be long before these gentlemen in the back are well and truly concealed.'

They drove carefully along the ramp the dump trucks had been using. The heavily laden vehicles would just dump at the very end. Bulldozers would then push the fill over the edge, creating an ever-longer ridge across the valley. When they reached the end, the two friends considered driving back and down to the base of the fill for a hiding spot. Eventually, they decided against it because their tyre tracks might be visible in the morning, even if it rained.

Instead, they peered over the edge, looking for any hollow where they could safely secrete the bodies. Finding nothing suitable, Sean clambered down the slope a few feet and soon discovered the ideal location. There was a large sheet of concrete masonry—probably a prefabricated wall, lying on its side in a horizontal position amid all the rubble. Beneath the huge sheet there was an empty space large enough to contain the two bodies.

Again the two men looked carefully around, to ensure that they were not being observed. Then, without delay, they manhandled the bodies down the difficult slope and lodged them under the concrete sheet. Sean got one of the shovels they had brought and filled in the face of the opening with rocks and soil so that both bodies were entirely concealed.

They clambered up the slope and left as quickly as possible, confident that one half of the day's work had been successfully completed.

The next week was full of tension and took ages to go by.

Sean went back to work and found it almost impossible to concentrate.

Roxy found it especially difficult at the diner by herself, but thought she could cope. On the Wednesday, Rolf drove along the interstate past the land-fill site. Even from a distance, he could see that tonnes and tonnes of further rubble covered the bodies.

Eventually, Friday night came around and Sean returned to Lancaster.

That evening, he and Rolf continued their discussion on what to do with the bikes. Still they couldn't come up with a solution. Marianne poured them another cup of coffee and talked with Roxy about Roxy's difficult week at the diner.

Suddenly, there was a breakthrough. As he gazed at the red-hot coals glowing in the hearth, Sean surprised them all by saying he had the answer. He explained his idea to the others and they agreed that it could work.

At 9:30 that night, Sean made the phone call to put his plan in motion. He dialled the home number of his long-time army buddy, Mike Pradonavic. The others remained quiet and listened intently as he made the fateful call.

'Say, Mike, this is Sean. How the devil are you these days?'

Mike was obviously pleased to hear from Sean. They laughed and joked for a couple of minutes before Sean continued more seriously, 'Mike, are you still the super over at that smelting joint near Harrisburg?'

The reply was apparently affirmative, and Sean went on, 'Listen, Mike, I need you to do me a big favour. One of the guys in our old unit has managed to get himself in a corner with the Feds. The damn fool has gotten involved in counterfeiting bank notes. Bottom line is that he needs to get rid of the plates and he's desperate to get them destroyed. You see, without the plates as evidence they can't charge him with anything. You'll understand that I wouldn't like to tell you who he is, but any chance we could chuck the plates into the mix at the smelter? There'll be 500 dollars in it for you.'

Rolf, Marianne and Roxy waited on the edge of their seats for news of the man's reaction. Sean listened carefully for about three minutes and then hung up with the words, 'Thanks a million, Mike. We will only be there for the 10 minutes we've agreed and let's never speak of this again. God bless you, pal!'

'It's okay,' said Sean, with a big sigh of relief.

'He's agreed to leave the gate open for us on Sunday while they go to lunch, but doesn't want any further involvement at all. Also, I've agreed that if we get caught, we won't implicate him in any way. Now, let me explain things a bit more. This smelter we just talked about is a place where they melt down car bodies and all kinds of scrap metal in a big electric crucible. After an hour or so, they drain off the molten steel and extrude it into rods for concrete re-enforcement mesh. The plant is shut for maintenance tomorrow but works on Sunday. The whole crew goes to lunch from 12:30 to 1:15. For safety reasons, the canteen is about 150 metres away from the smelter and entirely hidden from view behind some enclosed loading bays. Mike will unlock the padlock on the main gate at 12:30 and leave the key in the industrial lift that goes up to the top of the crucible. He wants us in and out in 10 minutes and says the plates will melt in about ten seconds flat.'

On Saturday night, Sean phoned Mike once more to double check that everything was okay. Mike confirmed their earlier arrangement, but said he thought it was worth a thousand bucks. Sean agreed, with a little hesitation.

By 10:20 on Sunday morning, Sean and Rolf had arrived at the dreaded picnic spot where the shootings had taken place only a week earlier. Dark clouds were rumbling in the sky and it looked as if rain would come tumbling down any minute. Using a wide plank they had kept from the land-fill site, they pushed the two bikes up onto the pick-up, lashed them down and completely covered the load with the tarpaulin.

When the smoke belching from the steel smelter came into sight the time was only 12:15, so Rolf slowed down and pulled off by the side of the road. At about 12:28 he moved forward again so that they arrived at the gate at exactly 12:32. As expected, the padlock was undone, so they drove directly over to the lift tower. Rolf backed the pick-up so that it was adjacent to the access doors.

Sean looked around in all directions. When he was satisfied no-one was watching, he yelled to Rolf that he would open the doors. The noise around them was deafening. Energy expended in the cauldron produced a massive amount of heat. The giant crucible caused old car engines and such to literally explode in its molten core. The smelter was like a giant electric jug, about 15 metres high. In the centre were three enormous electric probes that provided the heat for decomposition of metal. The whole scene was like Dante's inferno, heat, noise and smoke all combining to create a highly dangerous and intimidating environment. The two friends agreed not to bother with protective clothing, but to get in and out as fast as possible.

In an instant, they backed the two bikes into the lift. Frantically they searched for the lift controls. Behind a pair of leather gloves hanging on a pillar, Sean found two buttons. He pressed the green one. Slowly they ascended. Already, the radiated heat was enormous. As the lift continued its ponderously slow journey upwards, they knew they should have donned protective coats.

Wringing with perspiration, they arrived at the top. They kicked open the double doors. Before them was a steel chute leading straight down into the bubbling cauldron of molten steel. Ignoring as best they could the incredible heat, the two friends quickly sent the two Harleys to a fiery end in the glowing mix below. Both machines completely disappeared in seconds.

Sean threw in a dirty, leather side bag from one of the bikes. It contained a corduroy jacket, a leather wristband, two wallets, a wedding ring, a watch, three medals and various newspaper clippings. Such was the heat of the cauldron that the bag was alight even before it hit the molten surface.

They shut the doors and descended, both saturated in grimy perspiration. It was 12:43 as they padlocked the gate. The whole operation had taken just 11 minutes.

Both were silent and introspective on the way back to Lancaster, their minds racing with the drama of it all. Now at least there was some quiet satisfaction that all the physical evidence was squared away. Rolf was very relieved. Sean decided that he would get the thousand-dollar payment to Mike Pradonavic without delay. There could be no loose ends.

Chapter 12

Decision time

When Rolf and old Jim pulled into the diner around noon the next day, Roxy was in a state. Clearly agitated, she beckoned Rolf to come out the back. She blurted out that she was a bundle of nerves, unable to concentrate on anything. Try as she might, she could not suppress the violent images of the past week. Things were catching up with her.

Sobbing into Rolf's shoulder, she begged him to agree that she resign immediately. For a moment he was inclined to go along with her, but he persuaded her to stay on for the afternoon. They both decided it would be best that she see out the day. However, they also agreed that the next morning Marianne would call the proprietor. On the pretence of being a distraught family member, she would explain that Roxy must return to Australia immediately because of family illness. Moreover, Rolf agreed with Roxy that he, too, would finish on the coming Friday. Reasonably satisfied with these arrangements, she dried her eyes and went back to her duties, consoled but not content.

While Marianne was grateful for Roxy's company for the remainder of the week, Friday was a long time coming for Rolf. Old Jim was disappointed to lose him, but their arrangement was on a casual basis, so he could scarcely complain.

Marianne and Roxy had driven up to Reading to collect Rolf on the Friday afternoon. When he handed the keys of the pick-up back to old Jim, Rolf took $200 from his pocket.

'Jim, I'm sorry, but I must have left it unlocked at some stage because that rifle under the seat seems to be missing. Will 200 cover it?'

'No, 200 is too much for that old girl. I haven't used that piece for years. Not even sure the bloody thing would still be working. Just gimme 100.'

Rolf handed over the 100-dollar bill, ruefully thinking to himself that the rifle had worked just fine.

Christmas was soon upon them. That year it was a very sober affair in the Gleeson household, despite the magic of snow flurries that arrived just in time to wrap Lancaster County in a blanket of white.

Sean was comfortable in the knowledge that his parents were now domiciled down in Florida, among their friends and relatives. After all, they had their own lives to lead.

However, he was troubled by a couple of developments in the Army. His buddy Patrick and several of his Washington friends had been transferred to Korea a few days earlier. Apparently the UN forces were losing the battle. North Korea, strongly supported by China, was pushing further south— perilously close to Seoul. While he missed Patrick, Sean was more annoyed that his personal workload was gradually increasing. He felt that unless he took some action, he wouldn't be able to get home every weekend. The shootings also weighed heavily on his mind, as did his long-term goal to make out a living off the land.

In serious discussions with Marianne, Sean realised he was moving inexorably towards resigning from the Army. Deep down, they both wanted to move away from Lancaster and its chilling memories.

Roxy had settled down somewhat after her ordeal. She and Marianne became closer as they recovered from the nightmare of the Susquehanna.

On the one hand, Roxy desperately wanted to get back home to Australia. But, at the same time, she felt a growing love and respect for the big, blond German who had come into her life. She and Rolf enjoyed each other's company immensely.

Rolf never tired of Roxy's stories about her childhood on outback properties. He discovered to his delight that this girl of his knew a lot about farming. More and more, her recollections and anecdotes intrigued him: tales of massive sheep stations, wild shearers, yabbying in dams, rabbit casseroles, and so on. At times he wondered whether she was stretching the truth a bit, talking of earning pocket money by shooting crows, whistling up foxes at night, skinning rabbits and driving a Land Rover at the age of 12. These were strange things indeed to one born and raised in the cloistered environment of the Bavarian mountains. Several times, they talked about what to do next with their lives, more often than not skirting around the issue. Both felt uncomfortable to be living together unmarried, but neither wanted to put their partnership at risk.

Rolf's whole outlook was starting to change. After all he had experienced, he felt it was time to take charge of his life, to dictate the course of his future and take charge. The shootings played on his mind every day. He needed an escape. To start again somewhere, and build a new life for himself. At length, therefore, it was Rolf who brought the matter to a resolution.

'Roxy, I have come to a decision,' he started. 'We both want to move away from Lancaster. You're anxious to get back home and I want to settle down soon and work a farm of my own. I've decided I'm not going back to settle down in Germany.

My mother is my only blood relative there, and she has the means to visit me wherever I am. Marianne and I each have a half stake in our property in Germany. I think it's time to put a stake in the ground. My plan is to sell the farm in Bavaria as soon as I can and move to Australia, then to marry you, my dear. To buy us a farm so we can settle down and raise a couple of girls with your green eyes. What do you think?'

Roxy was beside herself with joy to hear from Rolf's lips the very thoughts she had only dared to dream. She wrapped her arms around him and hugged him tightly for a long time. Tears of happiness spilled down her face. 'Rolf, you'll love it in Australia. I can't wait for you to meet Mum and Dad. Let's get married around Easter time. I've got lots of friends to invite. Oh, this is so exciting! You'll have dozens of new things to learn about farming. Let's tell the other two about it.'

Over dinner that evening, they explained everything to Sean and Marianne.

Predictably, Marianne immediately agreed Rolf could sell the farm property back home. She was pleased to see Rolf and Roxy so happy and anxious to tie the knot and carve out a new future for themselves.

'When exactly would you be heading off to Australia?' Sean asked.

'Well, Roxy is already ticketed to go back from New York in about three weeks, so I thought I'd book on the same flight. Why do you ask?'

'Just curious,' Sean replied, winking at Marianne.

That night, as they lay in bed, Sean said, 'Marianne, you know those two tickets your mother sent us a few weeks ago? Let's give them to Rolf. Then he can take Roxy to see your mother before they head off to Australia.'

'Sean, how thoughtful of you. I didn't think of that. Are you sure we wouldn't want to use them ourselves?'

'Well, not in the short-term, anyway. I'm going to be flat out at work until about March and then I think I'll resign and be done with it. I'll get a pretty good pay-out, and we could go to Germany for a visit then, if you like.'

'Sean Gleeson, you're a great guy!' she responded.

The next evening the phone in Lancaster rang red-hot. First, Roxy called her parents in the outback town of Macarthur Creek in New South Wales. Her mother, Natalie, knew she was going out with Rolf, but it was a pleasant surprise to hear that the two were now planning an Easter wedding.

'Roxy, are you sure about this man, Rolf? You've only known each other for a few weeks,' Natalie said.

'Don't worry, Mum. I know what I'm doing. I want to spend my life with Rolf. He's a good man and we've really clicked, I liked him from the minute I first met him at the diner. I'm sure you and Dad will like him too. As I told you last time I rang, he's a big guy, but very gentle and considerate. A farmer as well. I'll put a photo in the mail tomorrow. By the way, can you check if they can put him up at the hotel for a couple of months? I know they usually have a couple of rooms available. Is Dad there?'

'No, he's away at the moment on a fishing trip down south for three days. I'll see if I can ring him tomorrow. Roxy, as long as you are sure, my dear, then I'm very happy for you. Don't worry about the hotel, I'll make sure they have a room.'

Natalie Regan put the phone down and immediately called many of her friends and relatives to break the good news. Several called Roxy to wish her the best and give assurances that they would be at the wedding, whenever or wherever it was to be held.

When the phone was eventually free, Rolf made a call to Munich.

Brigitte was very happy to hear that her only son had found his bride-to-be. She was disappointed to hear that the wedding would be in Australia, but pleased to know that Rolf and Roxy would be visiting Germany soon.

Five days later, in the middle of January 1951, Rolf and Roxy were on their way to Munich. They had a full day in New York before the main flight, so they went to the jewellery area of mid-town Manhattan and selected a diamond engagement ring. Then they fixed up Rolf's visa application for Australia. To celebrate their engagement, they splashed out on lunch at the Plaza Hotel.

They booked Rolf's ticket to Australia, at the airport.

It was freezing in New York. They were tired and glad to climb on board the plane to Germany.

During the flight, the pilot put a special announcement over the speaker system. North Korean forces had captured the giant city of Seoul. Rolf hoped that Sean's friend Patrick O'Connor would be safe in that far-off conflict.

Rolf and Roxy stayed only six days in Munich. Although Brigitte made them very welcome, she was very pre-occupied with Wolfgang's health and well-being. Despite the fact that the pair walked twice each day in the English Garden, it was clear that Wolfgang was losing strength.

Rolf took Roxy for a nostalgic drive out to the farmhouse. He found to his surprise that he no longer felt the same affinity for the area. It was as if that chapter of his life had closed. They called in at the Salzburg office and had lunch with Martin Kohl and his fiancee, Renate Becke.

Renate gave Rolf's hand a playful squeeze as they said hello again. Rolf thought she looked even more attractive than when had they danced together at the wedding.

Fortunately, with Roxy by his side, he had the good sense to keep these thoughts entirely to himself.

Martin explained how the business was still expanding in some areas, despite losing the benefit of Wolfgang's direct involvement.

Rolf felt comfortable that although he was moving to Australia, his mother's business interests would be well served by this likeable young dynamo, Martin Kohl.

The visit to Germany confirmed in Rolf's mind that it was the right time to move. Roxy wanted to get home. Besides, his mother was coping well and needed time alone with Wolfgang. Rolf looked forward to a new beginning.

They phoned Sean and Marianne to tell them they would be leaving for Sydney the next day. Sean advised that there had been no news in any of the local papers.

Marianne told her brother that Sean had made up his mind to leave the Army as soon as possible. Also, they were both still worried that there might be a knock on their door. They would seek out a property a long way from Lancaster, Pennsylvania. But that wasn't all. She also told him that she was definitely pregnant. The Gleeson household would increase by one in another 30 weeks' time.

Chapter 13

A new beginning

At the end of February 1951, Rolf and Roxy arrived in Sydney, Australia, after the long flight from Europe. They caught a train west for four hours, then changed onto a narrow-gauge line for the shorter journey south to Macarthur Creek.

Natalie and Alan Regan, who had booked two rooms at the Macarthur Creek Hotel for their prospective son-in-law, made Rolf very welcome. He was given every courtesy on his arrival and introduced to many family friends, but Rolf still found the culture shock overwhelming.

First, there was the heat. It was an unrelenting heat that began early in the morning, shimmered all day and lingered on even when the sun went down. It was nothing like he had ever experienced before. There was just no escape from it. Even under the gum trees that dotted the Regan property, the shade was scant relief from the sun's rays. Then there were the flies. Sheep properties always attract flies—big, heavy blowies that swarm around anything that moves. Every door and every window in the Regan homestead was fitted with flywire screens to keep the pests at bay.

The Regan property was a sprawling farm of more than a thousand hectares, dominated by a homestead in the centre. Near the big house were many outbuildings and a new shearing shed. The property was gently undulating, with scattered gums for shade and a few cypresses along the fence lines. It was divided into 22 paddocks, each with its own dam. A small creek ran along one boundary, but the flow was merely a trickle—not enough for irrigation and barely enough to sustain a line of willow trees that grew in crooked symmetry along its crusty banks.

Soon after he arrived, Rolf went into town with Alan Regan, to meet the local stock-and-station agent. Rolf explained that he wanted to buy a small wool-growing property. He would work it with his new wife Roxy, who was familiar with sheep farming. The agent's eyes lit up when Rolf told him how much ready capital he could put into the purchase. He took down details on what kind of house Rolf wanted, preferred locations and so forth. The agent promised to get back to Rolf as soon as possible with the available options.

The culture clash notwithstanding, Rolf made new friends quickly and Roxy's family made him feel an important part of their household. The property had 10 horses and Rolf often enjoyed a ride with Roxy. The best time was in the early morning, before the sun inched over the horizon.

On a Saturday afternoon in the middle of March, the agent came out and told the young couple he had found a farm that might be just the ticket for them. It was a sprawling river frontage property of around 600 hectares being sold on a WIWO basis.

'What does WIWO mean?' Rolf asked.

'Well, Rolf, it means walk in, walk out. That is to say, the previous owner just leaves the property and you take possession of everything left behind. The land, the buildings, furniture, tools, any other improvements and the stock.'

'All right, where is it?' asked Roxy.

The agent pulled a small map from his pocket and continued, 'As I said, the property has a river frontage along the northern side. It's this coloured part of the map. The land is very flat and could be irrigated because the water supply is strong all year round. Lucerne or clover would grow exceptionally well along the river flats. There's a two-bedroom, bluestone cottage in good condition and various machinery sheds. Some of those outbuildings are in need of repair. Included in the deal would be 700 merino ewes, a few rams, three workhorses and some chooks. Good layers, I'm told. There's an old Bedford truck, a Massey Ferguson tractor, a stump-jump plough and a motor bike. The motor bike doesn't run, but it's not very old, so maybe it can be fixed. The tractor has a re-conditioned motor and good tyres. Just needs a battery charge. External fences are all solid, but the internal ones need work. All fencing is red-gum posts with steel droppers.'

'Can you tell us who owns it now and why they are selling?' Rolf asked.

'Sure. Ron Moore—a single bloke—has owned it for 11 years. Thing is, he has a twin brother Jack, down at Lakes Entrance in Victoria. Jack wants Ron to go into business with him fishing for sharks in Bass Strait. As it happens, Ron is sick of living by himself, with only sheep for company. He wants to make the change. He'll use the proceeds from the sale to help Jack pay for an ocean-going trawler and go fifty-fifty with him on each catch.'

'Well, sounds as if this place might be worth looking at,' said Rolf.

'Righto! We could go down there for a drive today if you like. It's only twelve miles from here. Personally, I think it's a pretty good buy because it has potential for more than just wool. The flats right next to the river are rich, alluvial soil.

You could grow veggies, an orchard or anything along the river there.'

'Okay, okay,' protested Rolf. 'You can back off on the selling for a while. Let's go and take a look.'

Rolf and Roxy fell in love with the property as soon as they saw it—not so much for its present condition, but for the potential it offered.

The bluestone cottage with a white picket fence all round was in livable condition, but would benefit enormously from a woman's touch. The agent was right about the land. It was flat—dead flat. But that could be a bonus if they chose to irrigate. The flow of water in the river was strong, even in March at the very end of summer. The rye grass was burned and brown from the summer heat. Roxy assured Rolf it would turn green overnight with the first of the autumn rains. They inspected the sheep that stood motionless under scraggly red-gum trees to escape the heat. Roxy thought they were in fairly good condition, considering the lack of rain lately.

Over the next couple of weeks they sorted through more of the details. Rolf was able to buy the property outright without a bank loan. He even had about £20,000 left over for working capital. They looked forward to moving in and building new lives, on the other side of the Earth to the Susquehanna river.

When the title search verified that Ron Moore was the legal owner, Rolf and Roxy signed the sale note on the 3rd April, just three weeks before their wedding.

On a glorious sunny day in April 1951, Roxy Regan became Mrs Bauer.

The ceremony was held in a quaint brick church nestled beneath a huge *magnolia grandiflora* in the centre of Macarthur Creek. The whole town turned out and many others came from surrounding properties, but Rolf was disappointed that neither his sister nor his mother could attend.

Marianne was reluctant to travel while pregnant. Besides, Sean could only get five days leave from the Army.

Brigitte would have loved to have come, but she needed to stand by Wolfgang.

The wedding reception in the community hall was a boisterous affair that went on until 2:30 in the morning. With a bit of help from his new family and friends, Rolf managed to get himself so drunk he couldn't stand.

Roxy was annoyed with him for getting in such a state. However, a few drinks later and she was starting to get merry.

The newlyweds had a short honeymoon of five days, roughing it on a camping trip in the outback territory to the west of Macarthur Creek. They enjoyed the solitude of it all, the simple pleasure of each other's company.

Too soon, it was time to return and put their investment in order.

It was a hot and muggy day towards the end of April when the couple took possession of their new farm. The first thing they did was to explore the whole property. At one of the dams they stopped and had a paddle in the muddy shallows. It was good to feel the soft mud squishing up between their toes.

They rested for a while on the bank under the shade of a willow tree. Rolf said, 'Well, we'd better rinse some of this mud off our feet before we get going.'

'I've got a better idea, Rolf. Let's have a dip and cool off as well.'

'In our undies, you mean?'

'No, silly. There's no need for them out here, unless of course you're worried about a few magpies seeing you. Come on— strip off. Are you a man or a mouse?'

With that, she took off all her clothes and dived naked into the muddy dam. Roxy squealed with girlish surprise because the water was colder than she expected.

Rolf didn't need a second invitation. He joined her in the water, making an enormous splash. They played about like young children, enjoying the blissful isolation of it all.

Rolf slept well that night. He was well satisfied: he owned a property, and also satisfied with the headstrong companion who would share his life.

The next day, Roxy started work on the cottage with a vengeance. She peeled off all the dark wallpaper and started repainting the interior in light, pastel colours.

Rolf ripped out the old carpets and sanded the floorboards. Then they varnished all the boards and bought some Indian mats to give the floor a lift. Roxy's mother gave her some basic furniture and made up new curtains for the whole house.

Later, Roxy turned her attention to the garden. She ripped out all the geraniums that attracted so many snails, and planted creepers next to the bluestone walls.

The place was looking better in no time. Soon Roxy turned her attention to the vegetable garden. The soil was rock hard, so she started pestering Rolf to start an old rotary hoe lying idle and unloved out in the shed.

Rolf had plenty to do himself. He first checked the perimeter fences and made all necessary repairs. Most of the posts were sound; the wires just had to be re-strained. It wasn't long before he had the tractor running.

He figured out how to hook a crosscut saw up to the power take-off. The saw would be ideal for cutting firewood.

By the end of April the autumn rains still hadn't arrived. Sheep had eaten much of the pasture down to ground level. Occasionally, the wind would whip up swirling clouds of reddish dust. Rolf started to feed the sheep baled hay, with a ration of grain every couple of days. He wanted to maintain their condition right through to lambing in the springtime. During May, Rolf mended the shedding and cut plenty of firewood for the winter. He also got to know his neighbours— all of them sheep graziers, too.

In the first week of June the rains came. Not heavy showers, but steady, unrelenting rain. Within nine days all the dams were full. The rain freshened up the garden and brought that first flush of green to the pasture. Small puddles started to appear. The sheep huddled together in mobs. Soon the soil became muddied. More and more pools of water scattered the paddocks.

Rolf and Roxy still had plenty of work they could do, in the house or in the shelter of the outside sheds. A wood fire in the cottage lounge room kept the whole house cosy and warm.

Still, the rain continued. The small puddles turned into bigger pools that spread out over the flat land, submerging much of the grass. The whole property became waterlogged before the showers started to ease.

As winter set in, Rolf found the weather very mild compared to Germany. He could work outdoors with just a pullover. It was wet, but it wasn't cold. He generally wore rubber boots because the soil remained soggy with more rain falling every few days.

Rolf was determined to make a success of the farm. Although he missed his mother and sister, he and Roxy wanted the satisfaction of building up the farm by themselves. Most of all, Rolf enjoyed the challenge of it all.

For her part, Roxy thought her man was adapting well to his new environment. Every day he learned more about sheep and the skills required to succeed with wool.

Towards the end of July, Rolf decided to ask John Clarkson, his closest neighbour, about sharing his shearing shed before the lambing season was upon them.

The Clarkson property was bigger than Rolf's, about 800 hectares. Although adjacent to Rolf's, it was on higher ground with better run-off, so John didn't have the same problems with muddy soil.

Rolf got to know John Clarkson and his wife Veronica very well. John was a man aged about 60 who knew all there was to know about wool production. John said it would be no problem at all for Rolf to use his shed. In fact, he could use his shearing crew as well. They would do all Rolf's sheep in about eight hours flat.

One day, Rolf asked John, 'How long exactly have you been on the land, John?'

'We bought this place about 30 years ago, Rolf. Been on it ever since. Actually, we started out with wheat and barley, but changed to wool just after the war. It's hard yakka now for an old guy like me, but Veronica helps me a lot. We are thinking of selling up soon and moving to Queensland. Our eldest son has a big caravan park up there, right on the beach. Great spot. He wants us to move up there and help him run the place. I've got to say I'm tempted. Biggest problem out here is drought. If there's no rain for a few months, the sheep chew the grass down to the ground and the paddocks turn to dustbowls. The mobs sometimes lose so much condition that you have to shoot half of them so the rest can survive. Breaks your heart, mate.'

'What about all your dams? Couldn't you irrigate during the dry spells?'

'No, unfortunately, it's not that easy, Rolf. When it's really dry, evaporation takes its toll. The dam levels drop dramatically and big cracks open up in the paddocks. Even if you did irrigate, it's not effective—the water just gets sucked under and the topsoil stays dry. Actually, you're lucky being right next to the river. You could plant some lucerne along there, and rotate the sheep onto it in the dry spells. Besides, irrigation might just work next to the bank there. You should give it a try, Rolf. Anyway, one day I should come down and have a look at your sheep. I'll be able to tell you straight off then whether we'll be able to get through them in one day or two. How about next week some time?'

'Okay, any time,' Rolf said. As he returned home, he wondered to himself what price John would want to sell his property.

Brigitte phoned Rolf in early August to say that Wolfgang's blood-sugar condition had worsened. Further hospital tests revealed the onset of pancreatic cancer. Sobbing, Brigitte went on to say that the condition was generally fatal. It was only a matter of time. Wolfgang was in reasonable spirits, though. He had already instructed Martin Kohl to initiate the sale of the transport arm of Europa Constructions so that Brigitte was financially protected. Despite Wolfgang's illness, the company business remained strong and they all expected a very healthy return on the sale of Europa Trucking.

Marianne called also to say she was getting bigger every week. They had decided on Rachel if it was a girl or Patrick for a boy. Sean liked Biblical names. He favoured Patrick, because his good friend Patrick O'Connor had been killed a week earlier by friendly fire in a night skirmish on the Korean peninsula.

Sean was due to leave the Army at the end of September— by which time their baby should be about three weeks old. He had put in a request for discharge at the end of August, but wasn't confident the earlier date would be approved. They still worried about that dark day on the river.

Back at the farm, Roxy had done wonders to improve the cottage. The garden was looking a picture. She had built a barbecue from leftover bluestone cobblers. Roxy relished the opportunity to use her accumulated knowledge and to share with Rolf the joy of it all.

Rolf eventually got the rotary-hoe working. He spent two weeks preparing the vegetable garden. There was a bag of seed potatoes left behind in one of the sheds. He planted the whole bag, as well as onions, cabbages, beetroot and some carrots.

When John Clarkson finally came to look at the sheep, Rolf was pleased, because he hadn't checked on them himself for two weeks.

As they approached the main mob, John said, 'Well, Rolf, we could shear your flock next week some time. That would give the ewes a few weeks to recover before they start lambing. You'd need to bring them over to the shed the day before and we'll keep them in a holding yard overnight. Saves the wool from getting damp. Shearers won't touch wet sheep, you know.'

He paused for a moment and looked intently at the flock. 'Listen, mate. I think we've got a problem here.'

'What do you mean, John? Is something wrong?'

John Clarkson stopped the vehicle, got out and walked over to the closest mob of sheep. Some of them were standing on three legs, with one foot off the ground. John leaned down on one knee and examined some of their feet.

Rising slowly to his feet, he shook his head and said, 'Rolf, I'm sorry to tell you this, but I can't shear your sheep. They've all got footrot.'

Chapter 14

Footrot

R olf's face turned white. Back in Germany, he had heard of footrot in cattle, but didn't know that it could affect sheep. John grabbed one of the ewes and wrestled it over on its back.

'Have a look at this one, Rolf. Do you see—both the back feet are infected. It's not too bad, though. This one's treatable, but we'd have to pare a lot of that hoof away.'

'John, I don't know what to say. This is such a shock and a bad one at that. Where do we go from here?'

'All right, Rolf. Let me give it to you straight. First of all, we can't shear these sheep until the infection is cleared up. That will probably take about a month. You should leave the shearing now until after lambing. I would wait until November, just to make sure all of it is gone. I can't let you bring them over to my shearing shed because this disease is so damn contagious. But I do have a couple of portable shearing machines we use for crutching. I could get some of my crew to come over here, I guess.'

'But what causes the infection in the first place?' interjected Rolf.

'In your case I would say it was almost certainly a result of your paddocks being water-logged for few weeks. Footrot is caused by a bacterium, which is fairly contagious and hard to eradicate. Unfortunately, by the look of them, it seems like about half your flock may be infected. The signs are swelling of the feet, reddish tissue around the hoof, lameness and spreading of the toes. When the condition is well-advanced, the foot might abscess above the hoof. Horrible smell, I can tell you. I know it's a bad situation, Rolf, but I think we have caught it in time. I doubt that any of yours would have had time to get to the severe stage yet. The bad news is that unless we treat the whole flock quickly, the infection will work into the joints and cause serious arthritis.'

'Well, who can I get to help? I still have some cash left and—'

John interrupted him saying, 'No, no, Rolf. Out here in the country we don't call in outsiders. We help each other get over problems like this. Here's what I think. We need to work quickly. Tonight I'll make a couple of calls and organise four others to help us from lunchtime tomorrow. In the morning, you get Roxy to go into town and pick up what we need from the vet. He'll know what to give her. While she's doing that, you and I will build three wooden trestles. They each need to be about three feet high—a bit like a cradle. We'll need those so we can turn the sheep upside down and work on them. We should aim to start treating them by about one o'clock so we get a good four hours in tomorrow before it starts to get dark. We'll work in three teams of two. It would be good if Roxy can keep us supplied with tea and sandwiches. I think we'll probably get through them in about three days. Depends how bad they are, really. Anyway, how does all that sound?'

'How can I ever thank you?' Rolf replied.

'You could buy my farm off me if you like, so I can give all this away and head off to Queensland,' John said jokingly.

'I'll tell you what. If I had the money, I would. I envy you those hilly paddocks.'

'Well, I hope one day you do win the lottery, then. Oh, one more thing. When we've done the sheep, we should move them onto the driest of your other paddocks so they don't get re-infected. Those that have no infection at all, we will need to isolate in a separate paddock. The bacteria stays in the soil for a while, so you'll need to leave these paddocks fallow for a while.'

When John returned home, Rolf told Roxy all that had happened.

He expected her to be very upset, but she said, 'Well, that's what farming is like our here, Rolf. When it's tough it's really tough and when it's not tough it's bloody hard going. We'll get through it.'

By noon the next day the three makeshift trestles were ready. John and Rolf herded the first batch of sheep into a nearby holding pen. John introduced Rolf to the four other farmers who had just arrived to help. Soon, Roxy got back from her trip into town. She took the groceries inside and told the men that the vet was only a few minutes behind her with all his supplies.

In a cloud of dust Michael Farrell, the congenial vet from Macarthur Creek, pulled up in his utility. Dressed in khaki, he was a stout man of about 35 years with a ruddy face. A pair of spectacles was perched precariously on the bridge of his nose. Michael was well-liked in the area, because did his best for everyone in the community, whether they could pay or not.

Nothing was too much trouble for him where the welfare of animals was concerned. Despite his bulk, he swivelled expertly from the driver's seat and said hellos all round. Then he pulled a folding metal table from the back of his vehicle. He filled three steel billycans with disinfectant solution and laid out six gleaming new paring shears. He mixed up three batches of zinc sulphate solution in water and left several small paintbrushes on the table. Finally, he laid a number of thick, coloured markers on the table. He surveyed his preparations and said, 'Rolf, with your permission, I'll now give some instructions.'

'Please go ahead, Michael. I appreciate all your help.'

'All right, fellas. Listen carefully! First, mark any sheep that has no evidence of footrot with a green marker. Every hour or so we'll take a break, and isolate them. Second, for those that are infected, you must trim away the diseased hoof area so the solution I've prepared can reach the harmful organisms. Between each sheep you must, I repeat, must, dip the shears in the disinfectant. Use the little paintbrushes to apply the zinc solution, then mark the sheep with a yellow marker. All right so far?'

They all nodded in silent agreement, so he went on. 'Now, if you find any sheep where the disease is very advanced and in your opinion untreatable, just mark them with red. Those we'll destroy. Any questions?'

'Will this treatment cure the problem altogether?' Rolf asked.

'Probably not, Rolf. I'll come out every week for a few weeks and we'll figure out what action to take each time. If you want to avoid this problem in future you simply have to buy some land where you can move the sheep in these extra wet spells. Anyway, let's get started. By the way, Roxy, mine is milk with two sugars.'

For four solid hours they went about their distasteful task, in three teams of two each, with the vet providing advice as required. After each treatment he gave each ewe a combination penicillin injection just behind the ear. The work was difficult and at times sickening, but it had to be done. Each team soon settled into its own routine. First, one man would bring a sheep over and turn it upside down. Then both would lift it into the cradle. One would hold the legs while the other inspected, cut away bits of hoof and brushed on the applied the zinc solution. They would lift the sheep down, hold it still for the jab of penicillin, mark it on the back and then herd the distressed ewe into the appropriate pen. Fortunately, almost every second sheep had no symptoms at all. They moved these directly into the quarantine pen.

At a little after five o'clock they called a halt for the day. The count was 205 examined with 96 cleared of any symptoms. Of the remainder, three had red slashes on their backs. All three had difficulty standing.

'Rolf, you'll have to shoot those three straight away,' the vet said.

'But, I don't have a gun,' Rolf replied. He shuddered at the very thought of using a firearm again and stole a quick glance at Roxy. She looked away.

'No worries, then. I've got one in my ute,' the vet responded. 'Put them into the back for me. There's an old quarry up the road that the Department of Agriculture uses for diseased stock. I'll shoot them up there and torch the carcases in a few days.'

Rolf was thankful that the matter was settled. He went to each man and shook his hand in appreciation. The vet said he couldn't come for the first two hours the next morning, so he showed Roxy how to give the penicillin doses.

As they lay in bed that evening, Rolf remarked, 'Gee, it's amazing, Roxy, what has happened in the last eight or nine months. Who'd have thought we'd finish up together fighting footrot on a farm in Australia?'

'Well, I'm not complaining,' she replied, giving him a playful elbow to the ribcage. 'Besides, I'm glad we're both in

Australia. It's good to be so isolated from the troubles of the world. Now go to sleep, you big ox. We've got an even bigger day before us tomorrow.'

Two hours later the phone rang. It was Sean. He told them that Rachel Mary Gleeson had just been born. She was the spitting image of her mother. They were both fine. Marianne was breast-feeding the infant okay. She'd be staying in hospital for another four days, then they would phone again. Sean also advised that because Korean cease-fire negotiations had started in Panmunjom, he had been successful with his early discharge.

Rolf and Roxy had two bottles of beer to celebrate. At length, they wearily climbed back to bed—still aching all over from the day's toil.

The next day they all started at eight in the morning and worked through non-stop until noon. The work was no less distasteful, but again progress was steady. Unfortunately the red marker had been applied to a further six sheep by the time the vet arrived.

'Can we save any of those six, Michael?' Rolf asked.

Michael Farrell gave each sheep a cursory examination and replied, 'No, Rolf. We've got to cull the worst of them to contain the infection. As a matter of fact, I'll take this six straight down to the quarry now and join you guys after you've had some lunch.'

The afternoon session was very good. There were no more reds and a much higher proportion with no symptoms at all. At day's end they were again careful to keep all the non-infected ewes quarantined in a separate paddock.

Day three and another early start! It looked like rain was on the way, so they planned to work through midday and finish the whole mob by 2 pm.

Soon after nine, one of the men accidentally cut his finger with the paring shears. The vet advised him to go to the doctor and get a couple of stitches and a tetanus shot. He would drive, himself, but that left them one man short.

Roxy stepped forward and said, 'I'll take his place. I've done this work before and I can keep up with any of you guys.'

No-one dared argue with her, and they pressed on without further delay.

Rolf felt proud of his Roxy in her tight blue jeans and gingham blouse. Her long black hair cascaded over her face as she worked. By 2:40 pm they had finished. Again the red marker had not been required. Carefully, they raked up all the pieces of hoof on the ground and put them in a drum. They threw in the used paintbrushes, splashed on some kerosene and burned the lot.

As they washed up, Roxy brought out a supply of toasted ham sandwiches and a carton of beer. Feeling humbled by the whole experience, Rolf started to make a short thank-you speech. He didn't get very far because everyone shouted at him to sit down and have a drink. They were all aching and exhausted. Rolf thought—no wonder the farmers survived the tough times when they pitched in and helped each other so.

Before he left, Michael Farrell worked out a schedule with Rolf for the pair of them to conduct regular inspections over the next six weeks. He said, 'Rolf, don't worry now. Your flock will be all right. But learn a lesson from this. You must take some action to prevent a re-occurrence. A real problem with footrot is that once the bacteria gets into the soil, it may persist for a long time. It might flare up again next winter. The best answer is prevention—not control. I think the only way out for you is to acquire more land, so whenever yours looks like getting waterlogged, you can take some pre-emptive action. At the moment, you can't. Think about it. If I hear of anything going, I'll let you know. Another thing, before next winter let's run your sheep through a few footbaths of copper sulphate or formalin. I'll show you how to set it up. In the meantime, drop into my office any time if you need help with anything. All right, so long! Nice to have met you and Roxy.'

Rolf shook his hand warmly and was close to tears with his thanks. Meanwhile Roxy slipped a carton of beer into the back of the vet's utility.

Michael Farrell struggled into his vehicle and disappeared in a cloud of dust. Rolf felt like a weight had been taken from his shoulders now that they had broken the back of the problem.

Two days later, Rolf phoned his mother to tell her all about the whole episode.

Brigitte was distressed when he called. She had just visited Wolfgang. He was no longer at home, but confined to a hospital bed. She told her son that Wolfgang was not expected to survive until Christmas.

Rolf offered what words of consolation he could. He assured Brigitte that he would try to come over to visit immediately after lambing.

'I'll send you two tickets, Rolf, so you don't have to worry about the cost. Might do the same for Mari, too, because I'd love to see her baby. Now tell me more about that property you mentioned. The one near yours that might be up for sale. Is it the kind of place you want and how much are they asking?'

'Mother, don't you bother about that for the moment, you just concentrate on looking after Wolfgang.'

'Nonsense, Rolf. Wolfgang is getting the best of care in the hospital and I visit him twice each day. I am perfectly capable of handling several things at the moment, and I want to keep as busy as I can. So what's your answer? Do you want the property and how much will it cost?'

'Well, the place is owned by a nice old guy named John Clarkson. His farm is adjacent to mine. Whereas mine is dead flat, his land is undulating to hilly. He's got about two thousand acres altogether, so it's more than twice the size of what I have now. The house is fairly run down, but it has a giant shearing shed. I know he's keen to sell and I figure he would take about £90,000 Australian for it. But, mother, I do feel awkward about all this. You should be saving every penny for later on.'

'Rolf, listen to me for a minute. My problem is not going to be a shortage of money. It'll be more a question of how to wisely invest what I've got now and what I'll inherit. You see, our holding company Europa Constructions now consists of nine organisations—each of which is profitable in its own right. Since Wolfgang has no relatives, he's leaving most of it to me. On the first of January next year Martin Kohl and Renate will start working for me personally, purely to manage my financial interests. Now, as you may know, we've already put the transport company up for sale because forward projections show a slowdown in growth. Rolf, last week we got a written offer of 27 million marks. I'll discuss things with Martin and get back to you. Perhaps you could find out from this Mr Clarkson exactly what figure he would accept. You are my only son, Rolf. Allow me the pleasure of helping you out where I can.'

'All right, Mother. God bless you! I do hope Wolfgang isn't suffering too much. He's a nice man and he certainly gave you a new lease of life.'

'That he did, Rolf, that he did. When he dies I'll have him buried at Berchtesgaden in the same cemetery as my dear Joachim.'

There was a pause. Rolf could hear his mother weeping.

She continued, 'I'll send you those tickets, Rolf. Come over if you can. He doesn't have long to go.'

'We'll come around the end of September, Mother. You can be sure of that. Stay calm. I think of you both every day.'

Chapter 15

The family re-united

The first of the lambs was born in the second week of September. After the frosty chill of the mornings, spring sunshine bathed the paddocks in warmth. The soil had dried out and the farm was covered in new growth. Rolf was surprised at how many sets of twins were born. Roxy explained that this was no accident, but the result of planned animal husbandry to improve productivity.

A week later about 200 lambs were prancing about, chasing one another, getting lost and bleating for their mothers. Every morning Rolf and Roxy inspected their growing flock. The footrot was almost completely gone. The young couple felt happy with the world. Even their vegetable garden was looking good as the new plants responded to the glorious sunshine.

Then disaster struck. As they did their regular inspection one morning, they came across the bloodied carcases of four new lambs. Each had been pitifully mutilated and partly eaten.

'Foxes, I guess,' Rolf suggested, shaking his head in disbelief.

'They're generally too timid to go after lambs, Rolf. Foxes don't hunt in packs either—they're loners. Occasionally, with so much myxomatosis around and the rabbit population down, a fox will take a solitary lamb—if it's separated from the mob.

This is different. There was more than one attacker here. I'm thinking maybe there are still some of those Darcy dogs left.'

'What on earth is a Darcy dog? I've never heard you use that term before.'

'Well, it's a long story. Years ago an old vet called Darcy retired into the hills over there and became a hermit living in a cabin all by himself. He bred and studied dingos for a few years, then successfully crossed some dingos with a couple of black German Shepherd dogs. The crossbred pups grew up into a kind of black dingo—very powerful and aggressive. Anyway, when old Darcy died, his pure and cross-bred dogs all escaped into the bush. I thought all of them had been shot or died out by now. Maybe a couple have survived. Anyway, we'll have to get on top of this straight away or we'll lose a lot. There's two ways we can handle this—either by poison or shooting them. I think we should do both. Are you prepared to use a rifle again?'

'Sure, I'll do whatever I have to,' he replied.

'All right, let's go into town and pick up some poison and meat. We'll set up a string of baits late this afternoon. We should also ask my dad to help. He's the district expert in whistling up foxes. We should see if he can whistle up wild dogs too. Problem is, that his eyesight isn't so good any more, so you'd have to do the shooting. He's got a .22 rifle with a good scope on it. Looks like it'll be moonlight tonight, so we could try without a spotlight.'

By five o'clock they had laid out 17 baits, each embedded in a ball of mincemeat. Every one had been concealed under a piece of bark or down a hole to minimise the chances of being picked at by birds. They also made a note of where every bait was located. In a few days, they would retrieve all the remaining baits in case they were found by neighbouring farm dogs.

Rolf told John Clarkson what had happened and that he had laid out baits. John mentioned that he had momentarily seen a black dog only recently in his headlights.

Alan Regan arrived around six. He and Rolf set off for a spot beneath a red gum where there was a pile of old branches. They climbed into the middle and made themselves comfortable.

Alan loaded the magazine of the ten-shot repeater. 'Here, Rolf. This red catch is the safety and here's a box of shells. Over fifty yards the rifle shoots about an inch to the right—so allow for that. Must get it fixed one day. I've loaded soft-nosed bullets, so get him in the head or the chest area, and he'll die real quick. Once I start calling, take the safety off, but keep the rifle pointed away from us. If two of them come up, try to get them both. You'll have only about a second between each shot. Let's stay for two hours now and then come back at four in the morning for another go. All right?'

Rolf nodded. Alan Regan took a flat, round metal whistle from his pocket.

He wet his lips and started to blow. The noise was a high-pitched squeal—just like a rabbit crying in distress. In silence, they waited. Every few minutes Alan would blow the whistle again. The light was fading fast and visibility was down to about fifty metres. After 20 minutes Alan gently took hold of Rolf's arm and pointed to the left. There was a huge black dog, only 30 metres away with its head held high, sniffing the air. Rolf took aim with the cross hairs and started to squeeze.

'Fire!' said Alan.

Rolf pulled the trigger back further and the gun cracked.

'Good work, you got him!'

The dog died instantly with a bullet through the head. It was a male animal in fair condition, with an injured foot. They dragged the carcase into the logs and waited again. After an hour, dark clouds passed across the moon and they decided to give up for the night. Back a little after four the next morning, the pair tried again. This time they were unsuccessful. Inspecting the baits on the way back, they found two missing.

Following breakfast, Alan joined in the flock inspection. They found another two lambs killed and decided to try with the gun again that evening. This time, Alan said they would use a spotlight as well.

Just after dusk they climbed into the same pile of logs, carrying a fully charged car battery with them. They tested the light and waited for darkness to close in fully. Alan would use the whistle for a few minutes. Then they would wait a while and sweep the area ahead of them with the light. After two hours Alan picked up two sets of eyes in the distance. He held the spotlight hard against a branch so it didn't move. The eyes belonged to two black pups that stood still, curiously staring into the light.

'Shoot, shoot,' whispered Alan urgently.

'They're only pups.'

'They're killers. Shoot them both.'

Rolf fired and one pup went down. He fired again and missed. The second pup didn't move. Rolf's third shot despatched the second young predator. He felt wretched. As they started towards the bodies, they noticed a small light bobbing up and down in the distance. It was moving toward them.

'Rolf, it's me!' shouted Roxy through the darkness. Rolf knew something must be wrong and he headed towards the torchlight.

'It's Wolfgang, Rolf. Your mother just phoned to say he died about two hours ago.'

'Oh, God.' Rolf said. 'That's two husbands she's lost'

The trio returned promptly to the house. Roxy brought out some beers and they settled down in the lounge room to discuss things.

At length, they decided that Rolf would go to Germany for the funeral and that Roxy's father would help her out until he returned. Alan Regan had a reliable foreman who could look after his own property in such emergencies.

The next morning, Rolf phoned to make the travel bookings. He would not leave until late in the afternoon, so he dropped across to have a chat with John Clarkson. John advised that he did indeed want to sell. Further, he said he would take £95,000 on 90 days or £90,000 for 30-day settlement.

Rolf told him about the wild dogs and John said he would help Alan for the next couple of nights.

Rolf's sad journey to Europe again was tempered by the knowledge that he would meet Marianne and Sean again. He would see young Rachel for the first time.

On his arrival, he found Brigitte was remarkably composed for someone who had just lost her husband. When she told him how Wolfgang had died, he understood the situation better. Brigitte said that in the past couple of weeks, Wolfgang had known his time was fast running out. He'd instructed Martin to bring him all the necessary papers to sign.

Basically, his whole fortune was left to Brigitte, with a couple of caveats. She was required to employ Martin Kohl for at least five years to look after her financial affairs. Brigitte also was obliged to look after Karl Becke, the administrator at the Salzburg office. Wolfgang felt a great debt of gratitude to both these men, who had helped him build his industrial empire.

Brigitte was happy with both provisions, because she had a soft spot for the two men, as well as enormous respect for Martin's business acumen.

With these matters sorted out, Wolfgang had prayed a lot in the last few days and seemed at peace with himself. He passed away in his sleep in the dead of night. He had suffered discomfort, but no real pain throughout his illness.

Following Wolfgang's burial, in Berchtesgaden, Brigitte called a family conference in Munich two days later. The meeting was attended by Rolf, Sean and Marianne, and by Martin Kohl and Karl Becke.

Brigitte started proceedings by explaining that she had invited Martin and Karl because they would play a big part in managing her future affairs. She wanted her two children and Sean to get to know them better. Brigitte then gave a summary of her position, indicating that she had the wherewithal to make both immediate short and longer-terms investments.

Rolf was next. He told them all about his initial culture shock in Australia and how he now relished the challenges on the land. The small group was fascinated by his account of the footrot episode and the recent problem with the wild dogs. Rolf explained that in the longer term he needed to acquire more land to provide options whenever his farm's very flat acreage became waterlogged.

Sean followed. He talked about the joy of having a new baby with Marianne and a sense of relief that he was out of the Army. Soon he and Marianne would head south and look for a property of their own.

Martin said he was looking forward to the task of managing Brigitte's financial affairs and Karl said he would be happy to take on any role where he could help.

Before they adjourned for dinner, Brigitte told the group that she and Martin had decided to make an immediate gratis payment of £100,000 Australian to Rolf. The money would be drawn from a special family account that Wolfgang had established earlier. At any time in the future, Marianne and Sean could claim an equal amount from this special reserve.

As they retired for dinner and drinks, Rolf kissed his mother and said, 'Mother, thanks a million! You must make the journey Down Under soon and visit us. Roxy would love to see you again.'

'Let me think about it, Rolf. There's a lot to do at the moment. But I've read a lot about Australia and always wanted to go there. We'll see.'

After their meal, while Marianne fed her baby, Rolf took Sean aside for a few drinks.

'Any news at all about that business on the river?' Rolf asked anxiously.

'No, not a word. Forget about it, my friend. We've covered our tracks well. You're as bad as Marianne. She's absolutely paranoid about it. Put it all behind you. I have. Anyway, you're lucky being so far away from it and all.'

'Sean, that's something I want to talk about.'

'What do you mean, Rolf?'

'You heard my mother before. I've suddenly got the money to acquire another two thousand acres and about 1800 more sheep. To be honest Sean, Roxy and I are struggling to manage what we've got now. You and I have been good mates since the first time we met. I'm sure we'd work well together. It would be just fantastic if you and Marianne could come out for a year or so to help me out. We could go halves in everything, if you like. That way you might even stay on in

Australia. It's a great country once you get used to it. What do you say?'

'I don't know what to say, Rolf. I'll have to think about it and talk to Marianne. Off the top of my head, I wouldn't mind moving there for a while. Does the new place have a house on it?'

'Yes, of course! It's an older dwelling. You know—leadlight windows and that sort of thing. Plenty of room, though. There's a stable near the house and three or four horses. Ideal place to bring up a baby daughter.'

'All right, Rolf. Leave it with me. I'll talk to Marianne tonight and see what she thinks.'

That night, Marianne told Sean in no uncertain terms that the more distance she could put between herself and Pennsylvania, the better she would like it. She was delirious with joy about the prospect of moving to Australia.

The next day, Brigitte was delighted to hear that her two children would be living close together again, albeit in far-off Australia. She instructed Martin to make the formal offer for the Clarkson property on Rolf's behalf and to help Sean with all his visa arrangements. When John Clarkson's solicitor, Julie Pedersen, sent a telegram confirming acceptance of their offer, Brigitte broke open the champagne.

Soon it was time for Rolf to leave for home.

As he waited for the chauffeur to take him to the airport in Munich, his mother said, 'Well, I suppose I'll have to come to Australia now that both my children are down there, Rolf,'

'Damn right,' he replied.

When Rolf returned to Macarthur Creek, all the lambs had been born and the wild-dog problem was over. He gave Roxy all the details of his trip. She was overjoyed with the prospect of having Marianne as her neighbour. Roxy couldn't wait to see the baby.

John and Veronica Clarkson moved out the day after Christmas.

Roxy immediately set about preparing the house for Marianne.

One morning, when Rolf called in at about 10 am to check on her progress, he found her sitting on the back step—her face ashen.

'Are you all right, Roxy?' he asked anxiously

'Sure, Rolf. I'll be all right. Just a bit queasy for a minute. Actually, I've been a bit sick the last few mornings. Think I might have the same problem as the sheep.'

'What do you mean?'

'I might be pregnant, you big dummy,' she announced.

Rolf wrapped his arms around her and held her close.

'Roxy, that's wonderful. Just wonderful.'

Two days later the doctor confirmed that Roxy Bauer was six weeks' pregnant. She asked the doctor about the poliomyelitis epidemic that was always being mentioned in the newspapers. He assured her that the virus could spread only by direct contact, and that there had been no reported cases within 300 kilometres of Macarthur Creek.

Sean and his family arrived by train from Sydney on a stinking hot day in the middle of January, 1952.

Roxy was thrilled to see Marianne again. She immediately took baby Rachel and cradled her in her arms.

'I'll have to get used to this, Marianne.'

'What, don't tell me! You too!' she shrieked. 'Roxy, I was hoping you'd have a baby soon. This is just great. They'll be able to grow up together. Now let's get out to the house. Is it always so hot out here?'

'No, sometimes it gets a bloody lot hotter. I've left the fans running in your place so it'll be a bit cooler indoors.'

The next day, Rolf and Sean discussed how they would share the work on the two farms. They decided to keep the sheep entirely separate for a further six months because of the footrot problem. But they would share equipment, horses and hay. They would evenly share the workload and the profits.

That evening, they had a few drinks at Rolf's place. Every now and then they heard radio bulletins about bushfires sweeping out of control across New South Wales and Victoria. From the front verandah, they watched the crimson glow in the sky of fires in the far distance. Rolf and Sean agreed that they must include fire protection in their future planning.

Brigitte was impressed by reports of how well the two families were doing together and how much they enjoyed the Australian life. She called Martin in one day and surprised him by saying, 'Martin, are things under good control at the moment? How is Karl coming along?'

'Well, yes, Mrs Bauer. Things are in good shape. Your affairs are all in order. There're no outstanding issues aside from an overtime ban at one of our building sites. As for Karl, I have kept him involved as much as possible, so he has his finger on the pulse. Why do you ask?'

'Martin, I want you and Renate to take a working holiday. That is to say, it'll be work for you but a holiday for Renate. I'd like you to go to this Macarthur Creek and do some discreet research for me. Find out about the local economy. Who makes money and who doesn't? Are there any opportunities for investment? How do you think Rolf and Sean will fare in the years ahead? You know—give me a general run-down on your impressions of the place. I want to spread my investments outside Germany. If I can help my children along the way, well and good.'

'Should I tell Rolf and Sean what I'm doing?'

'Play it by ear, Martin. I'd prefer that they didn't know too much for the time being, because then they'll be disappointed if nothing happens. Use your own judgment. If you get backed into a corner, then fill them in for me.'

Martin and Renate enjoyed their two weeks at Macarthur Creek in April of 1952.

Martin said he wanted to get his hands dirty so he worked with Rolf and Sean for all the first week. During the second week he spent most of his time in the town. He bought all the local papers, spoke to many of the shopkeepers and visited the Titles Office to look at plans of the area.

When Renate met Rolf again, she gave his hand a wicked squeeze and held on for too long. On a couple of occasions when they chanced to be alone together, Renate and Rolf exchanged furtive smiles. Each of them was attracted to the other. There had been an unspoken chemistry between the two from the moment they had first danced together.

Most days Renate went horseback riding, with either Marianne or Roxy. She loved helping Marianne to look after Rachel and longed for a baby of her own.

The day after his return to Germany, Martin gave a full report to Brigitte. He stated that most farms in the area were badly managed and very few realised their full potential. Many concentrated wholly on wool production, so whenever wool prices went down, so did the farm. The owners themselves made poor use of equipment—a very expensive plough might be used for only two weeks a year. Water was important: too much or too little presented problems. The biggest problem, though, was the lack of diversity and few economies of scale.

Martin suggested that the best way to farm would be to have an enormous property so that resources could be equitably shared, and to have a spread of interests to offset market-price fluctuations. If 15 adjacent farms were combined, then wheat could grow in that area which most suited wheat production—regardless of the boundaries. Perhaps only one or two harvesters could be used across all 15 farms, with one shearing shed for everybody. The cost of drenches and fuel could be cut significantly through bulk buying.

Martin went on further to extol the virtues of his 'super' farm concept, arguing that sensible economic management was the key to success—not traditional practices. He showed Brigitte some of the plans he had brought back. She thanked him profusely for his efforts and analysis.

Two months later, Brigitte made the decision to spend two years in Australia and invest the sum of five million deutschmarks in building a farming enterprise near Macarthur Creek.

Once again the Bauer family would be united.

Chapter 16

Building the empire

B rigitte asked Karl Becke to look after her day-to-day business affairs in Europe while she and Martin set about planning the Australian operation.

The first order of business was to engage a local solicitor to handle their needs around Macarthur Creek and to provide them with local expertise, especially on taxation laws. Martin telephoned Julie Petersen, the solicitor who had handled the Clarkson sale, and asked if she would act for them on a range of commercial matters, starting almost immediately.

Business was slow, so Julie agreed without hesitation. When she went on to explain that her area of specialisation was real-estate transactions, Martin felt sure they had made the right choice. He queried her knowledge of taxation law and was reassured when she explained that country solicitors had to be up to the mark in all aspects of law.

Martin advised that, for reasons of confidentiality, he would not send her any information. He would travel to Australia in two weeks' time to give her a full briefing.

Carefully, Brigitte and Martin reviewed the properties surrounding Rolf's farm on the plans Martin had brought back from Australia. They marked 17 target farms that could provide the real estate for their new enterprise. Then they drew up a list of matters for Julie to research on each property: an independent valuation, the water supply, topography, soil type, stock numbers and so on.

As they would soon start to accrue costs in Australia, they decided Martin should ask Julie to immediately register Bavaria Enterprises as a business name in the state of New South Wales.

A few days before he left for Sydney, Martin phoned Julie and asked for a full day with her, to give her a complete explanation of their needs and to work on some specific action items.

Knowing that a good swag of business was likely to be coming her way, Julie met Martin at the airport in Sydney and drove him all the way to Macarthur Creek.

Julie Petersen was a single woman. Slim and well dressed, with a pageboy hairstyle, she used a heavy hand with the perfume bottle and always wore bright red lipstick. Julie was a quick thinker who oozed efficiency but tempered her business-like approach with a ready smile. She liked Martin from the moment she met him and hoped they would work together for a long time.

On the car journey, Martin explained what Brigitte Bauer and he had in mind. In essence, they wanted to acquire a number of targeted properties as soon as possible, then develop a super-farm using the latest management practices, as opposed to the more traditional Australian approaches. Martin acknowledged they would have their detractors along the way. They would proceed anyway—within the confines of their investment budget. Julie suggested she could probably help them a lot, since she was acutely aware why many farms were struggling.

Since they had covered the overall strategy fairly thoroughly in the car, they decided to spend the next day concentrating on short-term action. By mid-morning, they had concluded it would be too risky to have someone visit each farm for valuation and general assessment purposes. Word would soon get around and asking prices would skyrocket. Instead, they called the local real-estate agent, Jim Cassidy, and asked him to come to the solicitor's office.

Julie said they could trust him implicitly, because she had known him for years and could vouch for his reliability. The three of them squared away a few issues concerning commercial confidentiality. Then they discussed each farm in turn. They compiled an information sheet on every property and decided what was fair market value for each. Finally, they went for a drive past each farm and Jim gave further useful comments on each as they passed.

Martin and Julie thanked Jim for his contribution and reminded him to respect the confidentiality of the situation. In return, they would put as much business his way as possible.

After a counter-tea at the Macarthur Creek Hotel, Martin and Julie returned to her office to continue. They drew up a confidential written offer from Bavaria Enterprises for each of the seventeen properties with a price 25 per cent higher than the amount they had earlier calculated as fair market value. The only proviso was that the offer would have to be accepted within 14 days. To progress a sale transaction, the owner should contact Jim Cassidy, who would provide the contract-of-sale documents. Julie would send out each of the envelopes by registered post.

They called in at the hotel for a few drinks after an exhausting day.

Martin gave Julie the power-of-attorney the next morning to sign on behalf of Bavaria Enterprises for any offers which were accepted. He instructed Julie to send out, to those who didn't respond, a second and final offer at a further 10 percentage points above their original figure.

In the afternoon, the pair travelled to a nearby agricultural show to give Martin a first-hand perspective on the local farming scene. During that visit he made an appointment with a senior officer from the Department of Agriculture for an extended consultation the next day. In the evening, Martin and Julie had dinner and a few glasses of wine at the Outback Inn on the way back to Macarthur Creek.

Martin invited Julie to his meeting at the offices of the local offices of the Department of Agriculture. He explained that he wanted to discuss a future plan that may or may not come to fruition. Martin emphasised the point that his ideas were just that—ideas, at this stage. Specifically, he inquired if about 15 farms were merged into the one single enterprise, what kind of expertise would be needed to enable best management practices? After a couple of hours' discussion, they concluded that there were six areas which needed subject experts—stock, crops and/or pastures, equipment, buildings, labour and administration. Martin also asked about market trends in the prices of wool, lambs, beef cattle, wheat and barley, as well as the viability of any new crops. The department was very obliging, and what they could not provide immediately, they offered to post on to Julie as soon as possible.

Satisfied with how things were progressing, Martin phoned Brigitte with a progress report and then made plans to return to Germany two days later.

That evening Martin took Julie out to meet Rolf and Roxy. The four drove over to Marianne's, so they could all meet. Martin brought them up-to-date on Brigitte's thinking.

Although no-one else noticed, Rolf thought that Martin and Julie were on rather friendly terms for two people who had just met.

When it was time for his return, Julie was adamant that Martin should not catch the train to Sydney. She would drive him. As they were loading his cases into the car, Jim Cassidy pulled up to tell them that three farmers had already indicated they would sell. Martin was pleased. On arrival at Sydney Airport, the pair discovered Martin's flight had been delayed 24 hours. Apparently the aircraft had suffered damage when it struck some seagulls.

Julie drove Martin to a hotel with a view of the bustling water traffic and the famous Harbour Bridge. It was raining heavily as she parked out the front. They dashed inside to check availability. The receptionist asked, 'Will you be wanting a single or double room, Mr Kohl?'

Martin glanced at Julie for a moment.

'Make that a double,' she blurted out without a moment's hesitation.

Over the next three months, Martin made two more trips to Macarthur Creek. Bavaria Enterprises had now secured 11 of the 17 properties. Four were under negotiation and two they had abandoned because the acquisition cost was too high. Fortunately, these two were on the perimeter of their group of new holdings.

Martin rarely slept alone on his visits. While He cherished the stolen hours with Julie, but he still loved Renate as much as ever.

The Bauer household was filled with joy at the end of August when baby Mark was born. Whereas Marianne's daughter Rachel was fair, with white blonde hair, Mark Bauer had the same olive complexion as Roxy, as well as her dark hair. He was a big baby and it was a difficult birth, ending in forceps delivery.

Soon after, Roxy and Rolf remarked to the nurse in the ward that the baby's head seemed a little elongated.

'Happens all the time with forceps deliveries,' she said. 'A baby's head is very soft and can get pushed out of shape very easily. The good news is that it reverts to proper proportions very quickly. He'll be back to normal within 48 hours, I can assure you.'

Sure enough, within two days baby Mark Bauer looked just perfect.

In October of 1953, on his fourth trip, Martin finalised the purchase of all 15 properties and booked three rooms at the Macarthur Creek Hotel for the arrival of Brigitte Bauer. By now the whole town was abuzz with excitement and gossip. Word had gradually spread that a rich German woman was buying up farms to start a radical new venture near Macarthur Creek. The hotel refurbished the three rooms so they were spic and span for their important new guest. They also converted one of the rooms into a temporary office.

Marianne drove to Sydney to meet her mother, with baby Rachel in a bassinette on the back seat. Brigitte had travelled out with Renate Kohl. It was a joyous reunion and the three chatted incessantly on the journey back, while the baby slept.

There were a few sombre moments as Marianne and Brigitte talked about Wolfgang.

Renate really liked Marianne. They had remained close friends since their school days together. Renate decided that the very first time she was alone with Marianne, she would confide in her about the perfume smell on Martin's shirts.

Meanwhile, Rolf and Sean were out patrolling their paddocks. Each rode on horseback with a rifle and scope. A pack of crows had attacked some new lambs and pecked their eyes out. They had shot eleven of the crows already.

Martin had prepared one of the farmhouses vacated recently, for Renate and himself. He went to considerable trouble to make the house presentable, since the pangs of conscience were starting to gnaw at him.

Two days after Brigitte's arrival, Bavaria Enterprises had its first management meeting. Martin chaired the discussion, at Brigitte's request, with Rolf, Roxy, Sean and Marianne in attendance. Renate volunteered to stay home and baby-sit Rachel and Mark.

There were four main agenda items.

Martin was to give a summary of all their assets. He reported that the company had acquired 15 properties. Included were 22 dwellings, 38 machinery sheds, 46 hay sheds, six shearings sheds, 72 dams, 17 tractors, 11 trucks, 18 sundry motor vehicles, a large variety of farm implements, 22,000 sheep, 29 horses, 226 beef cattle and 1200 hectares of ripened wheat. In addition, he mentioned that about 10 kilometres of perimeter fencing needed to be replaced, some sheep urgently needed dipping and others were due for shearing. There were no obvious diseases present, but white cockatoos were starting to pick at the wheat crop. The total amount of real estate was just over 13 600 hectares—10 800 hectares of which was cleared and arable land.

Next Brigitte took over. She talked about the need to appoint specialist managers to concentrate on specific aspects of their enterprise. She said, 'Let me tell you all what I have in mind. We'll see if you agree. First, I'll take responsibility for all the buildings and facilities. That doesn't include farm equipment, but would cover dwellings, fences, roads, sheds and so forth. Rolf, I'd like you to look after stock. You've always had a way with animals. You and Roxy know more than the rest of us about sheep. Might be a good idea to get that nice vet you

mentioned on some kind of retainer. What was his name—
Farrell? Build a relationship with him so he gives us preventive
advice instead of just fixing things. Sean, I'd like you to manage
crops and pastures. I know you don't have a lot of experience,
but it's such an important area that I want someone in the family
to handle it. Get help and advice from the agriculture authorities
and see if you can enrol in some courses. Is everyone clear so
far?'

They all nodded. Brigitte knew Rolf would agree. She
breathed a sigh of relief when Sean smiled on hearing his new
assignment. She went on, 'Martin will work on commercial
strategies, forward planning and financial management. This
will be an important role too. Martin, you'll have to make
occasional trips back to Germany for me, of course. We still
have to keep an eye on our businesses over there. Now, for
general administration, I will ask Karl Becke to come out for
a couple of years. He has served our company well. His wife
has died and he will jump at the chance of being near his
daughter Renate again. Karl will keep the books and look after
purchasing, payroll, banking and so forth. The only other area
we need to get control of urgently is labour. We won't have
many permanent staff. But at different times of the year we'll
need to put contractors on for shearing, crutching and
harvesting. Martin, would Renate be able to take on labour?'

'No, Mrs Bauer. She has no experience in a supervisory
role at all. Besides I would like to use her to do some of my
work whenever I have to go back home. Might I suggest we
advertise the position in the local paper? There isn't a lot of
employment in small towns like Macarthur Creek. If we can
be seen to be helping the local community, that's a good thing.
I could get our solicitor to place an ad straight away, if we
agree. Incidentally, if we got the right man, maybe we could

combine labour and farm equipment. A self-starter should be able to handle both. Should we advertise it as the dual role and pay a bit extra?'

'Yes, good idea. Let's do that. Now, Martin, would you talk to the third agenda point? You know—immediate needs.'

'Surely. Now that we each have a specific area to work on, we thought it would be good to have another meeting in, say, a week's time, to go over what needs to be done immediately. So, could everybody please take a few days to analyse things and jot down anything you consider should be attended to urgently.'

A week later each of them made their report.

Brigitte was first. She said that three of the 22 dwellings in poor repair should be demolished and cleared for additional farming land. Four other smaller homes, which were relocatable, should be put up for sale and those areas cleared also. Brigitte presented a quotation for repair of all perimeter fences, arguing that internal fencing should not be touched until they made further decisions on land use.

Rolf followed. He said they needed to accelerate the shearing program before Christmas to maintain the local practice of getting two cuts a year. Rolf recommended they sell most of the 29 horses and replace them with three or four agricultural motorbikes, with utility trays at the back. This suggestion brought an immediate howl of protest from Roxy and Marianne, until Rolf assured them a few horses would be kept for recreational use.

Sean advised that he had commissioned a study of the soil types on the property and recommended pastures. He said he was anxious to diversify into other crops, but would review his findings and ideas in three weeks' time.

Martin reported that he had organised the newspaper advertisement agreed at their last meeting.

He also advised that one of the two property owners who had initially refused to sell now had now had a change of heart. They decided to proceed with the acquisition since the purchase was still within their investment budget. Besides, the property had excellent soil as well as a brand new shearing shed.

Martin suggested they plan on having a clearing sale in six weeks' time, to sell off all equipment they considered superfluous to the needs of the consolidated enterprise.

The management team accepted all recommendations put forward. Brigitte thanked them all for their efforts and declared, 'Small beginnings, but Bavaria Enterprises is up and running.'

Chapter 17

Renate's despair

Everyone was busy over the following months. Each played their own part in transforming the cluster of smaller properties into a super-farm.

A weekend clearing sale proved a great success. Superfluous tools and machinery were sold at a tidy profit, with some sheds that were no longer needed. However, the main benefit of the sale was the chance for the Bauer family to meet many of their neighbours and forge new relationships.

Things were moving along reasonably well, but Brigitte was worried sometimes about Martin's bullish approach. Martin had attended management-training sessions in Europe.

She called him in one day to confront the matter. 'Martin, you know I'm fond of you. You have been a great help first to Wolfgang and then to me, so I'll be frank with you. Since you aren't a member of my family, you need to be sensitive to the fact that Rolf and Sean will want to have some involvement in all major decisions. You need to go out of your way to find avenues for them to participate. If you take too much control, they'll resent you for it. Do you understand my point, Martin?'

'Indeed, Mrs Bauer. Thanks for being so direct with me. I appreciate your direct approach and agree that I could do more to engage the others. Here's an idea. For the last couple of days I've been thinking about a tree plan for the whole property. I could ask Sean to work with me in fleshing out the plan. That's a good way to start. What do you think?'

'Excellent, Martin. Now, any ideas for Rolf?'

Martin thought for a few seconds then replied, 'Well, as a matter of fact, I think we should consider buying some corriedales instead of just having merinos. The merinos are best for wool, but there's no doubt corriedales bring better prices as fat lambs. Having some of both would give us better protection against market-price fluctuations. I could work with Rolf to explore that option.'

'Another good idea, Martin. Just help Rolf to get started, then you back off when you can and let him run with it. I don't want to get you bogged down on any single exercise for too long.'

Martin took Brigitte's advice to heart and his relationships with Rolf and Sean improved immediately.

Meanwhile the two youngest members of the Bauer clan, Rachel and Mark, were now mobile. They required constant attention. Rachel was walking while baby Mark crawled and climbed everywhere. Both Marianne and Roxy had growing concerns that their property included 72 unfenced dams.

At least once each week the two girls would join Brigitte and Renate for tea and scones at the hotel. It was a pleasant escape from the day-to-day grind of farm life and an opportunity for them to share their worries.

One day they mentioned to Brigitte their concern about the dams. She replied, 'Don't worry. I'm way ahead of you on that. It's been worrying me too. Give me a couple of weeks and we'll come up with a solution. I've got some ideas I want to discuss with Karl when he arrives next week. Do me a favour and organise a babysitter for our next meeting. I want everyone to be there when we welcome Karl. He was such a good friend to Wolfgang, and I want to look after him.'

As expected, everyone attended the management meeting in early April of 1954.

Brigitte opened proceedings with a warm welcome for Karl Becke. Glowingly, she told how he had been a great support for Wolfgang, especially in the early days of his empire. Renate beamed in the background. She was so proud of her ageing father and delighted with his move to Macarthur Creek.

Brigitte continued, 'Before we get onto main reports, there are two matters I'd like to cover. It will only take a few minutes. First of all, you know that we've agreed Karl will be the admin manager. He'll look after the company books, make all the purchases, pay invoices, do payroll and so forth. For the first three or four months I've asked Karl to put on an assistant. I want him to spend about 50 percent of his time helping me on a special assignment. What I'd like to do is to look at the feasibility of building a big homestead. Probably with four separate wings of living quarters and a central area for the office, main meals, reception and so forth. There would be a garden of three or four acres, surrounded by a security fence so that all the children will be safe—especially from the dams. I'd also want to put up a big equipment shed so all our farm machinery is protected from the weather. Over the next week or two, think about what you'd like to have included and pass your ideas on to Karl. We should try to get some architectural sketches prepared within about three months. Then we can move on to the costing. Any initial comments?'

'Fantastic!' Roxy exclaimed.

Martin added, 'There'd be a big saving on fuel if we put in some tanks near the shed for petrol, diesel and oil and bought in bulk. What do you think, Sean?'

'Well, with all the bushfires lately, I must confess I worry about the fire danger over summer. If we had a green belt right around the house, we'd all be safe. We could put in a garden out the back and grow all our own vegetables. Have a big chook house as well, so no-one had to buy eggs.'

'All right, sounds good. Let's not spend too much time on it now, though,' Brigitte said.

'As I said, just think about it and give all your feedback to Karl. Now, for my second point. You all know I still have business interests in Europe. There are some tax problems that need to be sorted out urgently. The best person for the job is Martin. He has agreed to go over for about a month. Renate, will you be going with him?'

'No, Mrs Bauer. We've agreed that I will stay behind and help my father get settled in. Plus, I can help Marianne and Roxy with baby-sitting from time to time. I love looking after the children.'

'All right. It's probably just as well, because Martin will be very busy. Now, Rolf, do you have a report for us?'

Rolf advised that they had recently had another outbreak of footrot. Only a few sheep had been infected. The puzzling thing was that the bacteria had surfaced in sheep that had been kept in ideal conditions on dry soil which had not previously been contaminated. He had engaged the vet, Michael Farrell, to find the cause. But after two weeks Farrell hadn't come up with a scientific explanation, though he suspected one of the property trucks may have carried the bacteria. So Michael had invited a university friend of his, to investigate. His friend quickly discovered that the bacteria were in the floor of an old unregistered and run-down stock truck that was used occasionally to transfer the sheep into distant paddocks.

Rolf advised the management team that he would sell the seven old stock trucks they owned and buy two new ones, and a steam-cleaning machine.

He went on to explain that over time they would move from only having merinos to a mixture of merinos and corriedales.

Sean spoke next. He told them about the tree plan he had been working on with Martin. As well as new shelter trees, he wanted to try an experimental plot of fruit trees in the alluvial soil near the river on Rolf's place. And as well as planting hundreds of new trees, he proposed to clear a few bedraggled red gums which were obstacles in the grain-growing areas. Sean advised that he had arranged to trade-in three old tractors for a small Caterpillar bulldozer. Although it wouldn't be used all the time, it would save them paying out to contractors for earth moving, dam construction and stump removals.

After the meeting, they had a few drinks. Marianne and Povy told Brigitte they were excited at the prospect of the new homestead. They would give Karl plenty of ideas to consider.

Karl Becke had taken a room at the Macarthur Creek Hotel right next to Brigitte's office, so he could get started on his assignment without delay.

Renate decided to stay at home, by herself, while Martin was away. She wanted some time alone and planned to wallpaper three rooms that needed sprucing up.

After a couple of days she started to get depressed. She knew Martin had been having an affair, from the smell of his clothes every time he had returned from Australia. Moreover, she suspected it was still going on now they were both living in Macarthur Creek. Renate thought the other was probably the solicitor, Julie Petersen, but kept her views bottled up inside her. Her depression was compounded by loneliness. That loneliness turned to despair and she found solace in a bottle.

One day Roxy came to visit. Arriving at 11 in the morning, she found Renate still in bed. There were two empty rum bottles in the lounge and another in the bedroom. Roxy sat on the bed and started to question Renate.

Soon, Renate burst into tears. She told Roxy that she wanted to have a baby, like Roxy and Marianne, but she knew that Martin was on with another woman. She still loved Martin, but was troubled about having a baby to a man who had betrayed her.

In any event, she told Roxy, she had been trying without success for a year and a half to conceive.

Roxy consoled her as best she could and suggested to Renate that she stay at the hotel until Martin returned. They had a cup of tea together and Renate started to perk up a bit. Her troubles seemed a little lighter now they were shared.

In the late afternoon, as dusk closed in, Rolf returned home. He was tired after replacing the float valves on several drinking troughs.

As she fed baby Mark, Roxy told him about finding Renate depressed and half-drunk.

Rolf decided he should go over and check if Renate had taken Roxy's advice to move into town.

'Do you want to come, Roxy? We could take the pusher and walk over if you like.'

'No, Rolf. Mark's dead tired. I'll give him a bath and put him to bed. You go. Take the motorbike.'

Even before he got to the house around 9:30 pm, Rolf knew that Renate had not left. Most of the lights were still on. He knocked several times but no-one answered. Inside, a radio played country and western music. The front door was locked so he went around the back. It was locked too, but a back window was open. Rolf knocked again and shouted. Still no response! He dragged a drum over to the window and climbed in. Renate was lying face down on the bed. She was unconscious, dressed only in a flimsy nightie that was scrunched up around her waist. On a bookcase near the bedhead was an empty glass and an open pill bottle. He checked. Sure enough, it had had sleeping pills. The label said 25 tablets. It was empty.

Rolf knew he must act quickly. He raced to the bathroom and switched on the shower. Returning, he picked up Renate and carried her down the passage to the bathroom. Rolf kissed her on the forehead before he set her down on her feet. He shouted her name but still she wouldn't wake. Without hesitation, he held her in his arms and moved under the cold shower. She came to almost immediately but was very groggy. He walked her up and down the passage a few times, forcing her to use her legs. Gradually, she awoke. He held her head between his hands and looked straight into her eyes.

'Renate, how many pills did you take?' he demanded.

'Oh, don't shout at me, Rolf. I don't know. About ten, I think.'

'Look, we can't take any chances. I'll have to get you to a doctor. Can you stand up now?'

'Yes, I think so. Don't be angry with me, Rolf. I thought you liked me.'

'I do, Renate, I do. But we need to get you checked out.'

He kissed her on the cheek and gave her a comforting hug. 'Come on, we'll have to get you dressed. Take off that wet nightie. I'll get another towel from the bathroom.'

When he returned, Renate was naked. She leaned against a wardrobe for support. Her head was downcast and she started to doze off again. Unable to control himself, Rolf took her into his arms again, pushed her head back and kissed her full on the lips.

Instinctively, she responded. 'Oh, Rolf. Why didn't I marry you instead of Martin?'

'Well, for one thing, my dear, I was already wed to my Roxy. Now, come on, let's get you dressed,'

Reluctantly he disengaged his arms and briskly rubbed the towel over her. Grabbing a pair of sneakers nearby, he pushed each one on without bothering to lace them. He helped her struggle into a pair of jeans and a sloppy, mohair pullover. Finally, Rolf put the empty pill bottle in his pocket.

'I'll have to take you back to my place on the bike, then we'll get you to the doctor. Come on,'

Forty minutes later, Renate was safe in the care of the doctor. After treatment, he kept her at his house overnight for observation. She was discharged the next morning and took Roxy's advice to move into the hotel.

Rolf called on his mother and told her all about Renate's situation. He assured her he would be taking some initiatives to improve things. Rolf knew about the Julie Pedersen affair. Such news travelled like greased lightning in the bush. When Martin returned, he would tell him straight out to have nothing more to do with Julie Pedersen.

Henceforth, Rolf would have Karl handle all legal matters. Rolf would also encourage Martin to have Renate go with him on all his trips. Finally, Rolf said he would go out of his way to look after the young couple during their difficult time. He told Brigitte he thought that building the new farm was much more than economics. The people side of it had to work too.

Brigitte was pleased with her son's ideas and his leadership. 'Rolf, I like your thinking on this. Is there anything I can do?'

'Not in the short term, Mother, but I have a suggestion for later on. If we go ahead with the homestead, let's give one wing to Martin, Renate and her father. That way they'll feel part of the family more.'

'I agree, Rolf. You're a good boy, my son.'

Two weeks later when Martin returned from Germany, Rolf had a heart-to-heart talk with him.

Martin told Rolf that during his trip he had already decided to end it with Julie Pedersen. The next day he met Julie and told her he would not be seeing her again—either on business or socially.

She was livid. Julie felt used by Martin and at one stage during their fiery encounter she slapped his face in rage.

Martin was glad that it was over. On impulse, he went into Macarthur Creek. He resisted the urge to visit Julie a final time and bought a puppy for Renate. It was a border collie, seven weeks old with a glossy black coat, broken only by a splash of white over one eye.

Renate loved the little dog. It wagged its tail furiously when she picked it up and cradled it in her arms. The pup tried to lick Renate's face, but then the excitement of it all was too much and it peed on her arm. Martin and Renate burst out laughing. Things were better now. They decided to call their new pet Blackie.

Chapter 18

Bavaria homestead

Planning got under way in earnest for the new homestead in the winter of '55. Everyone was excited about the project. Even the townspeople were caught up in the drama of it all.

The architects working with Karl Becke achieved a sensible balance of function, style and comfort. As conceived originally, there would be four wings, each with three bedrooms. The two wings at the front would be for Rolf's and Marianne's families. Martin, Renate and Karl would occupy one at the rear, with Brigitte taking the other.

In the centre there would be a large complex combining business and leisure activities. On one side would be a spacious lounge room with a large dining room on the other. A new business office with all the latest furnishings and equipment would be included, with a modern kitchen.

The four wings would be connected to the centre by covered walkways, to be planted on both sides with wisteria. Each wing would have its own rainwater tank and private verandah.

The architects recommended that the main buildings should be constructed of Mt Gambier limestone. The white stone would be provided in large ashlars, allowing for rapid construction. Over time, the white calcium mortar between the blocks would blend with the limestone ashlars, making very solid walls. The grounds surrounding the homestead would be planted with sweeping green lawns, giving fire protection and a safe playing area for young children.

There were also plans for three additional areas at the back of the homestead compound. Immediately behind, there would be a large vegetable garden and orchard, fenced in for protection from stock. There would be a chook house and a stable for four or five horses. At the very back, there would be a giant machinery shed which would include a workshop, steam-cleaning bay, grease pit and a secure store for dangerous chemicals, Underground storage tanks for fuel would be outside.

Site levelling began in September. Brigitte and Rolf watched with pride as the concrete foundations were laid in late October. Karl Becke was assigned to liaise with the architects and builders throughout the construction period. They hoped to finish before the autumn rains the following April.

Meanwhile, Renate was happy that Martin had finished his assignment in Europe. She was happy too that he was no longer coming in contact with Julie Pedersen.

Renate and Martin took some time off in early November and drove to the Blue Mountains. The weather was simply glorious. Both of them relished the time alone and the chance to explore the rugged grandeur of the area.

Six weeks later Renate had the Christmas present she had wanted—confirmation from her doctor that she was pregnant.

The newspaper at Macarthur Creek began to take an interest in the new homestead. Every couple of weeks they printed a progress report and a new photograph. On weekends, visitors from the town would drive slowly past the building, looking on with a mixture of awe and envy.

The external walls were all up by Christmas. January was noisy as carpenters went to work on the roof trusses and flooring. The noise of their hammers echoed across the property. Every couple of days Marianne and Roxy would visit the site. Rachel and Mark loved to come, so that they could climb on the limestone ashlars, look for spare nails, play in the builder's sand and generally amuse themselves.

Rolf and Sean had little opportunity to get involved. There was much to do on the farm over the summer months.

Sean's experiment with stone fruits by the river was going well. He had planted apricot, plum, nectarine and peach trees. They were flourishing, with a little irrigation. He got some literature from the horticulture section of the Department of Agriculture on pruning and propagation techniques. Sean was attending night school once a week at an adult-education college nearby. One evening, an article in a *National Geographic* that one of his neighbours brought to class impressed him. It was a 10-page report that talked about a discovery related to wild-animal grazing in Africa. Observers had found that when a massive herd of wild stock, such antelopes, wildebeest or gnu grazed an area for only three days, the grasses recovered almost immediately. On the other hand, if they stayed in the area for weeks, the natural pasture would take months and sometimes a year to regrow. The article concluded that two factors contributed to rapid pasture improvement from concentrated grazing; first, there was an enormous amount of manure deposited on the soil, second, the scuffing and breaking of the surface by so many hooves.

Sean discussed the story with Rolf and Martin. The trio agreed that the idea was worth trying out on a small scale. Brigitte also supported the notion of a test. She encouraged them, remarking that just as her Wolfgang had changed some industrial practices in Europe, they should be prepared to try new farming approaches in Australia.

Rolf found the job of managing the summer shearing was a real challenge. He built a relationship with a good crew of subcontractors. They liked his flock because it was so large and gave them an opportunity to stay put for a while. The work was backbreaking for shearers in the hot weather. They appreciated the efforts Roxy had put in to improve their lot. She threw out all the old mattresses and bought inner-springs. She painted out their sleeping quarters and supplied them each with an electric fan. Best of all, she employed a shearer's cook who could cook. Roxy occasionally helped out with the wool classing and pressing. The work was hard, but prices for the wool clip were good.

Brigitte designed the garden around the homestead. She wanted low shrubs near the house, then the wide band of lawn with higher shrubs and trees running back to the fence. She insisted on having lots of honeysuckles, acacias and gums to attract the native birds. Just in front of the house she would have a fishpond with water lilies. The pond must have a safety grid of steel rods just below the water surface. She was ever conscious of her grandchildren.

Karl was grateful to Brigitte on two counts: bringing him out to Australia to be with his daughter, and for giving him so much responsibility. He kept an eye out for any gesture to show his appreciation. One day, he found the answer. There was an abandoned bridge near their farm that had some massive red-gum timbers, big, roughly sawn logs about 3.5 metres long. Karl decided he would surprise Brigitte by building an archway at the gateway to the new homestead. He got the builders to retrieve three of the best logs. Then he had them carve the words Bavaria Homestead across one of them. Finally, he instructed them to cut a mortice in the top of the other two so that the carved log could fit in securely. He decided that the next time Brigitte was away for a day, he would put in the two uprights and mount the carved log on top.

Three Saturdays later, Brigitte went with Sean, Marianne and Rachel on a picnic to Rainbow Falls, 100 kilometres away. Karl knew they would be gone most of the day. He decided to act quickly and explained his plan to Rolf. Rolf liked the idea. He attached the posthole digger to the tractor, drove to the front gate and bored two deep holes to take the uprights. Then he returned and put the hydraulic shovel on the front of the tractor, leaving the digger on the back as a counter-weight.

'Karl, are any of the builders working today?' Rolf asked.

'No, but there are two shearers just playing cards on the verandah over there. I'll ask them to give us a hand.'

The four men manhandled the three logs into the shovel. Rolf grabbed a spirit level and drove the tractor down to the entrance. It lurched under the heavy load. Then he returned and filled the shovel with rocks and building debris. Carefully they stood each of the timbers upright and checked for vertical. They filled in the holes with rocks and soil. As they filled, Karl rammed the debris home with a crowbar. While they discussed how to raise the top bar, Renate rode up on a motorbike with her dog Blackie perched on the back.

'Hey, Rolf, there's a ewe stuck up to its neck in our dam. I think it'll drown unless we haul it out soon. Martin isn't home. Can you come over?'

'Yeah, all right. What do you think of Karl's surprise for my mother? See that cross bar—Bavaria Homestead. Gives us some connection to back home.'

'How wonderful. Brigitte will be surprised.' Turning to Karl, she said, 'Great idea, Father!'

'Well, she's been very good to me. It's the least I could do. Rolf, do you want us to have a crack at putting up the top bar? We should be able to get it up there using the shovel.'

'No, wait. That thing weighs half a ton. We have to be careful. Anyway, doesn't take long to pull a sheep out. I'll be back as soon as I can.'

Rolf jumped on the bike behind Renate and the two sped off with the dog barking alongside.

Ten minutes went by and then 20. Still, there was no sign of Rolf.

Paul Jamieson, the younger of the two shearers, said, 'Come on, Karl. Let's put the damn thing up ourselves. I know how to work the hydraulics on the shovel. We'll surprise Rolf.'

'All right, then, let's have a go at it, but for God's sake be careful. We'll just take it one step at a time.'

Using crowbars, the trio managed to level the huge log onto the top of the shovel. Slowly Paul pushed back the hydraulic lever and raised the shovel higher and higher. Karl walked back about 20 paces.

'That's enough!' he shouted as soon as the log was high enough.

'All right, stand back, you blokes, This'll be a piece of cake,' Paul said.

Gently, he slowly moved the tractor forward and back until the log was lined up atop the two uprights. It was a difficult job because of the restricted space between the two poles. He lowered the log onto the top and it slotted into the two notches.

'Give that man a cigar,' the other shearer said.

'Yes, well done, Paul! Problem is it sticks out about a foot at one end and only a couple of inches at the other. Can you even it up a bit? Needs to go left.'

Paul nodded and manoeuvred the tractor under the log again. He raised the shovel to take weight and slowly pushed the log along. Thinking it was about centred, he punched the air excitedly and said, 'How's that?'

In that momentary lapse of concentration his foot slipped off the brake pedal and onto the accelerator. The tractor lurched forward about half a metre. It was enough to dislodge the log at one end and send it crashing down. It bounced off the rear mudguard of the tractor and hit Paul square across the back. The two others rushed forward. Despite the blow, he was still conscious but in considerable pain.

As the initial shock of it all receded, Paul tried to get down from the seat. He couldn't move. Turning to Karl with tears in his eyes, the young man gasped, 'Karl, get me to a doctor. I can't feel my legs. I can't move my feet.'

Three weeks later, Paul Jamieson was discharged from hospital in a wheelchair. He would never walk again. As soon the extent of the spinal damage was known, Rolf pondered all the options. He decided he should take some initiative. He felt a burden of responsibility because he had stayed chatting for a while to Renate at the dam, instead of returning promptly as he had promised.

Rolf also wanted to do something to make Karl feel more comfortable with things. Karl was distraught over the accident. Indeed, it affected him so much that his thinning dark hair turned white within one week. His interest in completing the homestead waned.

Paul Jamieson was 23 years old. Rolf discreetly researched his background and found that he had been an unusually bright student.

The school captain in his final years, he was described by teachers in school reports as a lad with enormous potential. Apparently, he was a real self-starter, capable of excellent work when he put his mind to it. Paul had always had good marks in maths, algebra and physics, so he had applied to become a pilot with the Royal Australian Air Force. Most of his results on the initial aptitude test were brilliant, but a pass in every one of the test elements was required and unfortunately for Paul he had completely failed in one section. Recognising his superb results in all other parts of the test, the Air Force had offered him entry to a non-pilot position, but he had declined, feeling bitter that failure in one single component of the overall test had disqualified him from flying.

Over the following years, he had drifted from job to job. He took on shearing because he liked the outdoors and the travel involved. Besides, with a little experience, he had found he wasn't a half-bad shearer.

Rolf visited Paul. They talked for three hours. Rolf started out by explaining to the young man that he wanted to have someone trained to become manager handling the administration of Bavaria Homestead. His mother, Brigitte, was withdrawing from day-to-day involvement, Martin would probably return to Europe eventually and Karl was due to retire. Moreover, if the enterprise were to be successful, he, Rolf, must continue to focus on the stock, while Sean looked after the pasture and crops.

Rolf said that if Paul was willing to accept the challenge of being groomed for the job, he would help him all the way. It would take about three years and most of the training would be on-the-job guidance. from Karl. However, Rolf would arrange for Paul to get any tuition required and give him some time off for studies. He would also provide accommodation on the property.

Paul thanked Rolf profusely for the offer. He said he was concerned about his own mobility. He didn't want to be stuck in an office all day. Rolf reassured the lad that it should not be a problem. He would immediately instruct the architects to provide ramps where necessary around the homestead and to widen certain doorways, if that was required. Rolf further explained to Paul that, at the end of the day, it was going to be up to Paul himself to decide what he could or could not achieve. But getting involved in a job which tested his mental and physical capabilities would provide a good starting point.

Rolf said that if Paul accepted the challenge, it would be effective immediately and that he should attend all management meetings to get first-hand exposure to the business side of farming.

This last point seemed to tip the balance for Paul. He shook hands with Rolf and accepted the job. When they reached agreement on starting salary, working hours and so forth, Rolf told Paul he would meet him for a one-on-one discussion every week to monitor his progress. Finally, Rolf said he would call on Paul's widowed mother to discuss their plan.

Brigitte was proud of the sympathetic way that her son had handled the situation. They both knew there was always the possibility that Paul would take some legal action. That prospect now seemed to be resolved in a manner acceptable to all concerned.

Brigitte travelled with Rolf down to the border town of Albury to meet with Paul's mother, Shirley Jamieson.

She was a frail-looking woman, aged 46 and very shy. A few wrinkles were etched at the side of her eyes and her dark hair was sprinkled with strands of grey. Shirley lived in a small weatherboard house on the outskirts of Albury with a dog and two blue-point Siamese cats. Despite her shyness, she made them welcome and insisted they all sit down for tea and scones.

Rolf expressed his regret over the accident and went on quickly to give a full account of the arrangements that he had negotiated with Paul.

Shirley was pleased to hear that so much had already been done for her injured son. She asked, 'Would you mind if I visit my son, every now and then? You see, I have no other children and my husband was killed in a car accident three years ago.'

'That will be fine,' Brigitte replied. She went on, 'If I might ask, what exactly are your own circumstances, Mrs Jamieson? Are you working yourself at the moment?'

'Please, call me Shirley. Yes, I am a cook. I have two part-time jobs—one at a hotel and the other at a nursing home. I own this house and I have a small car. So, I'm all right, thank you. Perhaps one day I'll move closer to your area. Then it won't be so far to visit Paul. I want to give him as much support as I can.'

'All right. Thank you for seeing us, Shirley,' Rolf said. 'We'll be off now. I'm glad we met you. As my mother said, you are welcome to visit whenever you like. In the meantime, please rest assured that we will take good care of your boy.'

When Rolf told Karl about his successful talks with Paul and his mother, the old man felt a load had been lifted from his shoulders. Karl knew very well he had been the senior man on the spot and that if he had told Paul to wait until Rolf returned, the lad would have done so.

He liked the idea of training someone for the administration and management. His part-time assistant wasn't working out and the support he had from Martin was interrupted by Martin's trips back to Europe. Karl was particularly pleased to hear that Paul would start in two weeks' time. He needed the help because he wanted to push the homestead project along again.

Over the next four months, the main building and the entire surrounding infrastructure was completed. A few last-minute changes were included. Two internal passageways were widened for improved wheelchair access.

Rolf insisted that a new steel gun cabinet should be relocated from the house to the dangerous-goods store in the equipment shed and that two padlocks be fitted to the cabinet. Rolf also got plumbers in to put extra hot water pipes around the slow-combustion stove in the kitchen to reduce electricity costs.

Whereas the original plan had been to have a mixture of carpet and linoleum floor coverings, they decided eventually to have all the floors sanded back, stained and polished.

Brigitte wanted wall fans installed in each wing with a larger one for the central living and office area. Two large rainwater tanks were set up at the back, to capture run-off from the galvanised-iron roofing. Cattle grids replaced the gates to the family compound and a sprinkler system was installed across the whole vegetable garden.

Paul Jamieson was a great help to Karl during the final stages. He looked after all the day-to-day accounts so that Karl could concentrate on ensuring proper finishing off by all the subcontractors involved.

The new homestead was occupied by the end of May 1956.

Brigitte had one of the back wings all to herself. The other at the rear was for Martin, Renate and her father Karl.

Renate was eight months' pregnant, so they decked out the smallest bedroom for the baby.

Rolf and Roxy moved into one of the front wings, with Sean and Marianne taking up the other. Between the two wings they put a swing, slippery dip and seesaw for Rachel and Mark. They also installed a sandpit for Mark, who was being spoiled by his uncle Sean with a shiny, new matchbox car every week.

Chapter 19

Brigitte leaves

For the next six months it was a joyous time at the homestead.

Renate Becke had a beautiful young daughter. The baby was named Martina. Her father, Martin, was so proud of his first child. Soon he extended his already impressive array of skills to include nappy changing. In the meantime, Renate bought everything pink she could lay her hands on.

In August, Marianne became pregnant again. Sean hoped that this time it would be a son.

Roxy's young boy, Mark, was a force to be reckoned with. At only three years of age he was a whirlwind of activity. He would talk to everyone, climb anything and generally take on things that would be daunting for children twice his age. Little Mark was mischief personified. The best time of day for Roxy was the minute the young fellow went off to sleep. Then she could get some peace.

Everyone at the homestead was disappointed towards the end of September to hear that Britain had exploded an atomic bomb in a test at Maralinga in South Australia. The radioactive cloud drifting across Australia passed well north of their property as it dissipated across Queensland. It was a grim reminder of the horror of war.

Further consolidation work took place on Bavaria Homestead. The paddocks were generally enlarged. Sean's notion of intensive grazing proved successful. None of the other farmers tried it, though. It was too much of a departure from tradition for those diehard battlers. The homestead pastures were progressively improved. Sean took maximum advantage of government subsidies for superphosphate.

Karl took on the job of driving the super spreader to give him a spell from the office. Whenever he climbed into the spreader truck, Blackie would jump on the back and bark continuously at the sight of the white powder being sprayed. Eventually, Karl bought some earmuffs. The experimental plot of fruit trees by the river was extended to a larger orchard with proper irrigation channels.

Rolf increased the number of beef cattle on the property and arranged for stronger stockyards to be built for handling his herd safely. They had already had two accidents while de-horning steers and he didn't want any more.

Brigitte's dream was almost realised. Australia had given her a new lease of life. The country life was so peaceful. Tanks had never crossed this land in anger. She relished the challenge of it all and she was winning.

The super-farm was a commercial success and a boon to the participants who enjoyed an enhanced quality of life. There were a few things still to be done. On Rolf's recommendation, she wanted to acquire two additional properties which carried a mixture of Angus and Murray Gray cattle. She asked Martin to make inquiries.

Then there was the question of the cook for the homestead. In the space of only a few months they had gone through three cooks, two of whom refused to do the extra work when the shearing gangs were on site. Brigitte asked Rolf to visit Paul's mother in Albury and see if she would be interested in the job.

If so, she could stay in the same farmhouse as her son, because there was plenty of room.

Brigitte also wanted to find out more about broad-acre farming. There were thousands of hectares of flat, arable land surrounding Bavaria Enterprises—most of it cleared of trees and stumps. It occurred to Brigitte that perhaps the notion of building a super-farm for wool could be replicated with wheat. She had many ideas for the future, but she was also getting tired and homesick.

Brigitte longed to see the snow-capped peaks of the Bavarian Alps again. She wanted to visit the grave of her beloved Joachim, and to spend some time in her Munich apartment and feel the presence of Wolfgang. She cherished the time with her children, but there was so much she missed. Also, she wanted to do something special for her family before she broached the subject of her return to Germany. Casually, she asked both Rolf and Sean whether they could be away from the farm for one week at the end of November.

Both gave the same answer—one week, but one week only. Brigitte then called them both in, with Roxy and Marianne. She said she would like to arrange for the four of them to take some time out and attend a few days of the Olympic Games due to start in Melbourne on 22nd November.

'Marvellous,' Roxy said. 'Marianne, we could visit the shops while we're down there.'

'Oh, I'd love to see Melbourne.' beamed Marianne. 'This will be my last chance to travel for a while. I'll be too big after Christmas. Come on, Sean. Let's do it. We could see some of the equestrian events. You know I love horses.'

'What about the kids?' Rolf interjected.

'What about them?' Brigitte retorted.

'They're both old enough to stay by themselves for a while Renate will be happy to look after them. It'll do them the world of good. You spoil them too much anyway. They can sleep in the spare room next to mine. I'm sure Renate and Shirley will love to help out. By the way, Marianne, you won't be able to see any of the horses. I read in the paper that the authorities won't let horses come into Australia because of quarantine restrictions. But there'll still be lots for you to see.' She continued, not waiting for any further comment. 'I'll get young Paul to get some pointers from Martin on how to arrange things and then let you know. It'll be good experience for Paul to coordinate it all.'

'Thanks, Mother,' Rolf said. He gave his mother a kiss and added, 'Say, Sean, we'd better sample a drop or two of that Fosters while we're down there. What do you think?'

'When in Rome!' Sean agreed with a grin.

Paul discovered that getting transport and Games' tickets arranged was easy. The problem was finding accommodation in Melbourne. Everything was booked out. He phoned several city hotels and arranged to go on a waiting list, taking Martin's advice to make the point that cost wasn't a problem. After a few days, a hotel in Little Collins Street called back to say they had two suites available for three nights only. Paul grabbed them.

Roxy and Marianne were looking forward to their trip down south. The journey in a light plane took just over two hours and was a little uncomfortable because Rolf and Sean were so tall and needed to push their seats back.

A hire care waited for them at Essendon Airport and whisked them into the city. Everywhere there were welcoming signs. The streets were bustling with visitors gawking at the city sights. Their hotel was right in the city centre. On the way in, Marianne observed they were in walking distance of the massive Myer department store.

That evening they had dinner in the hotel restaurant. Afterwards, the women drifted off to go window-shopping. Sean and Rolf strolled down to Young and Jackson's on Flinders and had a few beers. The four met back at the hotel lounge around ten o'clock for a nightcap. Each felt relaxed and excited about the day ahead.

In the morning, they decided to walk to the main Games venue. Most events were being conducted at the Melbourne Cricket Ground—less than a kilometre from the hotel. They set off down Swanston Street and crossed the busy Flinders Street intersection. Marianne asked them to wait a moment while she ducked into a store to get a straw sun hat that was on special. At Princes Bridge they turned left along the muddy Yarra River and followed the crowds. The sun already had a bite. Marianne was thankful for the shade of the elm trees on the riverbank. Fortunately, they already had tickets, so they were able to avoid the queues. With excitement building, they climbed flight after flight of concrete steps and emerged into the sunlight. Before them was a breathtaking scene. Built with seating all round, like a colosseum, the stadium was jam-packed with spectators. They wore hats of all colours and waved flags of many nationalities.

The arena itself was no less colourful. Many athletics events were being conducted at the same time. As luck would have it, their seats were in the finishing straight for the running. They watched in awe as the day's events unfolded. Many world records were broken. It was a wonderful day of struggle, pageantry and sporting drama, a day they would always remember. The highlight was Australian Betty Cuthbert's win in the 100-metre sprint. The crowd went absolutely wild at the local Australian victory.

At four o'clock they left the MCG and walked to the velodrome to watch some of the track cycling heats. They all found it thrilling to watch the colourful competitors race around the small track at full speed with their wheels only centimetres apart. The surface was made of boards set less than a centimetre apart. As the cyclists rode around their tyres created a rhythmic noise that reverberated through the stands, adding to the drama of it all. Since there were no finals scheduled till the evening, they stayed only an hour, and then started strolling back towards the city.

On the way, they made another stop, this time at the swimming stadium. For two hours they watched as men and women from all over the world sliced through the water.

A journalist sitting next to Rolf struck up a conversation. He told Rolf his paper had asked him to concentrate on a water-polo semi-final between Hungary and the Soviet Union. There was bad blood between the two teams following the attack on Budapest by the Soviets, and trouble during the match was expected.

Rolf thought even the Olympic Games were tarnished by the influence of war. As darkness fell, they ambled back under the elms to the city.

A cool breeze drifted across the Yarra River. Noisy trams rattled by, shuttling weary spectators back towards the city lights.

A welcome shower at the hotel and they were out on the streets again. It was cooler now. The four friends wanted to make the most of their visit. After looking around a while, they decided to eat at a Chinese restaurant in Little Bourke Street.

There was a wait of 10 minutes for a table, but it was worth it. Towards the end of their meal Rolf said, 'All right, we've talked a little bit today about what we might do tomorrow. Let's make a final decision.'

'Marianne and I are going to spend all day shopping,' Roxy replied firmly.

'All right, that'll be easy because there're so many stores all around the hotel. What about us, Sean? Do you want to go back to the stadium again?'

'As a matter of fact, Rolf, I'd prefer to go to the road race in the cycling. I heard someone at the velodrome say it's on tomorrow. It's at Broadfields or Broadmeadows—some name like that. I guess it must be a suburb somewhere. If the girls are shopping all day, we could take the hire car.'

'Good choice!' Rolf replied. 'I don't mind cycling because I used to see a bit of racing in Germany.'

Broadmeadows was a hilly rural area, just past the industrial suburbs to the north of Melbourne. The road race was held around a testing circuit with three successive hills along one side.

Rolf asked the driver to drop them at the top of the third hill. It was a perfect vantage point. They got a slow-motion look at the whole bunch every time the riders struggled to get over the third and steepest hill. All the riders looked extremely fit. None of them seemed to have an ounce of fat. Their tanned legs glistened in the sunshine as they simultaneously pushed down with one leg and pulled up with the other to crest the hill. On one lap, three riders fell near the top of the climb. Each tore skin off all over themselves as they crashed to the pavement—unable to break their falls with their feet firmly strapped to the pedals. At length all three managed to get to their feet, their knees and elbows bloodied. Each rider seemed more concerned about damage to his bike than to his own body. All three quickly re-mounted and took off in pursuit of the main bunch. Sean and Rolf stayed for the duration. A diminutive Italian rider named Ercole Baldini won the event, after nearly five and a half gruelling hours in the saddle.

Meanwhile, Roxy and Brigitte shopped in comparative comfort all day. They spent the whole morning at Myer, where they had a lunch with salad at the cafeteria. Then they went to Coles, Georges and back again to Myer.

Emerging on the Lonsdale Street side, Marianne noticed the small church of St Francis on the opposite corner. They were both tired. In the quiet coolness of the church they sat and rested a while. Marianne said a prayer for Joachim and Roxy thought about what she wanted to buy next.

When the two men returned to the hotel, hot from their day in the sun, their first priority was to have a shower. But it was not to be.

Roxy insisted on showing them all the presents they had bought. There were clothes for Rachel and Mark as well as some for Renate's baby, Martina. Marianne had got an opal brooch for her mother, three new shirts for Sean, a dress and two pairs of shoes for herself. Roxy also bought some clothes for herself, a book on farm management for Rolf and an electric train set for Mark.

That evening the four had dinner in the hotel dining room. They managed to get through three bottles of an agreeable red wine from the Barossa Valley.

When they were fairly sozzled, Rolf surprised the others by saying, 'Of course, you know this whole trip is a set-up, don't you?'

'What do you mean, Rolf?' Sean asked.

'I know my mother pretty well. This is a technique she picked up from Wolfgang. Whenever you want to ask something awkward, soften up your audience first and then pop the question.'

'What do you think it's about?' Sean asked.

'If I had to put money on it, I'd say she wants our blessing to let her go back to Germany for a while. Anyway, we'll cross that bridge when we come to it. Now, our plane leaves at three tomorrow afternoon, so we'd better leave for Essendon at about 1:30 to be sure.'

The day after their return, Brigitte told them she wanted to go back to Europe for Christmas, to escape the heat and to stay in her apartments. Furthermore, that she wanted to spend some time over there, now that Bavaria Enterprises was running successfully.

She talked it over at length with Rolf and Marianne. The three agreed that it would be a good idea for Brigitte to be in Europe for each winter, then return to Australia for the winter months in the southern hemisphere. That way she would never have to endure really hot weather.

That settled, they set a date for a party at Bavaria Homestead. Though she would only be away for five months, Rolf and Marianne were determined to give their mother a good send-off. Two weeks later they had a farewell banquet at the homestead. A local band provided the music. After a few drinks, Marianne gave them a few songs. Rolf had ordered in a keg of Foster's lager. The men were determined to drink the keg dry before the night was over.

As she was packing the next morning, Brigitte surprised Rolf by asking him to order four television sets for the homestead.

'It's tough being isolated out here sometime, Rolf' she explained.

'Give one set each to Marianne, Roxy and Renate and one to Paul. That boy is doing so well. He never complains. I agree with you, Rolf, at the rate he's learning, one day he'll run the place for us.'

Chapter 20

More heartbreak

When Rolf arose from a troubled sleep in early February of 1957, he sensed that something was wrong. The morning light that filtered through his bedroom window didn't seem quite right. He had listened to the radio well into the night and was well aware that hot northerlies were forecast with the mercury predicted to reach 40 degrees.

He stepped outside. The rising sun was hidden behind an orange haze but already he could feel its bite. He let the chickens out to run and turned on three sprinklers in the vegetable patch to give the plants an even chance against the midday sun. Occasional gusts of wind stirred up the dust and sent dry gum leaves swirling into the air. In the nearby trees a flock of white cockatoos jumped about restlessly on the upper branches. Rolf climbed up the windmill ladder and looked in all directions. There was no sign of any smoke but he could smell it in the air. He climbed down quickly. His left leg still made him wince.

While he was having a quick shave, Roxy called him into the kitchen. 'Quick, Rolf! On the wireless, they're talking about a fire just up north.'

They both listened intently, hanging on every word. A grassfire was burning on a five-kilometre front about 80 kilometres away. The gusty winds made it impossible to get under control and it was rapidly spreading south. The country fire brigade had decided to fall back to Barkers Road about 16 kilometres ahead of the front. There, they would start another fire to make a break and hopefully starve the fire of fuel.

Rolf called Sean. They got the others together for an emergency meeting. All agreed that a contingency plan was needed. The wind was becoming more violent so the chances of halting the fire at Barkers Road were becoming remote. They decided that the men would make a stand at the roadway along the northern perimeter of their property. If the fire got through, they would retreat to the homestead. In the meantime, the women would get as many sprinklers going as possible around the homestead building.

The smell of smoke in the air became more noticeable. They filled water tanks on the back of two trucks and six firefighters' knapsacks. Sean soaked about a dozen wheat bags in water and threw them onto the trucks as well. When they got to the perimeter road, they decided it was far too risky to try to burn a break themselves.

Although the air reeked, the clouds of smoke in the distance still seemed a long way away. Rolf asked two of the shearers on motorbikes to start herding all the sheep towards the dams. The smoke seemed to be moving to the east. Maybe the fire would miss them altogether. They watched and waited.

At the homestead, Roxy was making preparations too. She had seen bushfires before and knew what to do. Without delay, she and Marianne filled all the sinks and bathtubs with water, then every bucket and pot they could find as well. They blocked the downpipes and flooded the gutters. Next, they soaked all the towels in water and tried to calm the rest of the household. The sprinklers, going full blast around the homestead, provided them with a reasonable level of comfort. The area immediately surrounding the homestead was always kept mown and tidy.

There wasn't much natural fuel for a fire. They felt they should be safe.

The phone rang. The fire had got past the brigade up north on Barkers Road. Karl Becke drove off to tell the others.

'Just heard on the phone that it got past them. If it keeps coming this way, we'll have to stop it here. They said one or two trucks from down south will come and join you on this line. I'm going to tie the horses under the sprinklers and stay at the homestead. Good luck!'

The smoke in the air grew thicker and caught in their lungs. Above them, flocks of galahs and cockatoos screeched in protest as they winged their way south. In the distance they saw a mob of kangaroos jump the fence and cross the roadway. A pair of hares ran in panic along the fence line.

They soaked handkerchiefs in water and tied them across their faces. Forty minutes later they could see the flames in the distance. Now they could smell the fire, see the flames and hear it approaching. Out of the smoke ahead two fire-trucks came crashing towards them. Rolf jumped off his truck to open a nearby gate. The trucks just crashed through the fence.

'Where's the nearest dam?'

'About four hundred metres down there,' Sean replied, pointing to the closest water.

'Be back as quick as we can. It's down to a two-kilometre front, but headed this way. Don't tackle it before it gets to the road. Just try to stop it getting started on the other side. We've gotta go!'

As the two trucks sped off towards the dam, another two approached from the homestead. One was driven by Michael Farrell.

'Jees, Rolf. I'd have thought you've already had your share of bad luck. Still, maybe we can stop this one for you. Let's see. We should spread the trucks and men out about thirty metres inside the paddocks on this side. Give wet bags to any man who doesn't have a knapsack.'

The fire came closer. Soon it was only 200 metres away, but the wind seemed to be abating. More kangaroos came charging over the fences. The flames were only about a metre or so high but the front was so long. Still, they waited. When the blaze reached the roadway the wind mercifully died down further. A few sparks filled the air, but none reached the other side. The centre part of the front seemed to be under control. Towards the left, the flames were still approaching the roadway, so Rolf headed his truck in that direction. They kept the same vigil – watching for any sparks on the other side. Again the flames died down immediately they reached the roadway.

Rolf thought to himself, I think we've done it. I think we've actually beaten it.

He turned the truck around and headed towards the other end. Sean and two others were furiously squirting out the remaining flames with their knapsacks. Occasionally they would spray one of the tinder-dry wooden droppers along the fence that had caught fire. Rolf switched on his headlights. Even as the fire died down, the pall of smoke remained intense and suffocating. He drove on steadily, observing men swinging wet bags to douse the dying flames. He was feeling so pleased that their plan had worked. Then his heart sank. Through the smoke in the distance he could see that the fire had jumped the road. It was burning out of control on a 400-metre front across one of his north-east paddocks. Rolf pushed the accelerator and drove up next to Michael Farrell's truck.

'What happened?' he yelled.

'They couldn't start the pump engine on the truck at this end. Vapour block or something like that. You haven't got any stock in that top paddock, have you?'

'Damn right I have. About three hundred wethers. But maybe they'll be all right if they stay near the dam.'

'No,' Michael replied. 'Sheep are too dumb to do that. Let's head down there.'

Michael's truck took off across the paddock with Rolf's vehicle close behind. The fire seemed to have already passed through Rolf's paddock. It was now burning to the east on his neighbour's property. They could see the headlights of more fire-trucks in the distance, racing towards the flames.

As they drove across the blackened, smouldering landscape behind the fire, they came across the pitiful sight of dozens of burned sheep. Some were down and badly burned. Others were stumbling around in severe distress with burned legs. Some appeared uninjured but were coughing and gasping for air. They pulled up and observed that none of the sheep had stayed close to the dam at all. It was a heartbreaking spectacle.

'My God, Michael! What can we do?' pleaded Rolf.

'Sorry, Rolf. We'll have to destroy the lot. Those that aren't burned will have throat and lung damage anyway. The humane thing is to put the whole lot out of their suffering.'

Rolf didn't answer. He sat on the running board of his truck and buried his head in his hands.

Meanwhile, Michael climbed up onto the roof of his truck's cabin. He stood up, peering into the distance. 'Looks like they've got it all under control now. Can't see any more flames. Those extra trucks were a lifesaver. I'd better drive over and check because this tank has still got plenty of water. Rolf, you head home and collect some rifles and all the ammo you can. I'll meet you back here as soon as I can.'

With a heavy heart Rolf made his way back to the homestead. Roxy was bandaging Karl Beck's wrists as he came in the door.

'What happened, Karl?'

'It's no big deal. I was holding the horses with ropes and they started to panic. Had to wind them round my wrists and they tore the skin a bit. More importantly, how is it out there?'

'Bad news, I'm afraid,' Rolf replied. His voice trembled. 'About 300 sheep have been burned. We'll have to destroy them all. At least the fire is out, so no more stock will be lost.'

Roxy put her arms around Rolf. No words were necessary.

Half an hour later, Rolf met Michael back in the top paddock. The vet explained where to place the shot behind each animal's head so death would come quickly. He also suggested that once they started, they should keep going until the job was done. Sean arrived with an extra supply of ammunition.

'I heard what happened and thought we might need more bullets. Let's get on with it.'

The next 30 minutes were traumatic for Rolf. He hated the very thought of killing, yet had to continually aim, shoot and reload. Over and over again he did it. The only time they stopped was when they came across a dead fox with four dead pups beside her.

'Just look at that!' said Michael. 'She could have got away, but stayed and perished with her pups.'

They pressed on. Only seven sheep which seemed unharmed and breathing normally were spared.

That night, Rolf and Sean discussed the question of future fire prevention at great length. They decided to take up an earlier recommendation to plant lucerne along the perimeter of their property to provide a natural firebreak. The pair resolved to put in a strip of the evergreen crop about 150 metres wide right along the southern, western and northern boundaries. They would build a light five-wire fence using droppers only to control the access of stock. Rolf and Sean concluded that there was no need for any such protection on the eastern side, since the prevailing winds almost always came from the west. They also talked about what to do with all the carcases. Their first thoughts were to dump them all in an old creek bed that no longer carried any water. The problem would be finding soil to cover the bodies. At length they decided to use a long-abandoned limestone quarry in one of their far paddocks. The overgrown excavation was almost ten feet deep and large enough to hold all the carcases. Additionally, there was a huge pile of rubble nearby they could use to cover the bodies.

At first light the next day they began the grisly task of loading the burned and bloated carcases onto the tray truck and carting them off to the old quarry. That job took all day. They were exhausted when it was over. By early afternoon, Sean started the dozer and began pushing rubble over the dead animals. Rolf was visibly upset. He went to his truck, pulled out his gun and flung it onto the carcases.

Sean eased off the throttle and shouted, 'Why did you do that, Rolf? It was a perfectly good rifle.'

'I've killed enough, Sean. I've killed enough.'

Chapter 21

Life is sweet

In mid-December 1957, shortly after her arrival in Munich, Brigitte phoned Rolf to say that she would need Martin to come over for a couple of months after Christmas. There were some business issues that needed his attention.

'Tell him to bring Renate and the baby with him this time,' Brigitte said. 'They can use the apartment next to mine.'

'All right, I'll have them all on a plane in early January.'

On the day before Christmas, Rolf and Sean were planting a row of shelter trees along the front fence. It was a hot and humid day. Even the crows rested in the shade.

Rolf was on the tractor boring holes four metres apart with the post-hole auger. Whenever they worked together, Rolf would drive, because his leg still restricted him a little.

Sean thought that he sometimes made the most of this excuse, but went along with it. Sean's job was to drop in the trees and shovel back the soil. Rolf would add water from a tank on the tractor to give the trees a start.

After a while, a car pulled up alongside them. It was a police vehicle. Rolf's heart missed a beat. *Oh, My God!* He froze.

Sean, keeping his composure, said quietly but firmly, 'Take it easy, Rolf. Let's hear what he's got to say.'

'Hey, fellas! I'm Sergeant Kelly. I'm looking for a bloke named Rolf Bauer.'

'I'm Rolf Bauer, Sergeant. How can I help you?'

The policeman took a notebook from his back pocket. He pulled a folded sheet of paper from inside and said, 'Paul Jamieson. I understand he works on your property. Rolf, I have a warrant here for his arrest. He's got outstanding fines for speeding over the past three years. I'll have to take him with me.'

'Sergeant, do you know he's got a broken spine?' Sean said.

'No. What happened to him?'

'Let me explain it all to you,' Rolf said. 'Paul was working for us as part of a shearing gang. One day when he was trying to help us out, a log fell onto his back and crushed two vertebrae. He came out of hospital in a wheelchair. The lad will never walk again. I've given him a permanent job doing admin work for us. He's going very well. The boy works 10 hours a day, six days a week. On top of that, he spends one day each week on study and his mother has moved here to help him out and look after him. Sergeant, this young fellow is just starting to get his life together again. If you arrest him, it'll be a terrible experience for him and his mother. I'm prepared to look after the boy and keep him motivated. Is there any way you can help us out?'

The officer paused for a moment and went on, 'Listen, lads, I'm sorry to hear about the accident, but once an arrest warrant has been issued, it's a copper's duty to enforce that order. But I've got to tell you that my jurisdiction covers over 200 square miles. Every day I handle dozens of pieces of paper. Occasionally one gets lost.'

He ambled over to one of the empty holes.

'Are you going to be putting a tree in here?' he asked.

'Sure thing. We'll do this whole row today,' Sean replied.

Before their eyes, the sergeant tore the warrant into little pieces and dumped it down the hole. He winked at them and said, 'Happy Christmas, fellas!'

Rolf started to breathe normally again.

Over the holiday period, Rolf asked Martin to do him a favour. He wanted to establish some performance measures so he could better understand which farm activities were going well and which needed attention. He asked Martin to work with Karl and Paul to develop a number of performance charts.

It was an undertaking in which Paul Jamieson excelled. Guided by his two mentors, Paul established 22 graphs he would maintain for Rolf. They were all concerned with trend analysis. He dug deep into Karl's paperwork and pulled out as much historical data as possible. There were charts showing the prices for wool they had been paid for each successive clip, the price per beast for each batch of steers they sold at auction, and the price they were paid for each wheat crop. Paul also tracked costs. He had a graph showing each month's overall operating costs. It was supported by individual charts indicating fuel, labour, fertiliser, shearing and other breakdowns. Finally, Paul had comparison charts. These illustrated the difference between the prices paid to Bavaria Enterprises and the prevailing market prices that Paul looked up in the *Weekly Times*.

Two days before Martin was due to leave, they reviewed all the charts with Rolf. He was very impressed. Rolf emphasised with Paul the need to keep the charts up to date and as accurate as possible. He asked for additional charts to be maintained on the average market prices for Murray Grey and Angus cattle, and told Paul to check with Sean if he wanted anything else monitored.

Rolf thanked the trio and congratulated them on their efforts. As he left the room he knew his earlier decision had been vindicated. One day Paul Jamieson, a one-time shearer, would be appointed the manager of Bavaria Enterprises.

Before they left for Munich, Renate came to visit Rolf, with baby Martina on her hip.

'Rolf, a couple of things before we head off. My father says he will look after Blackie while we're away, but I don't want Blackie just hanging around the house all day. He loves exercise. So could you take him with you out on the farm sometimes and give him a run?'

'No problem. I'll take him on the back of my bike and make him run some of the way home.'

'That's good, Rolf. Also, I want to thank you for all you've done for me. Not just the sleeping-pill business, but I know you had something to do with getting Martin back on track. We are doing all right now and I just want you to know I appreciate it.'

'It was my pleasure, Renate. No trouble at all, really. I've always liked you, Renate. I feel I know you pretty well now, so if ever you need any more help, just give me a call.'

'Thanks, Rolf. You should know me well. After all, you've seen me naked,' she laughed.

'Get out of here, woman. I've got work to do,' he responded with a grin.

Meanwhile, Renate's father, Karl, had struck up a friendship with the new cook, Shirley Jamieson. He was almost 20 years her senior, but they enjoyed each other's company. They worked together to plant a herb garden at one end of the vegetable patch.

Karl put in a sprinkler system and dug in chook manure so the plants were always lush and green. Shirley liked to include fresh herbs in her cooking. Soon they got into the habit of going to the pictures every Saturday night at the Odeon Theatre in Macarthur Creek. It was a good escape for both, because the rest of the week was always so busy.

Sean and Marianne had decided to stay on indefinitely in Australia. Sean was experimenting with mobile electric fencing to make the radical practice of intensive grazing more effective. His New Year resolution for 1957 was to try and finish work earlier so he could be more help to Marianne with her second baby, due soon.

The original plan had been for Sean to concentrate on pastures and Rolf on the stock, but they found that they now shared all major decisions between them.

Their main objective for the first part of the year was to successfully assimilate the two new properties they had acquired, and their immediate priority was to replace some of the perimeter fencing that was in bad repair.

The Aberdeen Angus cattle they had bought with the land were healthy beasts in good condition. They would fetch a handsome price at the winter sales. Rolf and Sean considered it made little business sense to have poor fencing around such valuable stock. Strangely, most farmers in the area neglected their fences year in and year out.

Bavaria Homestead was establishing new farming standards in the Macarthur Creek area. Fresh, innovative practices were always being tried. Neither Rolf nor Sean shied away from experimentation. They had no hesitation in grazing sheep and cattle together—a departure from local convention.

What really set the homestead apart from neighbouring properties was the scope of the holdings. They had now successfully combined a total of 17 individual properties into the one concern and made dozens of economies of scale along the way.

Rolf and Sean thought it would be useful to subject their property to outside scrutiny. They decided that before the year was over they would have an open day. In addition to local farmers and stock agents, they would invite officers from the Department of Agriculture and students from the nearby agricultural college. Rolf and Sean were managing very well, but they both knew that there was still a lot to learn about Australian farming. But they loved the country, and the lifestyle—the burning sun creeping over the horizon on summer mornings, determined to scorch the earth and bleach the grass before it retreated ever so slowly out of sight again; the gum trees, green for the whole year, dropping their bark in a clutter around their trunks. They loved the peace and harmony of it all. The rural tranquillity was a substitute for the mountain solitude of Rolf's childhood.

During the rainy months of June and July, Sean and his family would make a trip to Florida to see his folks, then go on to Germany for a holiday.

Rolf planned to accompany his mother back to Europe in November for a well-earned break.

In the meantime, Rachel's fifth birthday was fast approaching. Word spread throughout the household that Rolf had bought something special. The weather was nice, so they had the birthday party on the lawn.

Marianne had invited eight children from nearby farms and they each brought a little present. The kids ate cake and ice-cream then played all around the homestead, shrieking and screaming like wild animals.

Roxy's boy, Mark, was the loudest. At the tender age of four, he already lived life to the full. Every day as soon as he woke, he was up and on the go. Mark led the charge as the young children raced around, exploring in wild abandon.

Marianne called them all together, to sing happy birthday to her daughter.

Rachel had heard the rumours, but, in the excitement of it all, she didn't notice she had not received a present from Rolf and Roxy.

When the singing died down, Rachel drew in a deep breath and blew the five candles out in one breath. As her mother handed her the knife to cut the cake, the side gate opened. Onto the lawn came Rolf leading a white Arabian pony. It was the most beautiful thing Rachel had ever seen.

'Happy birthday, Rachel,' Rolf said as he lifted her onto its back. 'Shall we put Mark up there with you, too?'

'Oh, yes, Uncle Rolf. Come on Mark. You can get on in front of me. I'm older than you are. I'm five years old now. I'll hold you on.'

The other children implored Rolf for a ride, too.

'All right, kids. You can all have a ride, but we'll have to take it in turns.'

'He's lovely, Uncle Rolf. But what's his name? What will we call him?' Rachel said.

Rolf put his sun-tanned arm around Marianne and pulled her towards him. Her eyes misted up with joy.

'We'll call him Kaiser, Rachel. We'll call him Kaiser.'